Catching On Fire
by
Sue Knott

Joan,
Thank you so much for your comments, proofreading and enthusiasm in helping me get this book to print. All proof helped improve the book tremendously.

Love,
Sue Knott
:)

Catching On Fire by Sue Knott 1st edition, April 2012, 1st print
edition May 2012

The visions are tattooed on my brain. I think they've been there since birth. Long before I could have ever understood the power of the elements, I'd seen the images in my mind's eye. Farmlands washed away by floods. Cities buried under mountains of snow. The forests of the world catching on fire…

Chapter 1

Autumn, 2008

I have hated my boobs my entire life. Well, maybe not all 24 years. I mean, they didn't show up until I was 12 – but at that time, they made a grand entrance practically overnight. I have definitely hated them since then. They're too big for my small frame. And they attract attention. I hate attention. Plus, they attract the wrong kind of attention. Case-in-point was closing in fast from across the bar: two lecherous jerks.

One of the guys had his eyes on my friend, Kim. The other had his fixed straight at my boobage. They were definitely giving off the jerk vibe. I could look at most people and tell what they were all about. There were some people I couldn't read, but these guys were very readable and they were radiating "jerk."

"You lovely ladies look thirsty. Can we buy you some drinks?" That was the tall one, who hadn't yet bothered to take his eyes off my chest.

I glanced pointedly at our full drinks. "Sorry, looks like we already have that covered."

Kim, oblivious to my attempt to brush these two off, blushed and smiled. "Maybe next round."

I closed my eyes to hide the fact that they were rolling up into my skull. This was just so typical of Kim. I could never understand how some people couldn't get a sense of someone by looking in their eyes. Kim was one of those people. She couldn't tell a jerk from a prince. She trusted everyone. Even after being burned by a series of losers, she still smiled at any self-centered jackass that made a move.

The trouble was, Kim was jaw-droppingly gorgeous. But, she didn't believe it. Her looks intimidated regular guys. But, jerks were bold enough to approach her.

If you don't realize how beautiful you are, I guess it's hard to realize that someone staring admiringly into your eyes could be a jerk. Now, me, if I can't "read" a guy, I can guess his intentions by the fact that his admiring gaze is falling about 10 inches below where it should be. That was one advantage – probably the only advantage – of having big boobs.

But, right now, I had to deal with the problem at hand. It had been about ten seconds and already the tall one put his arm around my shoulder – even though I hadn't indicated that would be in any way welcome. Truth be told, I was a little afraid of these guys.

"Jeepers creepers, Kim! Look at the time! We've gotta go." Damn. That was probably the worst acting job of the century. Could I possibly have been any more exaggerated when I looked at my watch?

I grabbed Kim by the sleeve and started pulling her off her barstool. She pouted in protest, but reluctantly complied. She trusted my judgment even if she wasn't always happy about it. She knew "jeepers creepers" was my code for "these guys are creeps."

"Aw, cutie, what's your hurry? We were just getting acquainted." The short one spoke in a drunken slur.

"Sorry, but we are really, really, really late." I barely bothered turning my head over my shoulder to shout my reply. I dragged Kim through the crowd. I hated bars. Too loud. Too crowded. Way too many jerks. The only reason we came was to hear the band. I breathed easier once we made it out the door.

Kim shook herself loose of my grip and grumbled in protest. "Honestly Rae, aren't there *any* guys you think are okay?"

"Sure. Not all guys are jerks. Unfortunately, the ones that are appear to hold their jerk conventions in bars on Friday nights. C'mon. Step up the pace."

"Why? Are we really running that late?" Her tone was more than a tad sarcastic.

Kim had come to a dead stop. I glanced back at her and saw, to my horror, the jerks coming out the bar. "Yes, we are. Those two are following us." I spit out between clenched teeth.

Kim immediately started into a trot, now looking as worried as me. I pulled my keys out of my pocket and hit the panic button. Nothing. We were too far away. Damn! Why did I leave my purse in the trunk? My mace was in my purse. I instinctively started arranging my keys between each knuckle like spikes – as if that would actually do any good. At 5'3", I wasn't exactly a powerhouse. And while Kim's lanky figure was the picture of perfection, she wasn't muscular at all. She deplored the gym and anything remotely connected to exercise.

"Ladies, ladies, why you hurrying off? Maybe we can give you a lift, huh?" The guys were hurrying our way.

I barely turned my head to reply. "Don't need a ride. Thanks anyway. Bye!" That sounded pretty good. I figured if we didn't show fear, we wouldn't force their hand.

The "Bye!" didn't insert the finality I had hoped for. The guys had nearly reached us. Stupid, stupid high heels! What idiot in the fashion world designed shoes to attract attackers rather than get away from them?

"Why in such a hurry, sweet cheeks?" The slurrer grabbed Kim's shoulders, forcing her to a halt. One of his hands dropped to her butt and gave it a lurid squeeze.

"Sis! Hey, Sis!" A total stranger was leaving the bar and half-jogging toward us. I was completely caught off guard. The two guys looked equally surprised – and pissed.

"Hey, you weren't going to leave without saying goodbye, were you?" The stranger caught up with us, slipping his arm protectively around the totally confused Kim's waist and steering her toward me.

I recovered and flashed our rescuer a warm smile. "Hey, sorry. We were running so late, we just didn't have time to look for you."

"Well, at least let me walk you to your car. I'm not interrupting anything, am I?" The stranger smoothly maneuvered his other arm around my waist, gliding us both away.

"Not at all." Kim took my lead in playing along. Finally, the two goons gave up and turned back toward the bar.

"Where are you parked?" The rather attractive stranger released us from his arms.

"The end of the street. Thanks for the escort." Damn. That came out a little more breathy than I intended.

"How'd you know we needed help?" Kim was trying to grasp the situation.

"I saw your friend dragging you out with a worried look on her face. Then I saw those two guys trailing behind and I got bad vibes off them."

"Bad vibes?" Kim got excited. "You sound like Rae! Do you pick up on vibes a lot?"

"Sort of."

"Do you rescue many damsels in distress?" I couldn't help but notice that our gallant protector had not once stared at my boobs.

"I think you may be my very first damsels." He flashed an incredibly charming smile.

I liked this guy better by the second. Caring. Charming. Brave. Definitely brave. Mid-size, he would have been no match for those two creeps if things hadn't gone smoothly. I'm pretty sure he was well aware of that fact, since his rather aggressive pace never slowed. We reached my car in no time.

"We were going to go grab a bite. Can I treat you to a burger or something?" I returned his smile, but I think I batted my eyes in the process. I stared down at the asphalt, totally mortified.

"By golly, that would be great. I'm starved. I'm broke. And I'm worried Boris and Igor might try to follow you."

"Do you know the Towne?" Everyone knew the Towne, but our intriguing rescuer didn't sound like a native. Rather than the harsh Buffalo, NY, twang, his voice had more of Midwestern lilt.

"Love the Towne!" Again with that smile. It was melting me. "I'm parked just a block away. I'll meet you there." He disappeared around the corner and I think I breathed for the first time in minutes.

Chapter 2

"I can't believe what just happened." Kim was still sort of hyperventilating as I turned on the car.

"Well, it's over now, so try to relax."

Kim put her hand on her chest, closed her eyes and took a couple slow, deep breaths. Then she turned on me with a fury.

"And *you*! I can't believe *you*! Ms. Safety Queen who's constantly harping about being careful and not trusting anyone...and you know this guy for thirty seconds and you're asking him out?!"

Okay, she had me there. I could feel the blood rising to my face. "It's not like I asked him 'out' out... I'm just repaying him for saving our butts."

"You think he's hot." Kim knew me all too well.

"Sooo...?"

"Sooo...you're not following your own rules. You're not being cautious. You're ignoring warning signs."

"What warning signs?"

"Well...being broke isn't exactly a good sign."

I had to admit, that bothered me a bit, too. And I hated that it did. I didn't consider myself materialistic. "Maybe he's broke 'cause he's paying his mother's hospital bills. He seems like the kind of guy who would do that." I couldn't believe I was wishing a sick mother on the poor guy.

Kim wracked her brain for more ammunition. "He was hanging out at a bar. You don't trust guys who hang out at bars."

"Maybe he doesn't always hang out at bars. I mean, we were there and we don't hang out at bars."

Kim sat quietly for a minute, thinking hard. I was falling into one of the traps I constantly lectured her about. She was not going to let this go.

"You know," she contemplated, "this would have been the perfect set up. Have two guys scare the girls, then the brave, gallant hero comes to the rescue. It would work every time."

I swelled with a combination of pride and disbelief at my own achievement. "Kimmy, I've succeeded! That is a brilliantly suspicious thought. You may now distrust men as much as I do."

"No one distrusts men as much as you do. But, I guess it's pretty easy to be suspicious when you're not the one involved," Kim smirked. "Shoe's on the other foot now, Raedar."

Hmm. Could Kim be right? Was my instant infatuation clouding my better judgment? No. That couldn't be it. I trusted the guy because he was wonderful. I could see it in his eyes. I could feel it in my bones.

"I just have good vibes about this guy."

She gave me her "reality check" look

"It's not like I go around having good feelings about guys all the time."

"I'll give you that. I can't remember you ever having good feelings about any guy for yourself." Kim sat quietly for awhile and then she started laughing hysterically.

"What?"

"It's just so funny to see you finally getting all hot and bothered." She started to snort the way she always did when she laughed really hard. "Thanks for the escort," she exaggerated my too-breathy delivery. "Are we your first damsels?" She batted her eyes profusely.

My cheeks were getting hotter by the minute.

"It's going to be fun watching you make your moves. I had no idea you were so..." she searched for the right word, "aggressive." Now she was laughing so hard she was crying as well as snorting.

I gripped the steering wheel harder. I had no idea I was so aggressive either. I can't believe I just flat out asked this guy to join us. And Kimmy was right. I had never been truly attracted to a guy. Sure, over the years there'd been a couple I'd wished would ask me out. But, I'd never felt this total, immediate, overwhelming attraction. And I felt like I had no control over my brain or my ridiculous batting eyelashes – and who knew what else I'd have no control over?

Funny, I could predict other people's reactions, but not my own. Though, I felt safe in predicting that I wasn't going to find this situation nearly as amusing as Kim was sure to.

Chapter 3

When we got to the Towne, our charming savior was standing by the door waiting for us. It was the perfect situation to get a good look at him. He was standing in the light, but we were walking through the dark – so he couldn't see me giving him the once-over.

He was even cuter than I'd thought: slightly wavy, tousled, dirty-blonde hair; a shy, little-boy smile that created a dimple on his left cheek; bright blue eyes that had a sort of twinkle to them –eyes that couldn't hide anything. You could tell he was genuinely glad to see us.

"Hey, damsels, I was starting to worry you ditched me."

"I've got this giant, old boat of a car. It takes me forever to find a spot big enough to park it." I hated that car and its gas-guzzling ways. I'd had a sort of strange obsession with ecology and climate change for as long as I could remember. Since childhood. I think since even before I could use words. Certainly long before anyone ever used the term "global warming."

But, the car was the only thing I could find in my price range that wasn't literally held together by duct tape. I rationalized the purchase knowing someone, somewhere would be driving the thing if I wasn't – and I substituted more eco-friendly transportation as often as I could.

"By the way, I'm Rachel Shannon and this is your 'sister,' Kim Laskowski," I stuck out my hand as a matter of habit. At my job, I did a lot of public relations work. Lots of hand shaking and formal greetings. Not exactly appropriate for this occasion. I immediately felt like an idiot.

"I'm Jim Kirkwood." He shook my hand with a rather bemused expression. Even though I was embarrassed to death by my ridiculous formality, I got a huge thrill from touching his hand. It was warm and felt surprisingly strong, yet soft. I swear I felt some sort of electric current travel up my arm, making every nerve ending stand at attention.

Kim, bless her heart, stuck out her hand, too, so I didn't have to look like a dolt all by myself. "Nice to meet you, 'bro.' One of us must be adopted, though." Kim had long, almost black hair and a slightly olive complexion that made Jim seem pale in comparison.

"I must have all the recessive genes."

"Recessive jeans? I thought those were only for guys a lot younger than you" Kim joked.

Jim stared at her blankly. You really had to know Kim before you could get her jokes. Her sense of humor was a bit odd.

"The boys these days? They wear their jeans way down low…receding down their butts? It was a joke. You know, one of those forms of speech that make you laugh unless they have to be explained to you?"

"Sorry. I'm sure I would have found that absolutely hilarious if I hadn't just gotten off an 18-hour shift. I'm not too sharp right now."

So, he did have a job! I was hoping my elation at this news wasn't radiating all over my face. But, I kind of think it was. Out of the corner of my eye, I could see Jim studying me out of the corner of his eye. He had a perplexed look on his face.

"Eighteen hours! Is that even legal? What kind of job do you have?" Kimmy was really coming through for me, asking the key questions so I didn't have to look like I was probing.

"I'm a surgical intern at Buffalo General…which basically means I'm slave labor. But, they do give us a cot, so we can catch a few winks when things are slow."

Okay, this was totally humiliating. Kim was giving me the "ooo he's a doctor" look. She could barely contain herself. I tried hiding behind my menu, but I could feel her eyes burning through it. And, of course, she was kicking my ankle under the table.

"Mrs. Laskowski always wanted a doctor in the family. As her new 'son, you'll be making her a very happy woman." I spoke with all the nonchalance I could muster as I folded my menu. "Where do you get the energy to go out after an 18 hour shift?"

"Spot Coffee." He smiled. "But it's just barely working. If it weren't for the promise of food, I'd be flat on my face by now. I'm not a late-night kind of person."

"So you're not a regular at McGee's?" Good ol' Kim was still filling in all the background info for me.

"By golly, no. Never been there before. It was one of the nurses' birthdays. I just stopped by to be sociable."

"We don't get out much either. Rachel works with one of the guys in the band, so we just dropped in to listen." Kim, I knew, felt it necessary to establish that we were not barflies either.

"The band was awesome! Which one was your friend?"

"David Moore...the one in the kilt." Jackdaw was a Celtic rock band, so the kilt wasn't as weird as it sounds. And he had great legs, so showing them off certainly wouldn't hurt the band's popularity. "He's really talented. A gifted art director by day, an equally gifted musician by night."

"Wow. Most people are lucky to do one thing well. Must be amazing to have two talents."

I could see Jim's eyes get a distant look. I knew he was imagining himself with two talents. I wondered what they might be, those talents he secretly desired? Surgeon and composer? Poet and drummer?

Who was I kidding? Intriguing as I found him, Jim was still a guy. Probably wished he was quarterback and a rockstar. I wouldn't shatter his dream by bringing up the realities of the multitalented. I mean, life is short. Very few could achieve greatness in two different pursuits. One or both would always be shortchanged...always suffering from whatever time you devoted to the other. It would be a maddening dilemma.

Of course, that was one dilemma I'd never have to deal with. Near as I could tell, I had no natural talent. So…what skill set was I supposed to pursue when nothing seemed to be rising to the forefront? The only talent I had, if you could call it that, was this weird sort of intuition. But, how do you build a career around intuition?

I thought the only obvious venues for exploiting that particular talent would be customs agent or airport security or something like that. And I just couldn't imagine myself doing any of those things. So, I was fumbling around trying to develop some sort of competency at marketing and public relations. But, most days, I felt like an imposter. An inexperienced kid pretending to be a professional.

"You look like you're pondering some deep life issue." Jim's comment brought me back to the moment.

"Actually, I was. I was thinking how I have not one, not two, but absolutely no talents." The smile in my voice was designed to deflect that sad reality.

"C'mon…you have at least two talents."

Oh no. Was this going to lead to a boob reference? Not when the night was going so well! I cringed internally.

"From what Kim's been telling me, you're a very good judge of character. And from what I've observed so far, I'd say you're durn good at interpersonal communications."

I wondered if he could see the wave of relief that swept through me. "Those aren't talents. At best, they're…traits."

"Traits, talents, same thing. And those are worth their weight in gold. My fiancée is brilliant. Top student in med school. But, she doesn't have any natural people skills. So, brilliant as she is, she pretty much sucks as a clinician."

"Wow. That's so sad for your fiancée." No wonder he never looked at my boobs. He was spoken for! I'd never gone from such a high to such a low so fast. Fortunately, if Jim picked up on my devastation, he could chalk it up to sympathy for his girlfriend's dilemma.

"Hey, don't worry your little head over Kiku. She's going into medical research. Lots of science. Very little patient contact. She loves it. And she'll probably save more lives than she would as a general practitioner."

"Kiku. That's an interesting name. Is your fiancée from abroad?" Kim was quick to take up the ball conversation-wise. She knew I could barely put a sentence together when I was feeling low.

"Isn't everyone?"

Kim stared at Jim blankly, but after years of Kim-speak, I knew where he was going. He was hiding the slightest smile that confirmed it for me. It was enough to bring me ever-so-slightly out of my bad mood. Though, it made me long to get to know this Jim Kirkwood even more.

"Aren't we all from a broad? You know…a woman who bore us? It's a joke. One of those forms of speech that make you laugh unless you have to explain them?" Wow. The fact that he picked up so perfectly on Kim's peculiar sense of humor was amazing.

"Oh." Kim was clearly dumbfounded by the first person ever to mirror her bizarre form of humor back at her.

"I thought after the recessive jeans crack, you'd find that one to be a knee slapper."

"I guess the fun's in making them up. Or maybe it's in the groan. Sorry. Next time I promise to groan."

"Maybe I'm not very good at it. Rachel groaned at yours, but not at mine."

"I was too busy being amazed that I had another Kim on my hands. Two at the same table. It's more than any one person should be expected to bear."

We all ordered chicken souvlaki and I somehow managed to muddle through the rest of the evening with some sense of pleasantness. But it wasn't easy.

It turned out that Jim's fiancée had immigrated to New York City from Japan when she was a little girl. How was anyone supposed to compete with that? Not only a brilliant doctor, but an Asian chick! What was it with American guys and Asian chicks? The men seemed to find them mysteriously alluring. I don't think the women were doing anything to cause it. It all had to do with the men. Granted, I didn't know if Jim fell into that stereotypical fascination with Asian women...but, it certainly helped to cement my new view that I did not stand a chance with this guy.

"I think it's time I got Rae home. Masochist that she is, she has a 7 a.m. Pilates class." Kim knew I was dejected and ready to leave.

We all got up to go, but ever "on the job," I remembered to add Jim to my contact list. In public relations, every acquaintance might be helpful in some way at some point.

"Can I get your contact info? I like to keep track of all the people who save my butt."

Kim rolled her eyes. "Beware of Rachel's list. You'll get roped into handing out water at charity marathons."

"I happen to be an experienced water-hander-outer..." Jim's easy smile disappeared as he stopped dead in his tracks. His mouth dropped open and his eyes fixed on the cover of the notebook I had just fished out of my purse.

Kim and I stared in confusion. Jim had the weirdest look on his face. It was a cross between shock, worry, fright...a whole range of emotions. Then he pulled a little memo pad out of his back pocket. There, scrawled across the cover of his memo pad, were the exact same doodles I had drawn on the cover of my notebook. Weird symbols that looked like hieroglyphics and equations. Jim and I dropped back into our seats, staring at each other.

Jim was the first to speak. And he did so cautiously. "Those...doodles...are yours?"

"Yeah."

"I think we need to talk."

Chapter 4

We were both too tired to have what was sure to be a long conversation that night. And we both had packed schedules. We arranged to get together the next weekend. That would give us a chance to come to grips with this new reality. To decide how much we dared to share with one another.

Kim went berserk in the car. She had no idea what was going on. This was a part of myself I kept secret even from her, my best friend, with whom I shared every other thought, emotion or event in my life. I had nearly confided in her hundreds of times, but this, this was just too weird to share.

No one knew. Not my parents, not my siblings. No one.

I was afraid people would think I was insane. Heck, *I* thought there was a chance I might be insane. I even asked my doctor if she thought I could be mentally ill. She assured me I was not...but then, I didn't tell her *why* I thought I might be insane.

I could tell Kim was deeply hurt that I had a secret I was keeping from her. But, I still couldn't tell her about it. I don't know how to explain it. It was too big. Too incomprehensible.

If I was crazy, I didn't want anyone to know. And if I wasn't crazy – and I really didn't think I was – I worried that having knowledge of those symbols could be dangerous. (Of course, I worry that everything is dangerous. I am a self-admitted safety nutcase. But, hey – just because you think every last little thing is hazardous, doesn't mean that it's not.)

I minimized our bizarre encounter as much as I could. "Of course I never told you about my doodles. What's to tell? I have this weird image that sticks in my head sometimes. I never thought much of it." I was, of course, lying through my teeth. To my best friend. Something I never would have thought myself capable of.

"But...when Jim had the same doodles...at that moment I realized this stupid, insignificant picture in my head might be something more than I thought it was." We sat in silence for a minute. "Kim, could you do me a huge favor?"

"Sure, what?"

"Never, ever tell *anyone* about the doodles?"

"Um...yeah...sure."

I could tell she thought that was a really weird request. But, then she brought up a whole other issue. "Do you think your attraction to Jim has something to do with the fact that you have identical doodles?"

I had been thinking that same thing. "It is strange that the first time I'm really, truly attracted to guy in anything more than a superficial way...that he turns out to have the same weird image in his head."

"Then, maybe he's attracted to you, too!" Kim was ever the optimist.

"I don't think so. I wasn't getting any attraction vibe off him. I mean, I thought he liked the both of us...in a 'friends' kind of way. But attraction, no. I think he's so committed to his fiancée that his thoughts don't even stray in another direction."

"Well...he's not married *yet*. And you *are* going to see him again. If you're still hot for him, you could let him know how you feel."

That was a dilemma. Do I make some sort of play for him? It didn't feel right to go after someone else's guy. But, I had never, ever, not once felt this way about anyone before.

"I don't know. I'm sure, no matter what my head tells me to do, that I'll end up being a puppet to some unconscious instinct. I mean, trust me, I certainly didn't choose to bat my eyes tonight."

We both broke into giggles at the memory of my shameless, uncharacteristic flirting.

"Kiku is probably some cute little thing that I don't stand a chance against anyway. I mean, a doctor doesn't want to be dragging around a wife with hooker boobs."

"You do *not* have hooker boobs! Hooker boobs hang out. You always keep yours neatly tucked away – completely hidden – under multiple layers. Really, Rae, you should loosen up a little…let those babies get some air now and then."

"Make the men drool like the dirty dogs that they are?"

"Exactly."

"I want them to drool over my mind. My personality. My sick jokes. Not my boobs."

And we both sat in silence the rest of the way home…wondering if there were any men who would ever care about the inner us.

Chapter 5

That week was the slowest week of my life. It dragged on and on. The days were spent second guessing myself. Rationalizing. Carefully planning exactly how much information I was willing to share. (Not much, it turns out.)

The nights were spent tossing and turning, my mind roiling with "what ifs" in a cauldron of conflicting emotions. Deep at the core of my being I knew that our shared vision was earth shatteringly important. That it was somehow tied up with something that would affect the future of the entire planet. I don't know how to explain it, but those symbols and the feelings about them were tied together. They came as a package. It wasn't like I saw the symbols and developed a feeling about them. I just knew they held a key to our survival and they must be shared with the world.

I also felt that the importance of those symbols put us in a position of danger. I was pretty sure that wariness was coming exclusively from me. But, I felt it was very rational to be afraid. Any knowledge crucial to earth's survival would give the possessor of that knowledge a great deal of power. And there was nothing powerful people wouldn't do to gain additional power.

Even though it seemed trivial in the face of earth-altering information, my personal future was at stake, too. That wasn't trivial to me. I was both living for seeing Jim again. And dreading it.

I gathered all the composure I could to prepare for our meeting. I threw on jeans and a baggie hoodie. To me, that definitely conveyed casual, disinterested, impersonal – the exact opposite of what I felt. And it had the dual advantage of minimizing the boobage. Even though it didn't appear that my chest was going to be an issue around Jim, *I* felt more comfortable when the ta-ta's were less noticeable.

We had agreed to meet at Chestnut Ridge Park. A bit of a drive for Jim, but we'd have lots of privacy there this time of year. And the casino – a big old lodge – was available in case it rained or got too cold.

As it was, we had no need to escape the weather. It was a perfect late September day. The air had a crisp coolness to it, but the sun shining on my brown hair kept me wonderfully warm. We didn't enjoy an overabundance of such glorious, cloudless days in Buffalo. It was exactly the kind of day you wouldn't want to waste inside.

Jim and I met at the casino as planned. When I first spotted him, I swear my heart jumped. He was exactly as I remembered: cute, though not achingly handsome. He radiated a warmth and genuineness that just had to make you smile. He was just as casually dressed as I, but I doubted he spent time and energy agonizing over *his* wardrobe choices.

Jim smiled, flashing that dimple that melted me. "Hey, there, damsel. This place is awesome."

Chestnut Ridge Park was set on the first ring of hills surrounding the flat, flat city. From the casino, you could see over the woods to the suburbs, to Lake Erie and the city. The view was spectacular. On a really clear day, you could see some of the Toronto skyline in the distance.

When I was in high school, my friends and I would pack coolers and spend all day picnicking here. But, that was slightly before every high schooler had a cell phone and Internet access. These days – at least in the fall – the park was largely empty except for big, planned picnic events and the ever-present joggers.

I took a deep breath of appreciation. It was a shame, really, that so few people were enjoying this wonderful place on such a glorious day.

"So, this is the casino?"

"Mmm-hhm."

"You had me worried. I thought you might be dragging me to some gaudy gambling den, not a grand, rustic lodge." He looked like he actually did think that.

"Around here, most of the park lodges are called casinos. Probably what they called 'em in the era they were built. I think this park was a WPA project…you know, 'The New Deal.' That was back when the government actually got something worthwhile for the money it spent. Funny…how the Depression was such a terrible thing, yet here's something good that came out of it…still providing a benefit seventy years later. It seems like everything bad has some good to it and everything good has some bad to it."

"So…do you think our…vision…is good or bad?"

"I think it's *about* something good. It feels…important. And it scares me."

Jim sighed. "I guess we should get down to business, kiddo."

We walked to an out-of-the-way picnic table where we'd have total privacy and got down to work. Both of us brought our notebooks…pages and pages of images scribbled like notes taken from blackboards embedded deep inside our heads

We spent a good hour pouring over each other's scribbles. It was perfectly clear that we were both seeing the same images in the same sequence…but, there were a lot of blank spots. We filled a few of those in for each other, but there were still plenty left. We agreed the images looked like they could be mathematic or scientific formulas – at least large parts of them. But, they were written in unfamiliar symbols that had no resemblance to any numbers or language on earth – we'd both done the research over the years and couldn't find anything that even remotely matched.

Once we got through the details it was time for the bigger issues. The issues we'd been avoiding. Jim broke the ice.

"Soooo…have you ever told anyone about this?"

"Not a soul. I'm assuming, since you don't appear to have been institutionalized, that you haven't either?"

"Nope. Not even Kiku…though, I've wanted to." Jim looked off into the distance.

"Where do you think…all this…is coming from?" I wondered if his theory matched mine.

"Well, my most promising theory used to be that I had some one-of-a-kind obsessive-compulsive disorder. But, you've sort of shot that theory to hell. I've been going through alternate theories all week. I think the ones that hold the most promise are that we're part of some government experiment with images implanted in the hospital at birth…or are brains are somehow able to pick up encrypted signals scientists are sending to each other."

"Those theories sound… rational…"

"Why is there a big 'but' in you tone…doesn't it make sense to assume the most reasonable answer is probably the right answer?"

"Maybe that's a good approach in medicine…but, we're not exactly dealing with a reasonable problem. Don't you have any…feelings…any gut sense…any intuition about this?"

"Uh…no." Jim shrugged. I looked at him, exasperated. How could men be so out of touch?

"But, if I did have a feeling…why would I give that any credence? Logic trumps feelings when it comes to…science. Wouldn't you have to say this falls into the science category?"

"Science fiction might be more like it. But, intuition isn't necessarily something separate from logic…it's complementary."

"I'm not following you. Intuition and logic are opposites." I could tell by the look on his face that he was dismissing me. Males! Start talking about feelings and they assume you are nuts.

"Let's take medicine for example. I'm guessing there are doctors who are excellent diagnosticians. And I'll bet some of them operate on a sort of intuition a lot of the time. All the symptoms might not necessarily line up exactly right, but they get a feeling that a certain diagnosis is the way to go. That intuition may not be a magical thing…it's probably based on cues so subtle that they can't identify them with their conscious minds."

"So, you're defining intuition as an internal logic you just can't put your finger on…well, that makes some sense."

"Good. Because I have a…feeling…as to what it's all about. A very strong feeling."

"Well, don't keep me here on my tiptoes chokin' on the rope…let's hear it!"

"'On my tiptoes chokin' on the rope?' Are you from some cowboy era? You have the most….archaic…way of speaking. You make a ninety year old sound like a whippersnapper." I couldn't help myself. The "goshes" and "gollies," I let slide. But, this just stopped me in my tracks and cracked me up.

"Me? Archaic? Well, now, I'd say that's the tiger calling the zebra striped, Missy. WPA…New Deal…you're beyond archaic…you're…encyclopedic! Who under sixty talks like that?"

We both admitted to being a little quirky. Apparently he was raised by New Age, tree-hugging parents who practiced a near-subsistence lifestyle on a farm in Wisconsin. They had no video games or cable TV. His relaxation time on long winter nights was spent watching old movies on whatever local stations their ancient, analog TV could pick up on its rabbit ears. (Okay, if you've never had to sit through your parents' olden days stories, rabbit ears were little portable antennas that sat on top of TVs to pick up the signal…and you usually had to adjust them for every station and sometimes put aluminum foil on them! Technology has come a long way in the last 40 years.)

Apparently his parents also had a treasure trove of VCR tapes featuring vintage TV shows…everything from "Gunsmoke" to "Leave It To Beaver"…whatever those were.

My story was surprisingly similar at its core. I stopped watching regular TV at about the time I entered high school. I guess I just didn't like having to center my entertainment around someone else's schedule (back in those days, there was no TiVo at our house…if it even existed then). I am a bit of a movie fanatic (only good ones, I'm picky about everything – especially stuff that steals my time.) But, even more than movies, I turned to reading. Fiction. Non-fiction. History. Science. Books. Magazines. I read anything and everything. It was something that always worked according to my schedule and my mood. That may have left me a bit 'encyclopedic.'

Finally, Jim forced me to stop stalling and tell him my theory. It was difficult, exposing my weird assumptions to the light of day. Even though Jim shared the same underlying vision, it seemed I had more stuff attached to it than he did. And with something this bizarre, you just didn't spill it out willy-nilly. With something this unusual, you never knew what might happen…you could be shipped off to an asylum…hauled away by the government…who knew what else?

Since Jim didn't seem to feel some of the other stuff attached to the vision, I couldn't just blurt out what I thought it was. I had to prepare him with a framework that would help him accept the new reality I was proposing.

The first thing to do was to shoot down his theories. "Where were you born?"

"Wisconsin, why?"

"Just a plausibility check on your theories. What kind of hospital?"

"A county hospital."

"Okay. I was born in Pennsylvania in a Catholic hospital in '84. What year were you born in?"

"1982.'

"Do you have any siblings?"

"Yes."

"Do they share the vision?"

"No."

"Same here. Doesn't exactly seem to support your government-implanted image theory…two different kinds of hospitals in different parts of the country at different times…other births not affected."

"Doesn't rule it out, but I get your point."

"The encrypted signal interception…don't you think the encryption seems weak? I mean, you and I aren't experts, but we agree these appear to be formulas. Doesn't it seem like the sender is trying to make the formulas easy to figure out? The entire first section feels like a math primer with all that methodical repetition."

"I hate to admit it, but it does feel like whoever is sending these wants me to figure out what they mean." So, he did have some *feelings* about these…Glyphs.

"I feel *obsessed* with these images. Judging by your notebook, so do you. I don't think we've chosen to be obsessed…I'd be happier to forget about them. I think some…entity…has somehow…" I had to choose my words carefully so as not to put him in instant denial, "imprinted this feeling of obsession on us."

He rolled his eyes. "I think you've read a little too much science fiction. People can't imprint obsessions onto other people from some remote location." He crossed his arms and looked totally exasperated with me.

I figured, as long as he was being so completely resistant to ideas outside the mainstream. (Which was really, quite frankly, stupid of him. I mean, the fact that we both shared this vision was so completely out of the mainstream, you'd think he'd be a bit more receptive), I'd just go ahead and lay out all the whacky details.

"Maybe *people* can't imprint obsessions. But, who said we're talking about people?"

He got up and started pacing. It looked like he suddenly felt caged in a place he did not want to be. And that place was with me.

"Now, you're definitely going off the deep end. The simplest, most likely explanation is almost always the correct explanation. What...do you think some space aliens have flown around planting images in our brains like 'Close Encounters of the Third Kind?'?"

"No. I don't think space aliens are flying around implanting images in our brains. But I think whoever came up with the storyline for 'Close Encounters of the Third Kind' probably has a notebook exactly like yours and mine."

That stopped his pacing. He obviously hadn't considered that there might be more of us. But, then again, he hadn't given the problem 24 years of intense scrutiny like I had. Until a week ago, he was writing this all off as an obsessive-compulsive disorder.

"Interesting, don't you think, that someone came up with a premise like an image – and an obsession with that image –being planted in someone's brain? Hmmm...I think you or I could come up with that premise pretty easily."

Jim sat back down, leaning his back against the picnic table, his hands up holding his head as if it might spiral away from his body if he let go.

"You're right. There should be others. I mean, why would it just be the two of us? There's nothing that connects us. We're just two random people. The odds of us finding each other if we were the only ones would be astronomical. There must be others."

I could tell that Jim had a very strong intuitive side. But, for some reason, he chose to suppress it. I was too trusting of my instincts for his taste. He wouldn't buy into my conclusions for a minute. Even if I felt, in every fiber of my being, that they were correct.

It would be waste of time to try to explain the rest of my theory to Jim at that point. I might totally scare him off. Who knows, he might even have me committed. I wondered if a med student had that power. Better if we focused on finding the others – since we now both realized that there must be others.

That would be our next step: to find the rest of us.

Chapter 6

I turned my cell phone off while I was meeting with Jim. I didn't want to be interrupted. I turn my cell phone off a lot. It drives people crazy, but I don't feel obligated to be available to the rest of the world every second of the day.

I had three messages from Kim. She was dying to hear how things went with Jim. That was going to be tough to explain. Once we got started talking about the symbols – we decided to call them the Glyphs– it was like the rest of the world melted away. I was so obsessed, I couldn't focus on anything beyond solving the puzzle of the Glyphs. Even my attraction to Jim sank into the background.

It wasn't until we said our goodbyes that the time spent so close to Jim had an effect on me. My heart started racing. I felt weak in the knees. I spent about ten minutes composing myself before I felt I could even drive home.

I called Kim and let her know that there were no new developments. I was still attracted to Jim. He was still not attracted to me. I was glad I was telling her this over the phone rather than in person. It allowed me to hide the emotional toll it was taking on me. It was weird…the emotional rollercoaster I was riding was *physically* exhausting. In the end, I had to go for an ice cream sundae to calm my nerves. You know things are stressful when you have to go for the full sundae.

Chapter 7

When I get back to my apartment, neither of my two roommates was home. Perfect. I'd have some quiet time to plan our next steps. I loved sitting alone in the apartment. It was a typical South Buffalo flat. High ceilings. Hardwood everywhere. Lots and lots of windows. An enclosed sun porch in the back and a big, open balcony on the front. We had an upper and the autumn sun was shining in, casting everything in a warm, golden glow. The beveled glass on the front windows projected dozens of little rainbows around the room.

We moved in about six months ago. It was my first apartment ever. Even though the apartment itself was lovely, it was in a non-trendy section (yes, there are trendy sections of Buffalo), so rent was relatively low. About $350 a month from each of us covered rent and utilities. (I was guessing it would be at least another $50 each when the furnace kicked on for the winter.)

The neighborhood was relatively safe, but it was slipping. I was glad we had the second floor. That way we could leave the windows open at night. Far as I knew, no one bothered with second-story crime in this neighborhood. No one would have anything valuable enough to make it worth the climb.

I sat down to work on a plan for our Glyphs project. Finding others who might share our "vision" was a tough assignment. How do you find people without being found out? I believed that knowledge of the Glyphs might put us in danger. Jim believed he'd be labeled a nut and thrown out of medical school. But, if we didn't want to call attention to ourselves, how were we going to call attention to the Glyphs?

With my advertising and public relations background, I thought this would be a piece of cake. But once I got into it, I realized how difficult it would be to get publicity while protecting our privacy. It was such a difficult project, I started foraging for food. Fortunately, my roommates and I didn't keep any junk food in the apartment. But, my quest for carbs did turn up half a box of Melba toast. I'd have to settle for that.

Chapter 8

I spent all Saturday night and most of Sunday trying to devise a plan. I wasn't totally happy with what I'd come up with, but I didn't feel like I was going to think up anything better.

The only way to reach a mass audience with no budget and complete anonymity was through the Web. I figured we could put a couple of our Glyphs on a website with the line, "Do you see what I see?"

Those who could input another of the symbols would be directed to a private message board. People who input an incorrect symbol would be directed to a page that looked like an ad. That way, only people who could "see" the Glyphs would know we were looking for "Seers." Everyone else would just think it was an ordinary, commercial website.

The problem was, I had no idea how to program it – nor how to maintain anonymity. Maybe Jim would have some thoughts. I called and left a message on his cell: "I have an idea for a website. How are your programming skills?"

He called me back Monday and we arranged to meet after work on Wednesday. I could tell he shared at least one feeling with me: paranoia. Our phone conversation was short and cryptic. I met him at the marina and we grabbed a nice, private bench.

He thought my idea was perfect and said his brother could handle the programming.

"I don't like the idea of bringing in your bother. We don't know what we're getting into. There is the chance…well…this could be dangerous."

"Don't worry. I'm not going to put Pete at risk. The only information I gave him is that we're looking for people who know the symbols. He knows he has to be careful. And that's all he knows. He's a bit of an underground nut. Ever since W got elected, he's gone out of his way to stay off the grid. Some of his friends hang out with hackers. He says he's got ways to keep things on the Q.T."

"Did he really say "Q.T."? That sounds a bit anachronistic."

"And 'anachronistic' sounds a bit encyclopedic."

"Touché"

"Oooo...you speak French?"

Did I detect just the faintest glimmer of flirt in his teasing? If it was there, it disappeared immediately and he got back to business. "My brother knows some guys who know some guys who can get fake electronic identities. With those we can set up bank accounts, PayPal accounts, domains...whatever we need. He can get us the identities pretty cheap.

"How cheap is cheap?" It wasn't like I had an excess of cash. And, as I recalled, neither did Jim.

"Under a hundred bucks for two -- and Pete's agreed to do the programming for free. He loves this kind of stuff – and the fact that it's undercover just gets him all the more jazzed. Getting money into the bank account is going to be the trickiest part. If anyone does look for us, they can find us when we make a deposit. I think we should put in as much as we can up front, so we won't need to make a deposit again."

We each put $250 in the account. That would be enough to finance the website for a couple years. We each bought a pay-as-you-go phone for exclusive "Glyphs" use and agreed not to contact each other on any other phone ever again. I made him promise that anything he did in connection with this would be totally anonymous. For instance, I made him promise his phone purchase would be made in cash, in disguise, without a car so that no video camera in the parking lot could be used to trace his identity.

"You know, you're sounding almost as paranoid as Pete."

"Haven't I told you about Rachel's First Law of Paranoia? Just because you think everyone is out to get you, doesn't mean they're not."

"Pete will like that one. I should get the two of you together." Hmmm. I wondered if Pete might have the same effect on me as Jim. Probably not a good idea to find out. One paranoid nutcase in a relationship is more than enough.

"He'll probably love my First Law of Peril."

"What's that?"

"Rachel's First Law of Peril: No matter how many precautions you take, something you could never anticipate will bring you down."

Jim frowned. "So you don't think our plan is failsafe?"

"I don't think a single thing on God's green earth is failsafe."

We sat for a few minutes in silence, lost in the worry of how true that was.

Chapter 9

I didn't see Jim much for quite awhile after that. I wrote the website and came up with a basic design Pete could follow. Jim drew out all the Glyphs, put that together with my files on a disk and snail-mailed it to Pete.

I was pretty proud of the domain name I came up with. First, it's crazy hard to even find a good domain name that's available. At least, it is if you want a "dot com" ending. And I felt we definitely needed to a "dot com" so the site looked commercial.

The name I picked was "CussedEmOuterwear.com." It was perfect. The symbols we were putting up looked a little like the way you'd type a swear word in a cartoon. We were even offering a free download you could use to make a t-shirt transfer. The whole thing could look like a totally legit commercial enterprise...at least until anyone figured out there were no Cussed Em Outerwear products or store.

The t-shirt transfer download featured some Glyphs. Under that it said, "Do you see what I see?" and under that, the web address. If we were lucky, the bizarreness of the message would strike a chord, kids would make some t-shirts, and we'd get our message out to an even broader audience.

It took over a month for Pete to do the programming. Inventing a way for site visitors to "draw" their symbol and coming up with a character reader to identify the symbols was a real challenge for him.

That downtime gave me a chance to figure out how I felt about Jim. Honestly, when we were working on this, I was so focused that I was like an automaton, completely immune to Jim's charms. I thought that maybe I was over him.

But, the days of waiting for Pete to finish the programming gave me time to breathe. And the same feelings were definitely there. I needed to find a way to shake them. Jim had talked frequently about Kiku and it was obvious that he was devoted to her.

I didn't get to meet Kiku because she was in New York City on her own internship. Jim visited her in New York, but she never came to Buffalo. Jim talked about her brilliance regularly. It didn't bother me at first, but I gradually came to find Kiku's amazingness rather annoying.

Jealousy was a new emotion for me. I didn't like it. It appeared to make me very cynical. I was finding Kiku to be pushy, selfish and cold. And I'd never even met her.

Finally, Pete finished the website. I had a computer, but being completely paranoid, I needed one that was untraceable. I drove across the Peace Bridge to Canada and bought the cheapest laptop I could find. (Of course, in disguise with my frickin' car parked blocks away. Can't be too careful, even in another country.) I threw away the box, slid the computer under the front seat and stuffed the instructions in the glove compartment. I wasn't even going to declare this baby. (Sooo unlike me. I follow every rule, always.)

I shipped the computer to Pete and he loaded the website programming and some anonymizer software onto it and shipped it back to me. I drove around looking for a Wi-Fi signal. I picked an upscale neighborhood, so it wasn't very difficult. The anonymizer software would let me surf the Web without anyone being able to trace it back to me. I figured, even if someone did take the trouble (and I understand it would mean obtaining warrants in multiple countries) to trace things back to my computer, they'd still have no idea who owned the computer. I didn't even mail in the warranty card. (Also very unlike me.)

I opened a PayPal account using the fake identity that Pete had purchased for us. Amazingly, it all went through smoothly. PayPal's computers couldn't see my flip-flopping stomach. I don't know why I was so nervous. What I was doing was deceptive, but I didn't think it was illegal. (Though, I could be wrong about that. I didn't check it out because I didn't want to know.) And it's not like I was going to cheat anyone out of any money.

I was doing most of the work even though Jim and I were supposed to be partners. But, no matter how many millions of hours I worked at my real job, it always seemed Jim put in even more hours at the hospital. And, honestly, I don't think Jim was quite as obsessed with the Glyphs as I was. Probably because he had no feeling for how big the consequences were. And I did. Or, at least, I thought I did. I didn't have any proof. Just that feeling. And so far in life, my feelings never proved to be wrong.

Once the financial stuff was in place, it was amazingly easy to purchase our domain name and web hosting service. Pete gave me explicit instruction on uploading the website, so even that wasn't too tough. Suddenly we were "out there." I'd never felt more hopeful – or more terrified – in my entire life.

Chapter 10

The responsibility of publicizing the site landed on my shoulders. I made a bunch of t-shirts from our download and gave them away at the University at Buffalo's (UB's) Student Union right before our website went live. UB had a huge population of international students and I tried to target them. (Though, deciding which students looked like they might be from abroad proved more difficult than I imagined. Apparently internationals have no problem assimilating quite nicely.)

I figured the t-shirts were one of the few ways I could reach an international audience – since I wasn't sure our website would be easily found in other countries. Of course, I wore huge sunglasses and bound my chest when I handed the T-shirts out. I was paranoid someone might recognize me and make the connection between the T's, the website, and me. Once the website went live the next day, I was never going to allow myself to be publicly associated with the Glyphs again.

I posted pictures of the t-shirt on flickr. I put a short video up on YouTube and a bunch of other video file sharing sites. And, of course, I made sure the Glyphs had their own pages on all the social networking sites.

Then, we waited.

I kind of hoped it would be awhile before our message boards really caught on. I had projects piled up to my ears at the ad agency where I worked.

My problem was, it took me three times longer than the more experienced copywriters to get my work done. How did those brilliant ideas fly out of their brains so quickly and consistently? I sat thinking for hours before I came up with anything good enough to present to my boss. I carried the same workload as everybody else…I just worked long into the night to get it all done.

Sometimes I worried that my employers would notice I was too slow and only marginally competent. To establish job security, I became extraordinarily attentive to detail. I even managed to catch several serious errors made by the more experienced staff members. It wasn't what I was hired to do, but I figured I'd at least earned my salary in the errors I helped the agency avert. Nobody was going to fire someone who saved their butt.

However, the time and attention I had been devoting to our website were definitely interfering with the quality of my work – and my quality of life. I wasn't getting enough sleep or exercise. I was grabbing whatever food was fast and easy. Kim, my family, and my other friends were starting to complain that they never got to see me. Worst of all, I really didn't have anyone to share my troubles with. The fleeting moments I had with Jim were mostly all business. I didn't tell another soul anything about the Glyphs. I wasn't used to shouldering such immense problems all by myself.

I didn't have much time to catch up at work because the week after the website went live, things really heated up.

Chapter 11

Our t-shirt transfer downloads became hugely popular. (Great...my first enormously successful ad campaign has to be one I can't put in my portfolio.) Aside from being a bit unusual, the download wasn't really all that exciting. I wondered if people might be attracted to it because deep in their subconscious, everyone saw the Glyphs – and just didn't realize it.

By the second week we were getting messages posted on our private boards. It appeared there were several different sections of Glyphs and that most people only "saw" one or two of them. Jim and I had been seeing the same two sections, but there were four more. At first, the Glyphs cyber community was fast and furious at filling in the blanks. By shortly after Thanksgiving, that pace was crawling to a halt. But, there were still plenty of blanks.

I put several questions up for a vote, with the community arriving at the following conclusions:

• The Glyphs we'd identified so far were accurate.

• The Glyphs had something to do with averting manmade climate change.

• The source of the vision came from somewhere within the "Horton Hears A Who" system.

Jim invited me to his place to discuss the results to date. He was going to NYC for the holidays and wouldn't be back for three weeks. I parked a couple blocks away. He answered the door on the first knock.

"Hey, you're right on time. Should I check your basement for pods?"

"Veeerrrry funny, Dr. Bennell...nice digs."

"An encyclopedic reference?"

"I don't think you can count movies as encyclopedic. Dr. Bennell was a character in the extremely old movie you just referred to – making your comment characteristically anachronistic."

I was surprised that his house truly was a house and not an apartment. Apparently, though poor, a med student has access to a considerable amount of credit. He owned his home. It was small, but cute and sparsely furnished in no discernable style. It looked like he picked up whatever was cheap, functional and comfortable.

"Patients don't like their physicians to live in hovels. Makes 'em nervous."

"Do I smell something wonderful?" I spied a table rather elegantly set for two. I didn't realize dinner was part of his plan. I mean, it was dinner time, but I didn't necessarily think that would have dawned on him. I guess I had to give him credit for better social etiquette than I'd imagined.

"You do smell something. Whether it's wonderful or not I can't predict. My cooking skills are…erratic."

"Erratic is better than nonexistent. You've got one up on me."

We had a very pleasant dinner, laughing and enjoying each other's company. The meal was delicious with the possible exception that it needed salt. I figured, being a doctor, Jim probably drastically reduced his salt intake. There wasn't even a shaker on the table. I could have really used some, but being polite (and fearing a lecture), I didn't ask for any.

Not only was dinner delicious, it was quite fancy. It obviously involved a lot of planning and work. The fact that he would go to all that effort melted me. He really was incredibly thoughtful, willing to put himself out for others.

Neither of us brought up the Glyphs during dinner, but after I helped Jim clear the dishes we got down to business.

"I'm guessing, since there hasn't been any uproar in the press, we might not have to be quite so concerned about security." Jim ventured.

"I wouldn't have parked only two blocks away if I didn't somewhat agree…but I do think it would be wise if we remained alert and careful. It could be that the website isn't yet on the radar of whatever natural enemies might be out there."

"I think you just like playing Mata Hari." He winked.

"No. I like being careful. Remember, Mata Hari didn't have a happy ending."

"I don't think it's entirely appropriate to talk about happy endings when the subject was also a prostitute." An off-color comment from the conservative Dr. Kirkwood! He was getting mighty comfortable around me.

"Ho, ho, ho." It was a really bad, really low pun, but I couldn't resist.

"Why, Ms. Shannon, I never!" Jim broke into mock horror.

"I'm sure you do some time." We both laughed.

"We're never going to get anything accomplished if you insist on having a personality." He teased.

"Hey, you started it. But, I agree. Strictly business from now on."

"Okay. We've got most of the formula. We even think we know it has something to do with averting man-made climate change. But…I don't get the whole 'Horton Hears A Who' thing you put up on the website. What the heck is that all about?"

I hadn't elaborated much when I posted that question. I figured those who got the same vibes I did would know what it meant. It wouldn't matter if anyone else understood. Amazingly, though, the vast majority understood.

"It's a concept that's been around forever. You see it in literature, science fiction. Even scientists have touched on it."

"Touched on what?"

"The idea of beings within a being...microscopic civilizations around us...within us...our civilization being housed within another living being. I was going to call it the 'Russian Nesting Doll Theory,' but I was worried the mention of a specific nationality might put some Seers off. Then, I thought of 'Horton Hears A Who.' Between the book and movie, that message has been translated into dozens of languages and reached billions of people." I could sense that he was going to find this very difficult to swallow.

"You're kidding, right?" He gave me that look that set me to wondering if he had the power to have me committed.

"No. Really. That book's got international recognition."

Jim gave me a look that said this was not something about which he wished to kid around.

"I'm dead serious. The Horton Theory is consistent with a lot of other theories out there. The Gaia theory. String theory. Christianity."

"By what twisted logic are you supporting your harebrained idea with science fiction, physics and religion?" Beyond disbelief, his voice was getting a perturbed edge to it.

"I didn't say those philosophies supported the idea. I said they were consistent with it." I shifted in my seat and leaned toward him. Maybe if I could get him to focus on what I was saying, rather than his internal opposition, he'd at least see I had a point.

"As I understand it, the Gaia theory suggests everything on Earth is part of a complex, self-regulating system designed to sustain life. To me, that sounds like Earth is functioning like a living organism – which would be consistent with us living within a larger being. And the Gaia theory isn't science fiction; it was first postulated by a scientist employed by NASA, for heaven's sake."

"String theory is a bit beyond my comprehension…and I'm not sure if the string part fits in exactly…but string theory requires the existence of at least nine dimensions –plus time – for it to be a workable theory. I figure those nine dimensions could be the levels of life within life. Are you familiar with string theory?"

"No. Not at all. I'm just the anachronism, remember? You're the encyclopedia."

"Ha. Ha."

Jim just sat there staring at me with a patronizing look on his face, so I soldiered on. "From what I understand, many of the older theories of physics break down at the atomic…or, I don't know…maybe it's subatomic…level. When you get that small, stuff that should be stationery isn't. At that level, stuff moves, almost like it's boiling. And string theory provides a plausible framework for how that is. I imagine that might be what our universe could look like if it were just a subatomic speck within a larger organism. I've even seen a scientist explain the dimensions as possibly being coiled around one another."

I could see that dragging hard science into the conversation loosened up his resistance just a tad. Though, quite honestly, I thought the whole string theory thing was the farthest stretch. But, perhaps that's because I couldn't get my tiny brain around physics to save my life. I didn't understand string theory. I just had a general notion that the Horton theory would not be inconsistent with string theory.

"And Christianity? How the heck is your Horton thing at all consistent with Christianity?"

"The mystery of the Divine Trinity…the Father, Son and Holy Ghost. Three people in one. It certainly explains how three people can be the same being. Maybe the Father is the main being, the Son lives inside Him and the Holy Spirit live inside the Son. I'm sure that no theologian would buy into that interpretation today…but, at one time, the Church wasn't too enthusiastic about the Earth revolving around the Sun either."

Surprisingly, Jim seemed to be finding the trinity example the most convincing of all. Maybe he was incredibly religious (with one helluva an open religious mind). He sat silent for awhile staring into his coffee.

He finally spoke, stirring his coffee slowly, still not looking at me. "We've got over a thousand people from the website who voted for your Horton theory. It could be mass hysteria, but…it really doesn't matter, does it?"

"No. As far as I'm concerned, all that matters is that we fill in the blanks and get the Glyphs to someone who can do something with them…but, I do think you sort of agree with 'Horton?'"

He finally looked up and, very earnestly, into my eyes. "What makes you say that?" It was as if he was looking to me to tell him what he felt. As if he thought I might hold a key he had lost access to.

"The fact that you're no longer so concerned about security. You've mentally ruled out that this is coming from anyone on Earth. So you must believe that the source is otherworldly."

"I think I may be avoiding admitting to anything so I don't have to doubt my sanity. Thank you very much for pointing out that I might be a whacko." A slight smile crossed his lips.

"You think I'm a whacko?" I raised my eyebrows in mock surprise.

"I think you are definitely whacky. Fortunately, I rather like that about you."

He smiled at me and I thought we might have had a moment of something akin to deep affection. But, Jim quickly shook it off.

"So," he picked up his pen, "what do we do now?"

Chapter 12

I was extremely agitated on the drive home. Jim and I had our first strong disagreement. I thought we should try to get the Glyphs info into the hands of the academics at UB. That way, Jim could monitor the interest level while he was working on his doctorate. He didn't want to even consider approaching anyone until we had every blank filled in. And he was uncomfortable with nosing around.

I was nervous about how long it might take to fill in the blanks. We were no longer making any headway on filling in the pieces to the puzzle. Most Seers visiting the website now had the same blank spots that we did. It seemed that some areas were just more difficult to visualize than the others.

Jim thought I should try to organize a face-to-face meeting of the community…that maybe we could somehow hammer it all out if we sat down together in a room. While I thought the idea had merit, I wasn't ready to abandon the layer of security that anonymity gave us.

When it came right down to it, I guess we were both protecting ourselves from the same thing: Publicly being associated with a bunch of screwy looking Glyphs. There was a high probability that non-Seers would think we were nuts, no matter how many people saw what they did not.

I had to come up with something, though. Basically, no one had filled in any blanks in the last week and a half. We had to find new people.

I decided to put a message out to the Glyphs community asking them to actively seek new Seers. It wasn't much of a plan. But, it was all I had. And it would have to wait until tomorrow. Kim and I were going to be driving way into the boonies. I'd post the message from there. No reason to get totally complacent about security.

Chapter 13

"He made you dinner?!" Kim looked at me like I'd just won the lottery.

"Don't get too excited. I had to listen to how great Kiku was through half the meal." I needed Kim to drop the notion that there might still be a chance for Jim and me to be more than friends. How was I going to banish that thought from my brain if she kept bringing it up?

"I met someone." Kim had a devilish glimmer in her eye.

"You did! Without me to vet him?"

"He's fine. You'll like him. He passes Rachel's First Law of Love with flying colors."

My First Law of Love was never to date someone you wouldn't want to marry. I was always explaining to Kimmy how her various boyfriends were totally unsuitable for marriage. It's a wonder she was willing to put up with me as a friend.

"Who, what, where, and when?" I wanted every detail. This was a nice mental distraction from the stress of work – and of the Glyphs.

"His name is Bill Burton. He's a rep with our computer service at work. He came by to install some upgrades. We got to talking. He invited me to lunch. And I'm going to dinner with him on Monday." I'd never seen Kim with such a huge smile. She usually worked hard to minimize her smile. She thought her teeth were too big. (Of course, they were not.)

Bill sounded like a great guy for Kim. Considerate, intelligent, gainfully employed – and apparently not all that funny. Since she snorted when she laughed, Kim hated dating funny guys. She didn't know how to get around the dilemma of either snorting, which embarrassed her to no end, or not laughing (if she could hold it in) and seeming dull. I wished Kim had more self confidence. Her snorty, little laugh was adorable.

During the long drive to Kim's uncle's Christmas tree farm Kim filled me in on every single detail about Bill. She'd never been so enthusiastic about a guy. Maybe, deep down, she realized all the other guys in her life had been losers. I think she honestly felt that was all she deserved. I could be wrong, but I thought I heard a spark of confidence in her conversation. I was liking this Bill already.

It didn't take us long to find perfect trees, saw them down and lug them back to the car. A thin blanket of snow made it easy to drag the trees…and really put me in the holiday mood. Everything was so beautiful out here. The air was fresh and crisp. The snow was still clinging to the pines, weighing their boughs down ever so slightly.

We stayed and visited with Kim's family for awhile. Kim's cousins were in middle school, so we started a snowball war with them. Mostly we just ran like hell trying not to get pelted. It was great exercise and the kids had a blast. Afterward, Kim's aunt put on a pot of hot chocolate and served us fresh biscuits with homemade preserves.

We chatted for over an hour. I think Kim's aunt was a little lonely for girl talk. They were isolated out here on the farm. She was probably too busy to notice most of the time. She farmed, raised three kids, canned, tended the animals and managed to find time to volunteer with an organization that assisted the elderly. It was an idyllic life. But, it was a hard life, too. Kim's uncle worked two jobs as well as tending the farm. At any given time, the family was just one health crisis away from disaster.

Kim and I fed the animals and helped her aunt peel a couple bushels of carrots for canning. But then it started to snow. Hard. We had to get on the road fast or risk being stuck in the middle of nowhere for who-knows-how long.

I was glad we took my car. It handled really well in the snow. And I like to be in control in tricky situations. Driving on slippery country roads through blinding snow was harrowing enough without someone else being at the wheel. Normally I wouldn't take my gas guzzler on such a long drive if I could help it. But, since we were picking up Christmas trees for both my apartment and Kim's family's house, we needed all the roof space we could get.

We had taken the back roads all the way down to the farm. It had been such a pretty and relaxing drive. Funny how all that gorgeous tranquility could suddenly turn treacherous. I headed for the highway and hoped the plows had beaten me to it. If they had, maybe I could crank it up to 10 miles an hour and stand half a chance of keeping ahead of the piling snow.

I remembered my EZ Pass and asked Kim to put it in its little foil pouch in my glove compartment so it wouldn't register my presence at the toll booth. I could tell she thought that was an odd request. I wasn't going to tell her that I posted to a top-secret website using her aunt's Wi-Fi and didn't want there to be any record of my being in the area. But, I didn't think she fully bought my story that I was having problems with my EZ Pass account.

The guy at the toll booth told us the plows had just come through, so we were in luck. If you can count driving with less than 2 feet of sight distance for an entire 50 miles "luck."

Chapter 14

After the harrowing drive back home on Saturday, I slept in late Sunday morning. I didn't think my roommates had made it home Saturday night. I looked out the window to see if their cars were around.

Mine was the only car on the street. And it had been plowed in and shoveled out. My walk and front porch were shoveled as well. That Mr. Laskowski. He was such a sweet guy. He and Kim must have come by to get their tree off the car after church and shoveled me out. That would have been no small task. There were easily four feet of wet, heavy snow on the ground.

I put on a pot of tea and flipped on both my computers. (I now felt comfortable enough to read the posts from my home Wi-Fi, but I still didn't trust posting from home. I had no idea if there was any sense to that; it's just what felt right.)

It would be a perfect day to catch up on work. I doubted my roommates would be home before Monday. Snow like this didn't get plowed very efficiently in the city. The only reason my street was plowed was because there was a fire station on it. The roomies were either stuck at friends' houses elsewhere in the city or enjoying driving freedom at their parents' houses in the suburbs. The suburbs always got plowed out right away. They had the tax dollars to do that kind of thing.

I was surprised at the response to my post on CussedEmOuterwear.com. Dozens of people said they'd print flyers and post them around their town or campus (in the dead of night while no one was watching…bless them, they were as paranoid as I was). And then there was one really strange post. "Truth Seeker," who identified himself as a well-to-do business owner, wanted to help finance a campaign. And he wanted me to meet him in Las Vegas the following weekend to work out the details.

That was exciting. And scary. Jim was still the only person I had face-to-face contact with regarding the Glyphs. But, if we had some money, we could post billboards or TV ads – something that would reach so many more people than the random hundreds that found us on the Web. Maybe we could even do some promotion internationally. (I thought there might be a small chance that "reception" of the Glyphs vision might vary geographically.)

Of course, how I was going to get to Vegas and how I was going to assure my safety there were entirely different matters. I called Jim on what we affectionately referred to as the "batphone" and left a message. Then I plowed into the assignments I brought home from work. If I was going to be traveling next weekend, I'd need to get caught up.

Chapter 15

Jim called back around 9 p.m. He was emphatic that I not go to Las Vegas. Unfortunately, by the time he called, I had made up my mind that I should meet with this guy somehow.

"It's too dangerous. You don't know what kind of nutcase this guy is. And *Las Vegas*…sin city for crying out loud!"

"There are security issues. I know that. I'll figure out some way to guarantee our safety." I could tell this was going to be a hard sell.

"It's not *our* safety I'm worried about, it's *your* safety."

"Look, I'm going to try to get the meeting moved someplace else. I can't afford to fly off for a weekend in Vegas. But, I really do think someone needs to meet with this guy."

"I don't care where the meeting is. I still don't like it."

"I don't think you understand. I can't keep up with what we're doing now – and we definitely need to do more. A lot more. And I can't do it. My work is suffering. My life is suffering. If I go on like this much longer, I'm going to end up with a nervous breakdown…or fired…or both. And that damn Wilkins Ice Shelf has been at risk of collapsing since April. We've had these visions since childhood. We may not have a lot of time left before the damage from climate change is irreparable."

"See if this guy can make it to New York and I'll meet with him. I don't want you to go. Okay?" I think Jim heard the desperation in my voice and realized the toll all this was taking on me.

"I'll see what I can do."

"Promise you won't do anything without letting me know?"

"Promise."

"Cross your heart and hope to die?" He definitely wanted our conversation to end on a lighter tone.

"I thought hoping to die was what I was trying to avoid."

"That's my girl. Good night, Rae."

"Good night." I couldn't help it, but it came out almost more of a whisper. I mean, 'that's my girl'…what was *that* all about?

Chapter 16

That night it started snowing again. By morning, there was another four feet on the ground at my house. Other parts of the city got it worse. Downtown got seven feet! That was unprecedented as far as I knew. It reminded me of the nightmares I used to have as a child: That it would snow and snow until we couldn't even open the doors and were trapped in the house under a mountain of snow.

They instituted a travel ban in the city, so my office was closed. (Though, I really would have liked to go downtown and see what seven feet of fresh snow looked like. By tomorrow, it would be settled down quite a bit, probably wouldn't look like more than five feet.)

I turned on my computer and dove into my work again first thing in the morning. By 3 p.m. I was actually almost caught up. My muscles were also starting to cramp after two days hunched over my computer in the cold (we kept our thermostat set at 65° since heat was a luxury we agreed we could not afford).

I was in no mood to hang around any longer in the cold all by myself. My street had been plowed and so had the main street at the corner. I decided to pack up and head to my parents' house in the suburbs. Surprisingly, they hadn't gotten half as much snow. (Surprising because they were in the traditional snowbelt south of the city. Contrary to its image, the city of Buffalo and the northern suburbs usually didn't get all that much snow. The snow was almost always concentrated in the southern suburbs. Could climate change be affecting the snowfall patterns? The thought made me shudder.)

I had no trouble getting to my parents' place. I lived near the city line, and even with a travel ban, the authorities didn't have a problem with people driving *out* of the city. Getting back in would be another matter, but I didn't plan to come back until the ban was lifted.

I used the opportunity to find a Wi-Fi signal and send Truth Seeker a message that I was interested, but would not have the resources to go to Vegas.

Walking in my parents' door was wonderful. It was warm. Mom was baking Christmas cookies with my sister, Kathy, so the house smelled delicious. Dad's workplace was closed, too, so he was outside futzing with the Christmas lights. We had an early dinner, decorated the tree and still had time to go Christmas shopping. The stores were nearly empty (of shoppers, not merchandise), so I finished my entire list that night.

Caught up on work and shopping! It felt like a giant weight had lifted from my shoulders. The only thing keeping this evening from being absolutely perfect was the fact that I had eaten waaay too many cookies.

My brother was still away at college, so I camped out in his bedroom. I called Kim. Bill had to cancel their date since he lived in the city. She wasn't too devastated because he rescheduled for Tuesday.

I flipped on my "stealth" computer to read the message boards. Nothing new in the general posts, but I did get a message from Truth Seeker. He gave me a pay-as-you-go phone number to call and requested I call immediately, no matter what the hour might be.

I dragged out the batphone and called. A woman answered and gave me another phone number to call. But, she instructed me to use a pay-as-you-go phone to make that call. This secrecy business was enough to drive me nuts.

The city was still closed the following day. I did as much research as I could on an upcoming project at work, then headed to the store. My mother wanted me to pick up some groceries. That would give me a chance to buy a new batphone.

I called Truth Seeker from my car. He had a sort of formal way of speaking and the slightest hint of an accent. I thought maybe he might be from India. He sounded very calm and rational. But he was emphatic that I meet him in Vegas on Saturday. Apparently he would be on a lengthy international trip after that.

Truth Seeker said he would cover the cost of flying me to Vegas. He was even more paranoid about security than I was. He asked me what city I lived in, then said he'd call me back the next day, after making arrangements.

I didn't know how he was going to make arrangements for me to fly to Las Vegas when he didn't know my name. Maybe he was getting me some fake I.D. I figured I'd better call Jim to let him know what was going on with Truth Seeker.

Jim, of course, was furious.

"Holy cow…what are you nuts?!"

"I know it's a little risky, but it's a calculated risk. No one's going to do anything to me. You know I'm going. And I'll write myself a letter and send it to my parents' house, so if anything happens to me, they'll be able to track down what happened."

"Oh. That makes me feel better. *After* you're dead we'll be able to find your killer. Glad you covered that base."

"No one is going to kill me if they know they'll be caught. Besides, I think this guy is sincere. I think he shares the devoted obsession that seems to come with the vision."

"I just don't like you going off by yourself."

"If you'd like to go instead of me, I could call him back and arrange that."

There was a long pause. Jim made some sort of weird groan and his breathing changed. It sounded like he was in torment.

"Jim? Are you all right?"

"I'm fine. I'm trying to think of a way I could go instead of you. I don't think I can. Things aren't great here."

"Why? What's wrong?"

"After I talked to you the other day, I decided I'd take a year off from med school. You're shouldering too much of the burden. And I can get enough credit to live without a paycheck for a year or so. When I told Kiku, she went through the roof. Wanted to cancel our engagement." You could hear the anguish in his voice.

"Oh, Jim...I'm so sorry."

"And beside all that drama, her parents are throwing a huge party in my honor on Saturday..."

"Listen. Don't worry about me. I will be safe. I will call you and let you know where I am at all times. And you don't have to quit school. We'll figure a way to handle this."

Jim was silent for awhile. "You're going on this Vegas trip no matter what I say, aren't you?"

"Yes."

"I don't seem to have any control over the women in my life."

"This is America. You're not supposed to." What I didn't say was that the women weren't supposed to have control over him either. Kiku's blowup had pretty much sealed my opinion that she was a controlling bitch.

"You'll call and let me know what's going on?"

"I promise. Everything will be fine."

"I think you're forgetting something."

"What?"

"Rachel's First Law of Peril."

"I'm not forgetting. I will be at a continual state of high alert."

"I care about you." The anguish was still in his voice. Was it over Kiku or over me? I couldn't tell.

"I care about me, too. I'll be fine."

Chapter 17

They lifted the travel ban on Wednesday. Even though the snow had settled, it was still amazing. Parking meters were completely buried. There was too much snow to simply plow away… they had to load it onto dump trucks and pile it into big mountains in selected parking lots and parks. I'd never seen so much snow.

Better yet, I'd never seen so little work on my agenda. I had enough to do to keep me busy, but I actually went out to lunch and still managed to go home on time. Was that how normal people got through their days? It almost felt like being on vacation. The absence of stress was so…freeing!

After work I went to my apartment rather than my parents' house. There was much shoveling that needed to be done. The snow had drifted so high in spots that you had to lift the shovel above your head to throw the snow over the drifts. My roommates and I shoveled the front walk (that was our deal with the landlord…we used the front entrance, so we kept in shoveled).

Then, we helped shovel out some of our neighbor's cars. It was like a little party on the street with everyone out shoveling and helping each other. That was the great thing about a snowstorm. It really brought city dwellers together. (On the flip side, it tended to isolate suburbanites who cocooned away in the deep snow, letting their plow services clear their driveways.)

That shoveling was the exercise I needed to get my endorphins going – or whatever the heck chemical it was that got going when you exercised. I hadn't felt so good, so relaxed, in so very long. I hadn't had time to go my Pilates class in weeks. I completely pushed right out of my head the fact that this was a false and temporary reprieve from my daily grind.

Our Christmas tree had blown off the front porch and was buried in a snow drift. We dug it out and put it back on the porch. No use dragging it inside with so much snow still clinging to it. With luck, most of it would evaporate by tomorrow and then we could bring it in.

Getting home in time to have dinner with my roommates was a real treat. Marilee was a great cook and whipped up some chili. I had picked up a box of cornbread mix at Big Lots a couple weeks before, so I made that. Olivia fixed a nice salad. We had a real dinner like real people. We lingered at the table after dinner laughing and catching up on each others' exploits. The fact that the oven had brought the kitchen temperature to something approaching comfortable was a real plus.

After getting ready for bed, I made my phone calls. Kim and Bill had finally gotten together for dinner. She said she had a wonderful time. He took her to the Left Bank, which was one of the city's hottest restaurants. I was a little jealous of that...I'd never been there. Kim said Bill was very attentive, didn't drink, and walked her to her car afterward (they met at the restaurant). He held her arm while they walked to the car, but he did not kiss her goodnight. She was seeing him again on Saturday.

Truth Seeker had made all his arrangements by the time I called. I was supposed to meet one of his female employees at the Galleria Mall after work on Friday. She would get me on a plane. I was not to bring a suitcase. I was to use valet parking and go straight into the dressing room at Urban Outfitters.

Jim found the whole meet-at-the-mall-no-suitcase thing bizarre. I did, too. But, I understood Truth Seeker's paranoia... I just couldn't figure out how the heck he was going to pull everything off.

Chapter 18

When Friday rolled around, my adrenaline was rushing. Half of me was scared stiff. The other half was kind of thrilled to be doing the cloak-and-dagger routine. (Hopefully, there'd be no daggers.) I wasn't sure what to expect, but I could never, in a zillion years, have foreseen what happened.

I was supposed to arrive at the mall's valet parking site at 5:30. I got there almost on the dot. A young, Middle-Eastern-looking valet greeted me with, "Ms. Hawn-Imus?" That was my username on our website, Anne Hawn-Imus. (Get it? Anonymous! Sometimes I crack myself up.)

I was floored. Truth Seeker didn't say anything about the valet expecting me. This was way more involved than I'd imagined. I started to get that feeling in my knees that I got when I was at the edge of a cliff. Or saw someone at the edge of a cliff. Edges of cliffs really got to me.

I was so shaky, I had to grab onto things to steady myself as I walked. It seemed to take forever to get to Urban Outfitters (but, it was just a couple stores from the valet). I walked into the dressing room. An attractive, young woman wearing a headscarf motioned me toward one of the stalls.

"Ms. Hawn-Imus?"

"Yes." My voice was as shaky as my knees.

"Please to come in."

She let me into the stall, closed the door...and opened an umbrella! At first that confused the heck out of me, but then I figured it must be to block any camera aimed at the dressing room.

"My name is Cala. I will be escorting you on your trip today. Mr. Kezal has provided a disguise to protect your identity. May I help you put on the hijab?"

"Um, sure. Thanks." There was no way I'd figure out how to get it on right.

"And please to put on this coat?"

She held out a conservative, but pricey-looking winter raincoat. I could see she had several matching coats in her bag. I suppose she had no way to know what size I'd be. She slipped my coat in her shopping bag.

"May I apply a foundation?"

I nodded and she proceeded to buff on some makeup that darkened my face a bit, followed by dark brown lipstick. The whole makeover took just a couple minutes.

"Did you want this?" She held up the outfit I brought in the dressing room. I shook my head and she placed the dress back on the hook.

"Please leave the store immediately. Another woman will meet you on the main concourse. I'll see you on the plane." She smiled and shook my hand formally. "Go. Go." She shooed me out of the stall.

As soon as I left the store a woman in headscarf and raincoat identical to mine came up to me like we were old friends.

"Anne! What? Again you didn't buy anything?" She took my arm and lead me into one of the mall's anchor stores. It was then that I noticed about a dozen women milling around the store, all dressed exactly like me. Same scarf. Same coat.

We walked quickly to the store entrance. A limousine was waiting. We hurried in and the driver took off – headed in the opposite direction of the airport! My handler must have noticed my alarm.

"Do not worry, miss. Faris will first make sure we are not being followed, then take us to our destination."

I assumed that destination would be the airport, but I didn't ask. Who knew – maybe there was a worry that the limo might be bugged. It was all a bit too much for me. For a paranoid guy, Truth Seeker…or, I guess, Mr. Kezal…trusted an awful lot of people. I wondered if I could be dealing with the Saudi Secret Service. At least I had all three of my phones on me. One in my person, one in my pocket and one in my bra (yet another advantage of big boobs, I suppose). I could call for help if I needed it.

We did finally circle around and head toward the airport. But, when we got there, we drove straight past it. At that moment, my heart nearly leapt out of my chest. But, the panic was short lived. We pulled into a private aviation company just past the airport…and straight up to a Lear jet!

I was hustled out of the limo and onto the jet. Cala was already onboard.

"I hope our little adventure wasn't too jarring for you?" Her smile was both warm and slightly amused.

"It was more…intriguing…than I imagined. But, I'm none the worse for wear."

"May I get you a drink?" Apparently she was going to be the flight stewardess.

"Thank you, no. But, would you mind if I made a phone call?" I wanted to assure my safety before we left the ground.

"Certainly. Mr. Kezal anticipated your needs. He asked that you use this phone."

I called Jim on the pay-as-you-go phone she handed me. I let him know that I was on some sort of private jet and that I'd call him again when I landed. I deleted the record of the call and handed the phone back to Cala. She removed the battery and dropped the phone in the trash.

"We have other phones if you need to make another call."

I would have liked to chat with Cala. She seemed very sweet and I had a million questions. But, I didn't know what Mr. Kezal had told her. Her knowing little smile led me to believe she thought I was on my way to a romantic rendezvous. I wondered if Mr. Kezal was married.

I was given the red carpet treatment during the flight. An elegant dinner had been catered in. Cala gave me an elaborate makeup kit so I could change back into myself. All I wore was lip-gloss and I had that in my purse. I tried to decline the kit, but Cala insisted I take it. She spent most of the flight in what I assumed was the cockpit, only popping in now and then to ask if I needed anything.

When we arrived in Las Vegas I called Jim and let him I know I'd be staying at the Venetian Hotel. Cala said Mr. Kezal was ready to see me and asked if I'd prefer to stop by my room first or meet with him directly. I didn't have any luggage, so I figured I might as well go straight to the big guy. Cala deposited me at a table in a magnificent garden and informed me Mr. Kezal would be down presently. As far as I could tell, we'd have the whole garden to ourselves. I wasn't exactly sure where I was, but I didn't think it was the hotel.

As I sat sipping my iced tea and nibbling on the most elegant fruit plate I'd ever seen in my life, I worried over what I was getting myself into. This was definitely a level far beyond anything I could have imagined. This guy must have immense wealth. And with immense wealth comes immense power. If he were a bad guy, I could find myself in immeasurable danger.

I didn't have much time to worry. Truth Seeker breezed across the patio. He was the proverbial tall, dark and handsome...except he wasn't that tall, he wasn't that dark, and handsome was an understatement. He wore khakis, a pink polo shirt and light jacket that looked exotic and expensive. His clothes hadn't the faintest hint of wrinkle anywhere. (Could it be that he hadn't sat down yet today?) His hair was thick and slightly wavy. Though he was young (maybe 28?), his hair had a few strands of grey worrying through it. His smile was quick and natural (and betrayed the slightest hint of a dimple – damn, I am such a sucker for dimples).

"Ms. Hawn-Imus! So good to see you!" In his enthusiasm he looked like he wanted to hug me. I extended my hand to maintain our distance. He grabbed my hand with both of his...and kissed it!

"It is good of you to come on such short notice. Are you up for a stroll?"

Actually, a stroll sounded perfect. Maybe I could walk off some of the adrenaline that had been piling up in my system all day. He took my arm and guided me down a well-lit path through the most amazing cactus collection I'd ever seen. (Granted, I'd only seen one or two other cactus collections in my entire life.)

"Ms. Hawn-Imus...."

"Please, call me Rachel."

"If you will call me Amir?"

"Sounds fair. Would you like to fill me in on who your people think I am so I don't make any stupid mistakes?"

"Ahhh. I am sure if you made a mistake, it would not be a stupid one. Especially since my staff members know nothing." He had a little twinkle in his eyes. And what eyes those were. Big, deep pools that a girl could fall into. I could get lost wading through those mysterious eyes

"Nothing?"

"Absolutely nothing."

"Do you do this kind of thing often?" I wondered if maybe he had women stashed all over the country that he flew in for trysts.

"No. I have never done anything of the kind. I'm sure my staff must realize you are a very special person."

"They have been treating me well. Would they think we're having an affair?"

"That is not beyond the realm of possibility. I assumed they might imagine we had some secret business dealing…a takeover, or something of the sort…but you have turned out to be so beautiful and charming, so exactly the kind of woman who might sweep me off my feet…that the staff could easily suspect a romantic liaison. Which is very good. They will make a great effort to keep knowledge of you from my family. The fewer people involved the better."

"Are you married?" Along with everything else, I sure didn't want to have to worry about a crazed wife attacking me.

"No. But in my country, a man and woman of such different backgrounds would be wise to keep their relationship discreet."

We walked and talked for at least a half an hour. I filled Amir in on my advertising background, but my limited resources to, what he called, "further the quest." He made it abundantly clear that his resources were virtually unlimited (for starters, his family owned vast oil fields). He was happy to find out that CussedEmOuterwear.com had just gotten started. He liked being in on the ground floor.

The sun had been down for hours. A chill was definitely settling in. My blazer was not up to the task of keeping me warm. (Cala took my coat from me earlier, when the temperature had been quite pleasant.) Amir made a call and Faris picked us up in a sort of limo/golf cart. Amir put his arm around me as we sat in the back of the cart...I assumed to further the ruse of our "affair." It was so cold, it didn't occur to me to protest. I snuggled in. It felt good to snuggle in. Extremely good.

It didn't take long to get to the Venetian. Who knows, maybe we had been on the grounds already. Everything was so grand around here, I was totally disoriented. Amir escorted me to my room, the Chairman Suite. Ohmigawd! It was more like a mansion than a hotel room. Fine art. Oriental rugs. An in-suite gym. Total opulence.

Best of all, there was a fireplace. Amir had the butler (yeah, the suite came with its own butler!) pull the couch and coffee table up close to the fire. We propped our feet up on what must have been a $10,000 coffee table.

The room was pure decadence. I protested that it was too much, but Amir assured me that as a business dealmaker or love interest, nothing less would be appropriate. I'd just have to make the sacrifice and live in the lap of luxury.

We stayed up late discussing our feelings about the Glyphs. (After all, an early night would blow our cover.) He was a lot more in touch with his intuitive side than Jim. He put great faith in his feelings, relying on them as strongly as I relied on mine.

Around 11:00 p.m. I realized that I had forgotten to call Jim. I excused myself and grabbed one of the phones laid out in the entryway. I thought I would just leave a message, but Jim picked up the phone. He was so worried he was still up waiting for my call. I felt terrible that I'd put him through all that worry. I assured him that I was safe and not to expect a call until Sunday morning. I didn't mention that Amir and I were still chatting in my room. Jim seemed to be fairly comfortable with my safety level by the time we hung up.

"Your partner, Jim…are you two…attached?"

"Like dating? No. Jim is engaged to another woman." At least I was assuming he was still engaged.

"Is there someone in your life?"

"A romantic interest? No." I was dying to ask him the same question, but figured it was a moot point. We were hoping to enter into a business relationship. Plus, he failed Rachel's First Law of Love. I'd never marry someone who lived in a country where women didn't have equal rights.

It was getting late and Amir had a business meeting in the morning. He said we could get together late Saturday afternoon. He figured he would have a plan to propose to me by then.

Amir recommended that I sleep in and order a massage after breakfast. He said it would be good for his image, but I think he mostly just wanted to pamper me. It seemed he got a kick out of exposing a regular person to the grand life.

I walked him to the door. When he opened it, there was Faris with the limo/golf cart thingie. I imagined it was for Faris's sake that Amir lifted my hand to his lips when he said goodbye…letting it slip ever so slowly from his grasp as he walked away. I made a mental note to get a manicure in the morning. My paws needed to be in better shape for all this hand kissing.

Funny, I had forgotten how cold I was, but after I was away from the fire for a bit, I realized I was still chilled to my core. I figured there must be a hot tub in the suite somewhere. (I cannot exaggerate this place…it was three times the size of my parents' house.) I hunted around for a master bedroom figuring there would probably be some sort of robe in there. With no suitcase, I figured I'd have to call the butler and see if he could get my outfit laundered. (Fortunately, I'd stuffed an extra pair of panties and a bra in my purse, so I wouldn't have to hand my unmetionables over to some strange guy.)

I was not prepared for what I found in the bedroom. Outfit after outfit had been laid out for me. Bathing suits. Casual wear. Business suits. Evening gowns. Undies. Bras. Purses. Accessories. It looked like a small store in there! Cala must have picked everything out. And she definitely must have thought we were having an affair. There were three negligees, but not a flannel pajama in sight.

Chapter 19

The next morning I picked out a casual outfit. I was pretty picky about my bras – I always purchased the same style. But, all of the bras Cala had picked out (at least, the ones that were my size) fit perfectly and offered great support. I guess, when you weren't selecting from bras stocked in boxes at Wal-Mart, you didn't have to be so picky.

Cala seemed to be fond of v-necks. She probably didn't realize the v-necks would act a whole lot different on me than they might on her. Or maybe she thought she'd be doing her boss a favor if I flashed more cleavage. Fortunately there were some square-necked camisoles I could wear underneath everything.

When I called to order breakfast Jeeves (I didn't call him that to his face) brought in a whole cart of goodies. I selected a couple items and made him take the cart back with him. I'm the kind of person where every package is a single serving if you leave it open in front of me. I shuddered to think how much of that cart I'd be able to down if I had to stare at it for any length of time.

A massage just seemed too decadent, but I did order a manicure. I got the manicurist to spill the names of a couple celebrities she's worked on, but getting any details about those stars out of her was impossible. Apparently this was a level of service where privacy was paid for and received.

I was afraid of how much the manicure might cost. I had gotten all my money out of my purse before the girl came in so that I wouldn't ruin my nails digging for it. When I asked how much I owed, the girl told me everything was to go on Mr. Kezal's bill. I asked if that included the tip as well and she said it did. The smile she got when she said that made me think that Amir was a very good tipper.

Having time to kill was a luxury for me. I figured I could still multi-task by getting some exercise while I saw Vegas. I asked Jeeves which way I'd go to see the fountains at the Bellagio. He informed me that they wouldn't be turned on until closer to the dinner hour, but if I could give him a moment perhaps he could arrange an early performance for me. My first reaction was to burst out laughing, but I stifled it. I figured if I acted like someone who was used to all this service, I'd be less likely to bring attention to myself.

"No, thank you. It's probably better to view them in the evening. That will be all." That will be all! I don't know how I managed to say that with a straight face. But it did seem the kind of thing you'd say to your en suite butler.

I'd never been to Las Vegas before. It was fun to explore. The whole place was over-the-top. Being early in the day there wasn't much of a crowd out on the main drag. It was blissfully cool, perfect for walking.

I'd only been out about 45 minutes when I noticed that a guy walking toward me was staring me up and down in an odd way. I was giving him my evil eye, but he probably didn't notice because I was wearing very dark sunglasses (my blue eyes just can't take much sun…and there had been such a stylish selection of shades laid out for me in my suite).

I saw his face sort of register a decision and then I watched out of the corner of my eye as he abruptly turned around when I passed. He was following me! Worse, the vibe I was getting off him was not good. I wasn't even carrying a purse, so robbery was not a likely option. I was pretty sure he was a rapist or maybe even a murderer. I could feel the evil intent radiating from him. (Don't ask me how I feel these things, I just do.)

I didn't panic. (And that's stupid of me. I should have been terrified and panicky.) I figured as long as I kept to public places, I'd be safe. I wanted to prove this guy was following me and have someone catch him. I didn't think this was the first time he spontaneously decided to rape or murder. I didn't think it would be the last. I had a chance to stop him. I had to try.

I took a lot of twists and turns and the guy was still behind me. He kept a good ten feet back. I had my eye out for a policeman, but didn't see any. I figured all these casinos had to be staffed with security. If I went in, I figured I could get someone to nab my stalker.

I turned into the nearest casino, the Mirage. Since my suite at the Venetian had its own private entrance, I hadn't actually set foot in a casino before. I wasn't prepared for the darkness, the barrage of bells and beeps, or the disconcerting layout. I looked around for someone who could help me. Everyone seemed occupied with other customers. Then I spotted some kind of slots worker on the floor. I walked up to her and asked her to please call security.

"What problem?" I was a bit taken aback. I figured employees would be trained to jump on a request for security.

"There's a man following me."

She couldn't have been any more obvious as she looked up and scanned the room. She found the right guy, though. He was still lurking about ten feet back, staring at me.

"He no follow you. He just lost." I couldn't believe it. She wasn't going to do anything. Maybe the fact that the guy was clean cut and well dressed threw her off. Still, I mean, she picked out the right guy. How could she know who was following me if he wasn't following me?

She stared over at him again. Since she wasn't going to do anything, I looked up, too. The guy completely freaked and walked out of there as quickly as he possibly could without making a scene.

Now, I was shaken. First, I felt terrible that this rapist or murderer or whatever was now free to rape or murder or whatever again. Next, having lost sight of him, I didn't know if he might still be following me. I figured I'd better call the Venetian and have them send a car for me. It was ridiculously embarrassing since the hotel was just a short walk away.

I hadn't brought my phone with me, but getting the hotel personnel to make a call proved infinitely easier than having them apprehend someone. I asked the concierge if they could call the Venetian and let them know the guest in the Chairman's suite needed a car. I wasn't sure how to tip for that. I gave the guy a five. He probably felt that was darn stingy for someone staying in the Chairman's suite. But, I only had $25 in my pocket and I sure as heck wasn't going to give him the twenty.

Faris appeared within minutes. I was surprised it was him. Maybe Amir arranged for him to lurk around the hotel waiting to ferry me around? I asked Faris to just drive around. I explained that I had been followed by a man with some sort of criminal intent and that I needed to be sure he wasn't somehow still on my tail.

Faris suggested we take a ride out to Red Rock Canyon. He thought I'd enjoy the scenery and it would be very easy to determine if we were being followed. That sounded good to me. While I didn't think the murderer/rapist would be bold enough to follow me, if I were wrong…and the guy had something to do with the Glyphs…who knows what lengths he might go to track me down.

I could see what Faris meant as we drove out of Vegas. Soon we were on a solitary highway winding through the desert. You could see the road for miles. There was only one other car out there. Faris let it pass. There was an entire family inside, complete with kids. And I did enjoy Red Rock. It was beautiful. A refreshing counterpoint to the amazing excess that was Vegas.

Of course, I noticed the terrain was mostly hills and gullies. The kind of place that might be prone to a flash flood in a sudden downpour? Funny how I could be paranoid about that, but walking around this morning – where apparently there were more immediate dangers present – I hadn't worried at all.

Chapter 20

When we arrived back at the Venetian, Amir was pacing frantically outside. It was too early for our meeting. Faris must have let Amir know of my little episode. He had gotten out of the car with me at Red Rock, but insisted on standing guard near the parking lot rather than joining me…giving him plenty of time to call. Amir looked relieved to see us pull up. He got me out of the car and waved Faris on.

"Are you alright? What happened? Tell me everything."

I was rather touched by the sincerity of his concern. I told him the whole story, exactly as it happened.

"I don't think this guy had anything to do with our business. When he was walking toward me, I could feel him making the decision to target me right there on the spot." I didn't bother to mention that I thought my boobs might have had something to do with it. Amir could probably draw that conclusion himself.

"Why did you not call the police? You could have done so without compromising our…privacy."

"I don't like to carry my phone all the time."

Amir shook his head in frustration. "Will you promise me that from now on you will always carry your phone? You don't have to turn it on. Just have it with you."

"I'm way ahead of you. I resolved to do that the minute I saw that guy turn around. In fact, I've resolved to get a camera phone. If I had a picture of the guy I could send it to the police."

"No. It would not be worth the risk for you to take the picture." He squeezed my hand and looked deep into my eyes. "But, I see from your eyes you will still get the camera phone regardless of my protests?"

"You read eyes well."

"And you are too stubborn for your own good."

"I'm a very cautious person. But when the stakes are high, you sometimes have to take calculated risks. Just like we're doing with the Glyphs."

With that, Amir became even more serious. He asked if I was too shaky to take a walk. Surprisingly, I wasn't at all shaky. I guess even though I had been at risk, I had not actually been in danger. I was in enough control of the situation that I had remained in safe, public places and out of "grabbing reach" of the creep. I'm sure I'd be in a whole different emotional state had that not been the case.

Amir summoned Faris and we went back to the garden we met at the night before. It was even more spectacular in the daylight. Amir held my hand as we walked. It didn't feel like the hand holding was for show. It also didn't feel like it was supposed to be romantic. I was guessing it was a cultural thing. I wouldn't be at all surprised if Amir took every business associates' hands into his when he was talking about something important. But, I could be wrong.

I had a suspicion that Amir liked to talk about the most sensitive aspects of the Glyphs in this garden for a reason. I guessed that he felt it was secure. No eavesdroppers or listening devices. Though, it could be that he liked the fresh air and exercise. I sure did. (It was going to be tough to have to face real winter weather after leaving Vegas.)

The plan that Amir had come up with blew me out of the water. I literally had to sit down. Stunned was too soft a term for my reaction. Amir paced, looking worried, while I tried to collect myself. I wondered if he realized that he had virtually dropped a bomb on me, exploding my world into little pieces.

After a few minutes my head stopped spinning enough for me to walk. Now it was *I* who took Amir's hand in mine.

"This is an awful lot to absorb. I...I'm not sure what to think. Can I take some time to think this over?"

"Only if you promise to let me talk you out of saying 'no'...if that's what you decide."

"I promise to let you argue your case. But, that's as far as I'll go."

"Fair enough."

We walked now in silence. I had too many thoughts swimming around in my head. Amir had offered to hire me to work on Glyphs full time. He would create a false identity and offshore accounts where he'd send my starting salary of $150,000. I'd have an unlimited expense account. I could work from home, or he would set me up with office space wherever I'd like. He would bankroll any advertising or promotion efforts I deemed necessary. And he wanted me to try to reach an international audience.

I finally had my head wrapped around this new reality enough to start asking questions.

"Amir…about security?"

"Yes?"

"I don't think that guy following me today had anything to do with the Glyphs, do you?"

He shook his head. "No. You have been very careful. I tried to find your identity before I contacted you. And with all my many resources, I could not. More importantly, I very much trust your instincts."

"I believe the Glyphs have something to do with thwarting climate change. Do you believe that as well?"

"Yes. I have had images of the Glyphs in my head since I was a small child. I have always associated them with my uneasiness regarding the weather. Like you, I've worried over climate change for as long as I can remember. Long before I ever heard the terms, 'global warming' or 'climate change.' Imagine it. A three year old boy who has never seen or heard of snow having nightmares about cities buried in it."

"That's why I am so anxious to uncover the meaning of the formula. We are losing ice shelves right and left. Farmlands are being baked into uselessness. Every day without a solution means lives lost."

"What do you propose we do with the Glyphs once we fill in the blanks?"

"In any given year there are several international conferences in various scientific fields. I can arrange for you – or someone else, if you prefer – to present the findings at one of these conferences. In this way, the entire world receives the results at the same time. As much as possible, that would remove egos, politics, and greed from the process. It would be my hope that scientists would either understand the Glyphs formula or be motivated to study it."

I felt Amir was telling me the truth. First, because I could see the sincerity in his eyes. And second, because I had the suspicion that a sort of magnanimous obsession came as part of the package with the vision.

I thought Amir's plan was both brilliant and noble. Still, it didn't make sense to me that his security measures were in such uber-drive.

"I've been security conscious because I have no idea what threats could be out there. I assume some other individuals or governments could be working on the project, too, and might not want anyone else on board. Are you worried specifically about any other potential dangers?"

"Because I believe this formula is the key to staving climate change…I believe it is most likely energy related. Perhaps it will unlock the power in an atom…or in a drop of salt water. Who can know?"

"But, unless it unlocks power from sand, such a formula would virtually put my country out of business. Oil is all we have. Any wealth…any power that we have… all flows from oil."

"If anyone were to realize I was working on a project which might make the need for oil obsolete, my government – or possibly even my family –might have me killed."

I stared at Amir in shock for a few seconds and then I did something I rarely ever do. I burst into tears.

Chapter 21

Amir deposited me back at the Venetian pretty quickly. He obviously wasn't used to dealing with sobbing women. I hoped that he wouldn't think I was an emotional basket case. After being stalked and then finding out someone was putting their life in my hands…all before lunchtime, I hoped Amir would realize a little meltdown wasn't totally out of order.

Back at the room (I still feel silly calling this mansion a room), I blasted some music and got on the treadmill. (It wasn't as easy as it sounds. It was some sort of high definition satellite radio with a million buttons. I had to have Jeeves show me how to work it.)

Usually I hate treadmills. I'd much rather walk outside. But, I wanted to work up a sweat to calm my nerves and the street was getting a little crowded for that kind of pace. Plus, I didn't want to be distracted by the sights or by having to keep an eye out for murderers.

The exercise did me good. It cleared my head. After my shower, my skin felt fresh and healthy. And I'd made my decision. I was not going to accept Amir's offer. Getting him killed was definitely something I didn't want to have to worry about.

Amir had asked if I'd mind going out for a formal dinner. I'm not normally one to get all dolled up, but since it was probably the only chance in my life to wear anything close to the evening gowns Cala picked out, I agreed. Amir was picking me up at six – early enough that I could skip lunch. That meant I could dive into my gourmet dinner without feeling too guilty. The decision to turn Amir down lifted a weight off my shoulders. Tonight I was going to enjoy myself.

Actually wearing one of the gowns was a completely different story from imagining wearing it. There was so little fabric! Only the skimpiest bra would fit under. That meant I had to worry about falling out of the bra as well as the dress. I was glad there was a large, gorgeous shall to mute the boob factor. Since I had the makeup case and the time, I tarted up the face a bit. And I had the salon send a stylist to do my hair. It was remarkably easy to splurge knowing that doing so was really a necessary part of the ruse. How often do you get that kind of excuse to be decadent?

Amir was impressed when he picked me up. He lingered over my hand when he kissed it.

"You look amazing...as always."

He looked pretty special in his tuxedo as well. I felt like we just stepped into a James Bond movie. Then I realized we were too close to that reality for my comfort.

As Faris held the limo door open for me Amir asked him:

"Tell me, Faris. How am I to remain inconspicuous when I am accompanied by the most dazzling jewel in the state?"

"I would not worry, Mr. Kezal. With Ms. Hawn-Imus at your side, no one will be looking at *you*."

Amir really didn't have to worry about appearing conspicuous. We arrived at a private entrance, took a private elevator, and sat at a private table in a private room with a spectacular view of the Vegas strip.

The host offered to take my wrap, but I waved him off. It was all I had to keep me from being chilly. I noticed Amir whispering an aside to the maître d' and felt the heat turn up enough that there was no chance of my being cold. Was Amir concerned about my comfort – or hoping to get a better view of my cleavage? He had not been one to ogle, but my suspicions of men's intentions were deeply ingrained.

"Are we to speak cryptically or casually here?" I had no idea how far to take caution.

"Ahhh – cryptic is the preferable always, everywhere. It adds to the intrigue, does it not?"

"I find you quite intriguing on your own, Mr. Kezal."

"And I you, Ms. Hawn-Imus."

"How am I registered at my hotel?"

"As the guest of Mr. Kezal. Does that suit you?"

"Yes. And what does your staff know of my name?"

"After they met you, they learned your first name was Rachel – but they may still think of you as Anne. Quite frankly, I presume they are quite confused and will choose to call you Ms. Hawn-Imus."

The wine steward came to the table to take my order. I declined. He didn't bother to ask Amir.

"They know you well here."

"In this town, business knows everyone well who has deep pockets."

"And you don't drink for religious reasons?"

"In a way. I am not what you would consider a practicing Muslim. I believe religion once existed to bring people together and make us better. But, religion – all religion – has too long been in the hands of men. Powerful men. And nothing gets mucked up worse than something in the hands of powerful men."

Amir stared in contemplation at the candle on the table. "Today, religions are riddled with foolish rules that I do not believe were intended by Allah…God. Today, religions drive people apart, which I also do not believe is intended by…God. I believe in the power of prayer. I believe in leading an honest and noble life. But the rest…not so much. I do not drink mainly because Arabs in America are highly scrutinized. I do my best to put forth an exemplary representation for the sake of my countrymen."

Amir pulled himself out of his introspection and looked at me with a twinkle in his eye. "And you do not drink because…?"

"I like to hang onto whatever brain cells I have for as long as I can."

"A wise choice."

"I've made another choice today, too."

Amir expectantly raised an eyebrow.

"I've decided to decline your most generous offer."

"On what grounds?"

"On the grounds that I cannot be responsible for…your life."

"That should not be your concern."

"But it is."

"If you will not accept my offer, every additional day you fail in your mission, you are responsible perhaps for the lives of many."

I hadn't thought of it that way. I looked into Amir's eyes. I could see he was enjoying the negotiation. He believed he would win.

"Damn, you're good."

"I am…prepared."

"I'm not prepared. Not for the responsibility."

"There are no guarantees…but, I sincerely believe you yourself will never be at risk."

"That isn't the issue."

Amir sighed. "If you do not accept my offer, I will have to find someone else. In seeking that person…I am…vulnerable. In working with that person – a person who I believe will never perform as well as you – I am vulnerable. So, you see, you will be responsible for more if you decline than if you accept."

"You are infuriating."

"It is only the truth. I am going to do this with or without you."

At that precise moment, U2's "With or Without You" began playing.

"Did you plan this?"

"I assure you, I did not."

"Is the table bugged?"

"I think, more likely, this is kismet. And kismet demands that we celebrate it. May I have this dance?"

I mumbled a protest as to my lack of dancing skills, but Amir was already gently pulling me out of my seat. He held me just a millimeter from too close. Once I settled into the rhythm of his dancing (or as close as I could come to it), Amir moved his hand up from my waist ever so slightly – so that it touched my bare back. The feel of that warm, soft hand, skin-to-skin against my back, took my breath away.

He seemed to sense my reaction. He pulled me even closer, brushed my hair away from my face and whispered into my ear.

"Please, my dear Rachel...I will never trust anyone to handle this...responsibility...as much as I trust you."

Chapter 22

I agreed to Amir's working arrangement and the rest of the evening was a blast. Dinner was fabulous. Amir tried to teach me how to dance some much fancier steps. He took me to a private terrace overlooking the Bellagio fountains for dessert. (Apparently nothing that went on between Jeeves and me was private.) Faris drove us the entire length of the strip with Amir providing a running commentary on whatever insider stories he was privy to.

Still, we arrived back at the Venetian before eleven. I wondered if there might be an agenda behind the timing...arriving home early enough that it seemed silly not to invite Amir in?

"Do you want me to come in, or are you just being polite?"

"I want you to come in."

"Are you sure?"

Now I was confused. Was Amir trying to get me to beg for his company for Faris's sake? Or did Amir think inviting him in was tantamount to an invitation to sex? Either way, I couldn't let the ambiguity linger.

"Amir, I'm not inviting you in to make love. I'm inviting you in to keep me company. There's nothing I'd rather do than spend time with you. I care for you very much. But, if you get too fresh, I will have Jeeves throw your sorry butt out the door."

Amir's face at that moment was priceless: A combination of surprise (or was it shock?), amusement, admiration, horror – and a big dose of dumbfounded. (I'd never seen dumbfounded before. I'd always wondered what it was. I think it must be one of those 'you'll know it when you see it' things.) I thought I heard some sort of choking sound coming from the driver's seat.

"Well, when you put it that way, how can I refuse?"

"I'm sorry. I guess you would look like a cad if you refuse. But, I think all men are cads, so my opinion of you would not be affected if you decline the invitation."

The choking sound from the front seat became more intense.

"Then, perhaps if I accept your invitation your opinion of me in this regard will change?"

"That will depend on how well you behave."

"I cannot go through life having you think me a cad. We had better go in before you give poor Faris convulsions."

Once inside I turned apologetic.

"I believe Faris and I both appreciated your honesty. There are no games with you, are there Ms. Hawn-Imus?"

"When the stakes are high, I believe in getting to the point. I hope that didn't blow your cover?"

"Quite the contrary. I think Faris knows me well enough to realize that you are exactly the type of woman I could fall deeply in love with."

He walked up behind me, and kissed my neck.

"I wasn't kidding when I said you wouldn't be getting lucky tonight."

"Nor I, when I said I could fall deeply in love with you."

"Amir, you're now my boss."

"Ahhh…I see you as an independent contractor. I am merely your client."

"If you're implying you want to take our relationship beyond the friendship stage, I'm afraid I'm going to have to disappoint you."

"But, why?"

I took his hand and looked into his eyes. I could see that he still felt this was a game he would win. Just like he won my employment. He thought he had an answer for whatever argument I might have. So I brought out the big one.

"Because of Rachel's First Law of Love."

"And what is this law?"

"Never date anyone you wouldn't marry."

"Ahhh. And, keeping in mind that this is not a proposal, what would be your objection to marrying me?

"Women don't have equal rights in your homeland."

"And you would reject me for a political situation beyond my control?"

"I would reject you for fear of living in repression."

"Ahhh. But I do not live in Saudi Arabia any longer. I live in Dubai. Women enjoy far greater freedom in Dubai."

"But, *home* is Saudi Arabia. Most people eventually long to go home. And my home is Buffalo. That's another conflict. Only one of us could live at home. Assuming your family would even allow you to marry me."

I could see I'd knocked the confidence out of Amir's eyes. My issues were more complex than he was prepared to deal with. How could he have foreseen he'd come across a girl who'd look ahead to the altar before the first date? Poor guy. I felt sorry for him.

"May I ask a personal question?"

"Shoot."

"Do you have feelings for your partner, Jim?"

Amir was extremely intuitive. Only way to deal with that was honesty.

"Jim and I have never been involved romantically...but, yes, I feel for him almost as strongly as I feel for you."

I hadn't realized I'd felt stronger for Amir than for Jim until I said that. But, it did feel true. Was that because Amir was here and Jim wasn't? Or because Amir wanted me and Jim didn't? I had no idea.

"I'm kind of worried about having feelings for the both of you. Do you think a mutual attraction could come with this vision thing?"

"My feeling is...no. But, if it did, what would it matter? Does it make a difference if love comes from the head, or the heart...or Horton?"

"I'm thinking it might be a Who rather than Horton, but it does make a difference. If all Seers were attracted to each other, we could seek out the most demographically suitable mates."

Amir roared with laughter. "I have found the only woman on the planet who approaches romance from the standpoint of logic. And it turns out to be not the ideal character trait a man might imagine."

It took a moment for Amir to compose himself. He literally was wiping away tears of laughter.

"So…you think the vision is sent up from the bottom rather than down from the top?"

"The bottom levels would assumingly be more evolved. They'd have gone through millions of more generations."

"Not necessarily. We have no way to know how many generations Horton's family has been around. And one would assume the Whos all have to start from scratch with the birth of each Horton. And if we're the Horton, how could it be that our Whos all use the same symbols?"

"Excellent point…you're absolutely right. If the vision was coming from within, it would be implausible for everyone to see the same thing. Then again, if we're talking plausibility, it's most likely the message would come from the same level we're on. Being in the same dimension – on the same space-time continuum – would sure make communication easier. They presumably wouldn't have to speed anything up or slow anything down."

"Ahhh…that might make it more dangerous for us. They would be more advanced while sharing our same space. Should their intentions change, they could come and obliterate us."

"If they could travel to us, they probably would have come and shown us what to do with their message in the first place."

"Another excellent point. Except for romantic applications, you make good use of logic."

"Do you think most people would throw us in the looney bin if they knew we were seriously talking about this? I mean, how logical is it to believe all this? It's bizarre. There's no way to prove it. We have only our feelings to base it on."

"Ahhh, but that sounds like an accurate description of religion. Religion has been embraced by mankind since the beginning of recorded history. It has nothing to do with logic. Yet, people aren't throwing each other in the looney bin over it."

"I'll mention that to the head shrink when they commit me."

"If anyone knew I was talking business to this most amazing woman on a Saturday night, they would commit me. And they would be right to do so."

"This isn't what you had in mind?"

"Not in the least."

"You knew you weren't going to score when you agreed to come in."

"True, but I thought I'd at least get to play the game." Amir slid dangerously close and began a trail of kisses up my arm."

"But this game isn't good for us."

"And why not? Will I crave your touch any less if you deny it to me? Quite the contrary! Will your fondness for me diminish if I sit across the room? Or leave the room? I think not. Why should we deny ourselves the pleasure of...proximity?" He put his arm around my waist and pulled me tight.

"You've been working on this angle in the back of your head the whole time, haven't you?"

"Of course. And it is irrefutable, is it not?" He stroked my hair.

"It is now that you're so close. I'm only human." I undid Amir's bow tie.

"Precisely what I was counting on." Amir kissed my neck.

"And I trust you will be gentleman enough not to attempt to cross the...goal line?" I undid the top few buttons of his tuxedo shirt.

"Ahhh...very good move. Put the onus on the other player." Amir ran his hand down my cheek and to my breast, letting it linger there ever so briefly.

"Mmmm-hmmm. You can't win, but you could lose." I brushed my teeth against his chest in little pseudo bites.

"I do not believe I will lose anything but my heart to you, Ms. Hawn-Imus." He lifted my chin, looking deep into my eyes.

Amir held to his word. When our cuddling risked growing intense, he got up to pour us some tea. We joked. We danced. We cuddled some more. I had an absolutely marvelous time. He kept it light, not even kissing me on the lips until we said goodbye at the door. But, that kiss was so loving, so soft, so filled with desire yet tempered by restraint, letting him leave felt...painful.

"You're very, very good at this game. I'm afraid I'm outmatched."

"Ahhh, coming from you, that is quite a compliment. I cannot imagine anyone outmatching a woman such as yourself."

Neither could I, until tonight. I was afraid my overconfidence had cost me dearly. I wasn't sure I'd have the strength to protect my heart from Amir.

I closed the door behind him and leaned against the wall, stifling an urge to scream. I felt like I'd just had the tiniest taste of the most delicious hot fudge sundae in the world...and I desperately wanted another. It took a half hour on the treadmill before I felt calm enough to go to bed.

Chapter 23

I called Jim in the morning. The big party with Kiku's family had gone well. Jim seemed both relieved and wary over my business arrangements with Amir. He was glad the issue with Kiku was now moot. But he was still worried about my safety. (I didn't let him know that it was my heart that was in the greatest jeopardy.)

I wanted to call Kim, but the thought of throwing another phone away was just too wasteful for my eco-minded conscience. Plus, what could I tell her? Nothing. She could never know about my trip to Vegas. I could never even admit knowing Amir, much less lusting over him. I was on my own, with no confidante to help me sort out my feelings.

Amir came by a bit before noon to take me to lunch and go over all the arrangements he'd made for my employment. He brought Cala with him. She had a full set of luggage. Against my protests, Amir insisted I take the clothes in my room home with me. I had sorted them into what fit and what did not. I told Cala to return or keep for herself the ones I didn't want. I put all of the negligees on that pile.

Cala packed my bags as Amir filled me in on the details of our working arrangement. He then drove to the airport with me. I had given Faris a little box to give Amir after I'd left. It was just a prettily wrapped box containing a single Hershey's kiss and a note that said, "I will miss you." But, I also wanted to say a proper goodbye in person before we got out of the limo.

"Faris, I don't mean to be rude, but there are things that are hard enough to say with one man listening, let alone two. Is there some kind of window thingie you can put up?"

"Of course, Ms. Hawn-Imus. I am sorry for any intrusion…"

Amir ended the apology with a wave of the hand. Faris got out of the car.

"I'm going to miss you, Amir."

"And I you. You are a most remarkable woman."

"You keep referring to me as a woman. I don't feel like a woman. I still feel like a girl."

"May I ask your age?"

"Twenty-four."

"Ahhh, you are on the cusp."

"The cusp?"

"It has been my experience that most people transition into what feels like adulthood sometime between 24 and 26."

"And how old are you?"

"I recently turned thirty."

"And do you feel like a boy or a man?"

"Both. I do not think the boy ever completely leaves the man."

"I don't think this girl will ever be able to completely leave the man either."

"I should hope not. Whatever the future holds, our brief past has been very special to me."

That didn't sound as promising as I would have liked.

"Do not frown, my Rachel. I am sure our future will be very special as well. We will see each other again. Often, I should hope."

He knocked on the window and Faris opened the door. Amir took my arm and walked me onto the plane. I didn't know what to expect. He seemed to be backing off emotionally. Should I tell him I was ready to throw Rachel's First Law of Love out the window? I couldn't find the courage for that, so I followed his lead. I extended my hand.

"Goodbye, Amir."

He shook my hand, reaching over to hold it in both of his when he was done.

"Goodbye. Good luck. Be careful."

"Please try not to worry. I understand the huge responsibility I bear. I'll be very, very careful."

Amir's face softened. He paused for a moment, wavering almost imperceptibly, then kissed my hand.

"I will miss you."
At that, he turned and left.

Chapter 24

It was going to take me the whole frickin' trip home to decipher what just occurred. During lunch, Amir had been all business, but there was so much we had to cover, there really wasn't time for any distractions. But, that goodbye. That goodbye was not what I'd expected after last night.

Amir was definitely turning off any emotional attachment. But why? Did he change his mind? Get a call from an old girlfriend this morning? Did his father read him the riot act about seeing an American? Was he following Rachel's First Law of Love because I didn't have the strength to? Did he not see that I was wavering on that law? Or was he just being practical?

I decided to give him the benefit of the doubt. Which was unlike me. I didn't go around giving men the benefit of the doubt when it came to relationships. But, I just didn't think Amir was a jerk.

But, jerk or no jerk, I got the sense he was definitely giving our personal relationship a sense of finality. Well, except when he wavered in our last seconds together. That gave me the sense that he was conflicted.

By the time I deplaned I had decided two things. Any romance between Amir and me was over. (It hadn't really even begun, had it?) And since there was no future in it, that was a good thing. It hurt, but I was surprised that it didn't hurt more.

Plus, with the job ahead of me, I wouldn't have any time to dwell on the situation anyway.

Chapter 25

We landed in Rochester. Amir had apologized all over the place about making my trip home longer, but I understood completely. It was a smart security move. It only added about an hour in a chauffeur-driven limo. I didn't consider that much of an inconvenience.

I was reunited with my car at a private storage facility. The car had been detailed inside and out, gassed up and kept safe in a garage. When I arrived, it was all warmed up for me. Which was nice – after a weekend in Vegas, I'd lost some of my winter hardiness.

The chauffeur could hardly fit the luggage in my car. It took up the entire trunk plus the back seat. When I got home, my roommates were out. That was a lucky break. I could drag the luggage up without a million questions. Fortunately, most of the clothes were too summery for a Buffalo winter, so I could take them straight to the attic.

No one besides Jim knew I had been out of town and I was going to try to keep it that way. This secret life was going to be hard to handle. Except for the Glyphs, I wasn't used to hiding things from my friends and family. And until recently, the Glyphs hadn't been that big a part of my life. Now, I was going to have to hide who my employer was and what I was actually working on. Worse, I couldn't tell Kim about Amir. I was going to have to bear all the emotional turmoil without an understanding ear to share it with. That sucked.

I called my parents and arranged to have dinner with them later in the week. I called Jim and left the message that I'd gotten home okay. He must not have been too worried since his phone was off.

Then I called Kim. I was dying to know how her date went with Bill. Apparently, things were going extremely well. They'd done dinner and a movie on Saturday and he took her snowboarding earlier in the day. No kiss yet, but he wanted to meet her friends. She asked if I could go out with them Friday night.

I thought that was perfect. I wanted to check this Bill out and make sure he was all Kim thought he was. I had to admit though, so far he sounded good. With Kim, I could often spot the losers before I even met them.

Then, I sat down and started strategizing how to allocate my new, huge Glyphs promotional budget. I stayed up way too late trying to figure it all out.

Chapter 26

The week passed quickly. Between my regular job and my Glyphs job, I was buried with work. I didn't want to give notice at the agency right away. Just on the chance that I let slip that I was whisked away over the weekend, I didn't want anyone to associate that with my new job. I really didn't know what to be careful about anymore, so I thought I'd best be careful about *everything*.

I did manage to take on less work at the ad agency. I told the traffic manager that I couldn't work nights for a couple weeks. She knew how many hours I had been putting in and was willing to cut back on the number of jobs assigned to me. However, I knew she couldn't get away with that too very long. The staff at the agency was lean and mean. Everyone had to pull their weight – and then some.

Then, on Friday morning when I was dressing for work, I found a box that had been tucked between two of the sweaters from Las Vegas. I was running late, as always (I was definitely not a morning person), so I slipped the box in my purse.

Being a typically hectic day, I didn't get a chance to open the box until after work. In it was an incredible necklace. It had diamonds, but it wasn't your standard diamond necklace. It was more like a funky work of art. I wouldn't be surprised if it were a one-of-a-kind piece.

Amir had inserted a note in the box:

My dear Rachel,

Once away from your intoxicating presence, I realized that I took unfair advantage of your vulnerability. Please forgive me.

You are correct that the obstacles to a lasting relationship are most likely insurmountable. It would be criminal for me to break your most wise First Law of Love.

I feared I might lose my resolve if I were to deliver this message within sight of your most beautiful, all-seeing eyes. I apologize for my cowardice.

You will forever hold a special place in my heart. I hope you can find the charity to forgive me. I would be most honored if I could remain your friend.

With great affection,
A

Somehow, the pain of loss felt far greater at that moment than it did on the plane. Was it because I was now dealing with certainty rather than speculation? Whatever the reason, I was glad that I was in the relative privacy of my car. I sobbed uncontrollably for a good five minutes. Geesh, tears twice in one week – what was becoming of me?

I wasn't at all sure if I should keep the necklace, but I put it on for safety's sake. I definitely didn't want to lose it. I assumed it cost a small fortune.

I was a mess and I was supposed to meet Kim and Bill in fifteen minutes. Fortunately, it had snowed a couple inches during the day. I grabbed a handful of fresh snow off the trunk of my car and rubbed my face in it. At least that evened out the blotchy red to an all-over red.

Chapter 27

Kim and Bill were already at Fat Bob's Smokehouse when I got there. Kim was sitting very close to Bill, leaning into him with a kind of proud ownership. I'd never seen her quite like that with a guy. She usually sort of slunk next to them like she imagined herself to be an unworthy tagalong.

"Rae! Did you walk here? Your face looks frozen!"

"Stupid me. I slid on a patch of ice and my head kerplunked right into the snow on my trunk."

"Are you alright?" Bill had stood up to greet me. (Points for good manners!) He extended his hand and I shook it. Like Amir, Bill seemed more a man than a guy.

"I'm fine. Just a little cold and embarrassed."

"Here, have my hot tea. It should just about be done steeping."

Kim was such the motherly type. Caring. Selfless. Generous. I hoped Bill was taking note.

"Thanks. You are a lifesaver. Have you been here long?"

It turned out that they'd only arrived about five minutes before me. Fat Bob's was a favorite of mine, so I knew exactly what I'd be ordering: the pulled pork platter with a couple of their homemade sides. Not having to look at the menu gave me a good opportunity to size Bill up.

He seemed like a nice guy. Kim was having trouble choosing between two items, so he ordered what she didn't so she could have some. He was wearing a nice suit even if the tie was a bit uninspired. He was very attractive. And he was very much attentive to other people. He hardly talked about himself. He kept the conversation going by asking Kim and I about ourselves. He really seemed interested, too.

"Kim tells me you're an advertising copywriter?"

"Yeah, I'm sort of a copywriter/PR/marketing catch-all grunt."

"What exactly does that mean?"

"Means I'm overworked and underpaid."

"Gee, I hope you're not having a problem making ends meet?"

"No. No more than anybody else."

Kim interjected: "Rachel can squeeze a nickel into a dime. She's one of the most frugal people I know."

"Hope it's not out of necessity?

"Nah. All my ends meet, unfortunately that includes the two ends of the candle I'm burning. The 'overworked' part of the equation is tougher to deal with than the 'underpaid' part."

I did get into a small argument with Bill about patriotism. He was sort of obsessed with patriotism, asking if we thought this person was patriotic or that action was unpatriotic. He seemed to think anyone who didn't have a flag hanging from their front porch should be shot.

I thought about Amir and how he worried his country would consider him a traitor for doing something he believed would ultimately benefit all people...but might reduce whatever power his nation held in the world at the moment. Amir was doing what would be right for his country in the long run, but from what I could tell, Bill wouldn't consider him a patriot.

I tried to explain to Bill that patriotism wasn't black and white. I pointed out that the flag-burning protesters of the seventies were at least as patriotic as, say, Senator Joseph McCarthy. That if memory served me correctly, John Wilkes Booth considered himself a patriot. And that if Lincoln had been a Hitler, maybe we'd all agree with Booth...and that wouldn't necessarily be right, either. Bill simply didn't "get" all these shades of grey.

I asked him if he thought the Patriot Act was, in fact, patriotic. (I personally worry about anything anyone tries to put an inspiring name to. The Patriot Act, Manifest Destiny...I think the more nasty stuff there is to hide, the more motivational the name.)

Bill couldn't see at all what I was getting at. He finally stuffed a sock in it when I asked him how he rationalized being so uber-patriotic with not having ever enlisted in the military.

I felt bad arguing with Bill. But, I figured he'd get his chance to pick a fight with me if I ever started babbling about climate change. That was my obsession…and I suppose I was probably more likely to see that as a black and white issue than I should. We all have our blind spots to the shades of grey in something.

At some point during dinner, Kim noticed my necklace and went ga-ga over it. I knew that was a big turning-point moment for me…coming up with my first huge lie. I told her I picked it up on clearance at T.J. Maxx. I said I intended to give it to my mother for Christmas, but decided that I liked it lot more than Mom would.

Bill leaned in to take a closer look at the necklace and reached out to lift it a little from my neck. I thought possibly he could have been trying to get closer to the boobage, but his eyes didn't seem to stray down. I gave him the benefit of the doubt. I figured maybe he was trying to be polite by showing interest.

Bill loved snowboarding and Kim said they'd had a blast at Holiday Valley the week before. He suggested we all go on Sunday. I tried to beg off due to the aforementioned "overworked," but they offered to go to Kissing Bridge instead. It was only a twenty minute drive, so I agreed to join them for a few hours.

When the waitress brought our bill, Bill insisted on paying the whole tab. I figured maybe he was still worried about my finances. I protested loudly, but he insisted.

"Hey, I invited you, so I'm picking up the tab. I'm underworked and overpaid."

"Really, let me chip in my share, please." I didn't want to be sponging off the guy the first time I met him.

"Sorry, won't hear of it."

He handed the waitress his credit card and the case was closed. So, apparently he was also very generous and perhaps even financially successful. He must have been a good tipper, too, because the waitress had a big smile on her face when she brought his card back.

"Thank you, Mr. Braxton."

"Thank *you*. Excellent meal. Excellent service."

I tried not to flinch or look up, but I did distinctly hear the waitress call Bill Burton, "Mr. Braxton." That would make the second big first for me. The necklace was my first big lie. "Mr. Braxton" was my first bout with real suspicion.

Chapter 28

The first thing I did when I got home was write Amir a note. I had an address where I could send him innocuous messages, as long as I assured that they could not be traced back to me.

> *Amir,*
> *I just found your much too generous gift today. Thank you so very much. I will treasure it always.*
> *I understand your feelings completely. You don't have to apologize. Sometimes #$%@ happens. This is one of those times.*
> *I don't regret having bended my First Law of Love on Saturday. I had an amazing time. You've now set the bar way too high for the next unsuspecting gentleman to stumble into my life.*
> *I will always be your devoted friend. With luck, time and distance will have cooled my passion for you by the next time we're together. (Sending a list of your faults might help, too. My top faults are: messy, constantly late, indecisive, and prone to pack on the pounds.)*
> *With great affection,*
> *R*

The message certainly wasn't as moving as Amir's elegant note. My everyday English seemed frivolous when compared to Amir's eloquent, formal way of speaking and writing. But, hopefully it would lighten up the situation and he'd know it was from the heart.

I'd mail the note from Kissing Bridge...and I'd pay cash for my lift ticket...if Bill let me pay at all.

Of course, the question of Bill was a whole 'nother matter. Did the waitress just slip up on his name? Who could slip up on Burton?

I didn't want to alarm Amir if this turned out to be nothing, but I wasn't going to make any major moves until I got the "Bill" question straightened out. Maybe I'd get the chance to peek at his credit card on Sunday. Or maybe Kim could clear the whole situation up. I wouldn't be able to call her until tomorrow. It was going to be a long night.

Chapter 29

I called Kim bright and early to tell her how much I liked Bill and how sorry I was that I'd argued with him. She didn't seem bothered by the argument. She pointed out that arguing is what I do. Constantly. She'd gotten used to it. She thought Bill would, too.

Between skiing and all my work, the weekend flew by. But, I'd been unsuccessful in finding out if Bill Burton was really Mr. Braxton. He didn't pull out a credit card on Sunday. And whitepages.com didn't have an appropriate listing for William Burton or William Braxton…assuming his first name really was "Bill."

By Monday night, I'd had enough worrying time to start getting really paranoid. I couldn't remember Bill getting near my purse or my coat, but I took my coat to the cleaners and gave my purse to Goodwill, carefully going over every single item that had been in it. (I used my secure computer to google listening devices on the Web. They looked like they should be easy enough to spot if you were actively looking for one.)

My work for Amir was really keeping me busy. By Friday, I'd ordered at least one billboard in every state, though most of them wouldn't actually be up for another six months. I had small space ads set to run in several English-speaking foreign countries. I got a post office box in yet another fictitious name and was having several different wigs delivered to it. I went to some discount stores and got XXL clothes along with a "fat suit." If I had to venture out on official Glyphs business, I was going to be a master of disguise, guaranteeing that I'd feel like a total idiot.

I sent Amir a Christmas card telling him I'd call him at 9 p.m. my time on Christmas day, which was at the end of the coming week. Cala had packed an entire suitcase with nothing but phones, all numbered in the order I should use them. I was still on number one. I checked it for messages each night, but there hadn't been any. (I really didn't expect any. After all, I'd be the one generating news, not Amir.)

If Amir was able to answer the phone, we could talk. If not, I'd leave a message. I hoped he could answer. I needed to let him know my worries about Bill and I was sure he'd have questions. I was determined to try to have some kind of answers before that call.

Bill and Kim and I were going to spend all day Saturday snowboarding in Ellicottville. It was over an hour's drive, so we'd have plenty of time to talk. Maybe I'd even get a chance to peek in Bill's glove compartment.

The drive down was a lot of fun. Bill had a fondness for Kim's bizarre puns. With encouragement like that, she tried even harder to come up with them. Of course, that made them all the worse. We were roaring with laughter before we'd even gotten halfway there. Even Kim was laughing. Snorting with laughter. And she didn't seem to be self conscious about it in front of Bill.

I could see that Bill was really good for Kim. She was happier than I'd ever known her to be. And she was changing in subtle ways. She was standing up for herself more often. Challenging other people's opinions when she didn't agree. Even being a little demanding now and then.

Some of our mutual friends had commented to me that they thought Kim was getting a little pushy. I didn't think she was getting pushy. I thought she was getting normal. Until I saw this new Kim, I didn't realize how much the old Kim had been treated like a doormat by so many people. Maybe even me at times.

I sure as heck hoped that Bill was for real. If his relationship with Kim was a ruse to spy on me, I didn't know what I'd do.

Bill seemed so enthralled with Kim, it was hard to imagine the relationship wasn't genuine. However, he still hadn't really kissed her, except on the cheek. That was a bit suspicious considering how much they'd been seeing each other.

I found out on the drive that Bill was having an early Christmas Eve dinner at the Laskowski's house before he drove home to Scranton to spend the holiday with his parents. That seemed to bode well. I mean, meeting the parents! And on Christmas Eve! What kind of spy would have the kahunas to do something like that?

Still, when we got out of the car at the ski resort, I managed to throw my gloves at Kim's head over some silly remark she made. They landed on the floor of the front seat. When I reached to pick them up, I knocked my elbow against the button on Bill's glove compartment. It didn't budge. It was locked. Who the heck locks their glove compartment?

Then, while we were having dinner in the lodge, Bill asked Kim how her computer was running. He had optimized it for her. She said it was faster than ever.

"Rachel, I'd be happy to optimize your computer, too. It just takes me a couple hours."

I said my computer was fairly new and ran great. Besides, I couldn't possibly impose on him like that.

"It's not an imposition at all. I love to optimize computers. Plus, I can load on some of that software you said you'd been wanting."

"The professional graphics suite? I can't afford that. I just lust after it."

"I've got copies. I can load it for free."

"You can load several thousand dollars worth of software on my computer? For free?"

"I'm the man."

"You know what. I'm not really comfortable with that. It can't possibly be legal."

"I guarantee you it is not illegal. I have promotional copies."

"Umm. Thanks, but no thanks. I'm not really comfortable with that."

"Rachel is like, the most straight laced person I know." Kim piped in. "She won't even let me rip her a CD."

Bill wasn't going to give up on this one, though. "I don't have to load the software if that's the way you feel…but at least let me optimize your laptop."

Kim agreed. "He really can perform miracles with a computer."

"You know what…I will take you up on that. I don't do much web surfing, but my mother uses my computer a lot and I know she'd love if it were a little faster."

If he was spying on me, I'd show him there was nothing to spy on. I'd load some of my boring personal and advertising files onto Mom's computer and have him optimize that.

Bill looked a little confused. "You live with your folks?"

"No…but I'm over there all the time. With two roommates, I get more peace and quiet there than at my apartment."

Kim laughed. "Peace and quiet, my butt. Her mom's a great cook."

On the drive home Kim and Bill made a date to have lunch on Monday. That gave me an idea. I'd do a little sleuthing on Monday.

At first I thought I'd find out where they were having lunch and follow Bill afterward. But, the more I thought about that, the colder my feet got. There was just too much of a chance that Bill would notice me following him.

So, I resolved to do the next best thing. The only place I could really think that Bill might be working for was the FBI. When I got to work on Monday morning, I took out my tape recorder and had one of our male college interns record himself saying "May I speak to Agent Braxton, please." I told him it was for a radio commercial I was working on. I had the interns recording parts for radio presentations all the time.

Just to be on the safe side, I went to the mall at lunchtime to make my call. I phoned the local FBI office and, as inconspicuously as possible, played the tape into the receiver. "May I speak to Agent Braxton?" played right on cue.

"One moment, please." The line rang and voicemail picked up...in Bill Burton's voice:"This is Special Agent Bill Braxton. I'm sorry I'm currently unavailable to take your call..." I hung up before the beep for the message. It took me a few minutes to stop shaking before I could drive back to work.

Chapter 30

Christmas was especially nice this year. Even though I told Amir not to pay me until January (letting me put off some sticky tax stuff 'til next year), I knew that a lot of money was going to be coming to me soon. That freed my gift spending. I couldn't go too crazy, or it would be suspicious, but still, it was nice to splurge a little... So, I went Christmas shopping a second time.

My brother was home from college and the whole family spent Christmas Eve and Christmas Day together. It felt so comfortable and safe. We laughed. We ate too much. We played jokes on each other.

Maybe the situation with Amir made me more appreciative of my ability to be with my family. Maybe my resolution to totally forget about everything for 24 hours did it. Whatever it was, I felt relaxed, happy and...I don't know...peaceful.

When I left for my apartment on Christmas night, I took a long, country drive. Satisfied that I wasn't being followed, I parked my car, got out, walked a ways and called Amir.

Amir answered on the first ring.

"Merry Christmas, Rachel."

"Okay, now you've embarrassed me in the first two seconds. I wanted to research Islam, but I didn't want to use my computer and never got to the library, so I'm just going to have to take a stab at this and say 'Happy Ramadan' and hope I'm close."

Amir chuckled and was kind, "Close enough." (I was months off.)

"Amir...we have a problem." As soon as I started to say it, I started shaking.

Amir turned very serious. "What is it? Rachel, are you all right?"

I told him all about Bill. Every detail. And I told him I hadn't given my notice at work, so we could shut everything down without a worry about me.

It was a good thirty seconds before Amir answered.

"Rachel…please to stop making that little croaking sound. This is not as serious as it might seem."

Amir went on to say that the FBI wasn't going to waste a lot of investigative money on someone like me. That Bill was probably the only agent on my case. And that at the rate he was moving, he probably wasn't all that concerned. He speculated that he may even be enjoying Kim's company so much that he was prolonging an investigation he might normally have wrapped up.

He advised me not to let Bill touch me, my purse, or anything he could bug. He said I should simply assume my car was bugged and never say anything sensitive in it.

"Where are you now?"

"Out in the middle of the country, a hundred feet from my car, freezing my toes off."

Amir laughed. "I knew you were the most cautious woman on the face of the earth. Good girl."

"I'm glad you can laugh about this."

"You have done nothing to warrant an arrest. And there is nothing yet to point toward me. I sincerely doubt the FBI is aware of our visit. You said this Bill started dating your friend before we met?"

"Yes."

"Do you have any idea how he might have taken interest in you?"

"Rachel's First Law of Peril."

This time Amir roared. "Your laws are the frustration of my existence! What is this law?"

"Something you could never have possibly foreseen will go wrong."

"That is a good law. Are you related to a Mr. Murphy?"

"Probably. The Irish are all interbred."

"I thought we agreed: no exchange of personal information."

"Are you telling me you could not tell I was Irish by looking at me?"

"Point well taken."

"So, where does all this leave us?"

"I am afraid you will have to be extra vigilant. Keep an eye on your watcher. Also, keep your computer with you as much as you possibly can. When it is not with you, hide it well. You must assume that your car and your home could be searched at any time without your knowledge. Find a place to hide your batphones, as you call them. Do not keep information about me or your partner, Jim, on your computers, ever. You need to give the appearance you are working alone. With luck, they will think you a kook and dismiss you."

"Great. Kook. Just what I want in some federal file."

"Do not worry. If you do these things. We should be safe. The FBI are not the ones hauling people off to Guantanamo."

"Guantanamo? This has nothing to do with terrorism!"

"I know, my little worry blossom. Please, do not fret. I merely meant that the fact that the FBI is involved suggests that they know nothing of your friendship with an Arab. I did not explain myself clearly. I apologize."

"Are you sure you don't want to terminate our business relationship?"

"I am as happy to continue our business relationship as I am to continue our friendship. I received your note. Thank you for…being so understanding."

"And thank you for the amazing necklace…I…oh, no! Oh, no! Oh no!"

"Rachel? What is it? What is wrong? Rachel!"

I didn't answer. I was too busy trying to tear off my necklace. I finally got it off and examined it thoroughly.

"Oh, Amir. I'm sorry. Thank God, everything is okay. I just realized Bill had touched my necklace. But, it's clean, there's nothing attached to it."

"Rachel, do not do this to me. Just now, the thought of you in danger…I feared I might have to leap from the roof of the building."

"Don't go all Romeo on me Amir…we agreed to just be friends."

"I would like you to keep yourself alive nonetheless."

"Ditto."

"Good night, Ms. Capulet."

"Merry Christmas, Mr. Montague."

Chapter 31

I gave my notice at work on Monday morning. I had wondered how they'd handle it. I gave two weeks' notice, but we were getting a day and a half off for New Year's…would they just tell me to pack up and go?

Surprisingly, the agency seemed to regret my leaving. They offered me a $3,000 raise to stay (okay, it wasn't like they were throwing serious money at me, but at least they made a gesture). They were letting me work the last two weeks (drat!). And I got the feeling I'd be welcome back in the future. All-in-all, my departure was going to be as friendly as I could possibly hope for.

I used the job change as part of a plan to throw Bill off my tail. When the three of us met for coffee, I sprang my new job on Kim and Bill simultaneously.

Kim thought I'd found nirvana. "You're getting more money and working from home? That's fantastic!"

Bill wanted all the details. "Who will you be working for?"

"I'll actually be kind of working for myself. I'm going to handle all the marketing for a startup company that's trying to break into the outerwear business. I'll be working as a consultant, doing a lot of guerilla marketing."

"What's your client's name?"

"I could tell you, but I'd have to kill you."

Bill seemed momentarily taken aback, but Kim was giggling. "Rachel's ad work always has all these nondisclosure clauses. She can never tell us what she's working on until after it's out running on TV or in the papers or wherever."

"I can tell you it's a company I did a little bit of freelance work for on the side already. They were really happy with what I'd done and they agreed to a one-year contract."

Bill played right into my plan. "So, Rachel, what exactly is 'guerilla marketing' anyway?"

"It's pretty much any promotional efforts that don't involve traditional media. Stuff like getting college students to wear t-shirts, hosting attention-getting events, creating viral e-mail campaigns."

"You send out computer viruses?"

I was kind of surprised Bill didn't know what viral marketing was about…or was he just pretending not to know? "Heavens, no! You try to create something that's so cool that people forward it to all their friends…then their friends forward it to all their friends. It travels like a virus, but it's not a virus. Usually it's just a funny picture or a link to a YouTube video…something like that."

"So, what did you do for the company so far?"

"Mostly just get some t-shirts designed and out there…plus a little bit of website work."

By the time we all said goodbye, Bill seemed pretty satisfied with the information I gave him. I was kind of hoping this would help throw him off my trail. I was giving him the information he was looking for openly and honestly. No need to skulk around digging it up.

Plus, I gave Bill the computer to optimize. Anyone tracking any activity on my mom's computer would get awfully bored awfully fast.

I was so darn proud of myself, I got worried. Being too cocky was dangerous. Rachel's First Law of Peril was bound to come into play again.

Chapter 32

Setting up the front to fool Bill gave me another idea. Why not make our dummy website more of a business itself? It might throw off anyone else who chose to investigate us…and maybe even help pay the bills.

I didn't expect to be too busy with new Glyphs input until the ads I placed ran…and that wouldn't be for another week or two. I used that time to find a web-based supplier who could actually print up some windbreakers on demand and fulfill any orders that came in for CussedEmOuterwear.com jackets.

I had a cool graphic designed for the jackets. Basically, the graphic incorporated the exact same message as the billboards. I had "Do you see what I see?" translated into seven languages so I could sell the merchandise around the globe. Anyone who ordered a jacket would become a walking billboard…so we'd get the message out at no cost to us. Plus, I contracted with Google Ad Words to put ads up on the commercial side of the website. We might get lucky and generate some income off of those.

To anyone who wasn't familiar with the Squiggle vision, we'd just look like another business. The only people I'd have to worry about were those that knew about Glyphs. And I did worry about those. Who knew if some crazy dictator somewhere would want the formula all to himself? A guy like that could come up with the means to knock me off. It wasn't like I had any security to protect me.

I trusted that I was able to keep myself untraceable. But, I realized that I couldn't be too careful.

Chapter 33

I was glad when Jim was finally back in town. His month-long semester break in NYC made me acutely aware of how much I needed him. He was the one person I didn't have to keep secrets from. I wanted to bring him up to speed on everything that was going on. He was eager to get together with me, too…to ream me a new one! We met at his house.

"You are never, ever to take a risk like running off to meet some stranger alone again. I lost five years off my life worrying about you."

"It's not like I just ran off. You knew I was going."

"I never should have let you go."

"It worked out fine."

"What if it hadn't?"

I could see I'd put him through a lot of anguish. And I felt terribly guilty over how lax I'd been in calling him from Vegas. I promised it wouldn't happen again.

Jim had mixed feelings about my new job, too. I was taking this to a level neither of us had previously imagined. Not having met Amir, Jim was naturally more nervous about his involvement. He calmed down a little when I pointed out that I was still in control of every step…and that Amir didn't know my real name or address, just that I was Rachel from Buffalo.

Then came the really hard part. I had to tell Jim about Bill and the FBI. He had a right to know. I thought he was going to explode.

"Are you out of your cotton-picking mind?"

I slunk down into my seat.

"You're in this neck deep, charging full speed ahead, and the FBI is surveiling you?!"

"I don't think they're actually following me. Just checking me out."

"Oh, this is priceless. I can't believe I'm sitting here with a…a…a person of interest to the federal government! Do you know what this could do to me?"

"What?"

"What do you mean, 'what?'?"

"What could it do to you?"

"Arrrgh! It could ruin my reputation!"

"I doubt that talking to a woman who runs a website full of Glyphs would make the front page."

"They could get you on identity theft."

"All of my identities are now non-real persons. I will be paying taxes on my income, albeit under another name. I took the website offshore. As far as I know, I'm not doing anything illegal."

"All of your identities? Offshore! Do you know how that would sound to Kiku? She'd think we were nuts. She'd leave me in a second."

"Why? Doesn't she trust you?"

"She trusts me."

"But, she controls you."

"What?"

"She wasn't going to let you take a year off. You think she won't let you do something you believe in if she'd find it strange. She treats you more like her lapdog than her fiancé."

Jim didn't answer. I'm guessing he was feeling so much rage, he thought best not to.

"I'm sorry you are unhappy with our situation. But, you really don't have to be involved. Your brother provided the groundwork we needed, but now I've got the resources to move forward without you. I don't want you to worry about ruining your opportunity to become a doctor. I won't bother you anymore. You are off the hook."

Before I walked away, I had to get in one, last word.

"I care about you, Jim. A lot. For your own sake, I'd like you to think about one thing: If Kiku told you she was taking a year off school to pursue something important to her, would you threaten to leave her?"

I bought a pint of Ben & Jerry's Cherry Garcia on my way home.

Chapter 34

I started working fulltime on my new "job" on the third week of January. I sat alone in my cold apartment after my roommates left for work and assessed my life. I was deeply attracted to two men. One I could never have a future with and one who pretty much hated me at the moment – and was engaged to someone else, no less. The FBI was watching me. My best friend, who thought she was in the first wonderful relationship of her life, was actually being used by the FBI to get to me. I couldn't warn my best friend about this guy. In fact, I had to lie to all my friends and family about half the goings on in my life.

All of this was my fault. I longed for a big bag of pretzels. Instead, I figured I'd better start working to turn the year around. I'd start off on the right foot, even if it was a few weeks late. I drove to the Southtowns YMCA and joined up.

It was a beautiful facility, just a few years old. I spent an hour on the treadmill and twenty minutes on the resistance machines. I hated dragging myself to the gym, but it was worth it. I felt so much better afterward.

Then, I went to my parents' house. They were both at work, but they kept their heat higher when they were away than my roommates and I did when we were home. I pulled out Mom's computer (the one Bill had "optimized") and wrote a script for a video promoting the website.

I shopped around on the web for production companies and sent the script out to three places for bidding…and to marketing@CustomEmOutterwear.com for approval. I had dinner ready for my parents and sister when they got home. Not bad for the first day on the job.

I was determined to keep to some kind of routine. The next day, I started at the Y (water aerobics), then went to Panera's. They had free Wi-Fi (and free heat). They also had a lot of bakery items, so I had to summon my self-restraint (which I don't have a lot of).

Fortunately, once I sat down and started working, I forgot all about the cheese Danish that had been trying to seduce me. I logged onto the Glyph's website through the public portal. (I didn't feel comfortable using any of my screen names or passwords on an unsecured Wi-Fi network.) I was shocked at the amount of recent activity.

Some of the ads had started to run, so responses were coming in from all over. I could tell we were getting a lot of foreign activity from the posts in broken English. Two of the holes in the formula had been filled in, but there were still plenty left.

I set up another poll asking visitors to vote on some random ideas I had. I replied to the email I'd sent myself from my mother's computer, approving the script. Then, I checked how our e-commerce business was doing.

My jaw dropped. I thought we'd sell maybe a couple jackets a week. We'd already sold 200! We weren't going to get rich off the jackets. I'd priced them low to encourage sales, so we only made a $5 profit on each one. But, if sales kept up at this pace, I could probably cut back on some of our advertising, saving us huge amounts of money.

Then I peeked at my offshore bank accounts for the first time. Amir had set up a personal checking account where my paycheck would be direct deposited, a savings account, and a business account. He had given me a $50,000 signing bonus that we had not discussed!

The $50,000 floored me, but it wasn't totally shocking. (At least, not after getting the necklace.) To Amir, it was a drop in the bucket. But, I wondered what he expected for it? Did he think that paid for all the work I'd done so far…so that this entire business was at his sole discretion? I considered myself a partner more than an employee. (Or, I guess, supplier by Amir's definition.)

I also wondered how he'd feel about that after seeing how much our business account had already been drawn down. But, that was silly. We'd agreed that I'd frontload our advertising. I knew how much money I was spending. But still, seeing it all deducted from the account made it seem a little more real. I wasn't used to being responsible for such a huge budget.

After my third cup of tea my nerves calmed and I returned to breathing normally. I rationalized that we were getting good results, so I was getting a nice return on the money invested. I still didn't know what to think about my $50,000 bonus.

Around three o'clock I packed up and headed to my parents' house. I used Mom's computer to read my personal e-mail, make a couple little adjustments on my video script and send myself more emails. Playing the role of both my boss and myself in a game of e-mail tag was confusing. I had to be extremely vigilant about what I knew as myself and what I knew as my boss…I didn't want the FBI, or anyone hacking my e-mails to suspect that I was my boss.

For the rest of the week…and the next…I spent every day working at my parents' house after exercising. (Okay, two days I slept in and skipped the gym.) I figured this way the FBI should get bored quickly with my innocuous routine. I hadn't even bothered to logon to CussedEmOuterwear.com with my stealth computer that entire time.

It was killing me not to know what was going on at the website, but I wanted to throw Bill off my trail as quickly as possible. It was heavy lugging my stealth computer around in my gym bag every day. Plus, the sooner the FBI lost interest, the sooner my nerves would calm down. It wasn't easy living on hyper-alert. Knowing that it wasn't just a cautionary measure, but a real necessity, made it that much more stressful.

I hadn't heard from Kim in awhile. I figured that was a good sign. I assumed Bill had stopped suggesting we all get together. Which would be wonderful. But, I worried Bill might have stopped calling her, which would be disastrous. If he just dumped her flat, I don't know how I'd ever forgive myself.

I decided to take matters into my own hands. I had to end the suspense! I called Kim to suggest that she and Bill and I go skiing that weekend. Kim apologized for not calling me in so long. Apparently she'd been really busy…with Bill! The two of them had been out almost every single night. And he'd kicked the relationship up to the next level, finally making the relationship more physical and telling her he adored her.

When I got off the phone, I could have screamed for joy. I assumed the FBI had some kind of code of ethics that would forbid entering into a physical relationship as part of an investigation…and that would mean Bill wasn't investigating me any longer. Best yet, rather than dumping Kim after the investigation, he kicked the relationship up a notch. So instead of being the cause of Kim's emotional ruin, I may have been the catalyst for her happiness. Phew! What a relief.

Skiing on Sunday was a lot of fun. Except, maybe for Kim and Bill being sooo kissy-huggy that it initiated by my gag reflex. But, I figured it was a long time coming for Kim and she deserved a little lovey-doveyness. It was nice not to get the Spanish Inquisition from Bill. He was a really sweet, funny (he had Kim snorting), earnest kind of guy…even if he was a little pompous and ultra conservative.

On Monday, I got up feeling relieved. I knew I couldn't let that lead to complacency, but it was so nice to shake off so much of the stress I'd been carrying around. After taking in a Zumba class at the Y, I went to my parents' house to dig the stealth computer out from where I'd hidden it. Then, I took a long drive out toward UB. On the way, I stopped at a car dealership. I needed a more fuel efficient and reliable car if I was going to be driving all over tarnation to make myself hard to pinpoint.

While I was at the car dealership I discovered that Rachel's First Law of Peril could easily be expanded to be my First Law of Life. I wasn't eligible for a car loan! Rachel Shannon didn't have a job...Rachel Shandling did.

This scenario had never occurred to me. It made me wonder what other ramifications there might be. Would I have trouble getting a job after this? How much would I be losing in social security benefits? (My fake name had its own fake social security number.) I definitely wouldn't be eligible for Workmen's Compensation or unemployment benefits if anything were to happen. And who knew how high my health insurance costs might be after my COBRA ran out?

Maybe Amir was thinking about all these complications when he gave me my signing bonus. Either way, I figured I'd better put the majority of the bonus into my savings account. I couldn't predict what kind of financial crises I might come across. So much for feeling rich.

Once I got near UB, I found a coffee shop with a Wi-Fi signal and logged onto CussedEmOuterwear.com for the first time in a couple weeks. Zowie! Traffic on both sides of the site had sky rocketed.

There wasn't all that much "news" on the Glyphs side of the site. One of the latest symbols that had been added to the formula was in hot contention. It looked like half the Glyphs community thought it was wrong, with the other half thinking it was right.

Independent discussions were springing up all over. Browsing through those, it looked like a big portion of the community still had the same feelings I did about the origin and meaning of the Glyphs. I posed the question of whether a person's intuition level had anything to do with their Glyphs assumptions. It would be interesting to see what the community had to say. I personally believed the two were connected.

I almost didn't notice a request for a personal meeting. It was short, but specific. "Seer" had information too sensitive to post. He (or she?) wanted to meet with me ASAP to discuss it. There was a number for me to call to make the arrangements.

I thought it was odd that someone would leave a phone number on the site. I assumed an obsession for security was part of the Glyphs package. Maybe I'd gotten that part wrong. I figured I'd wait to call "Seer" until after discussing it with Amir.

It wasn't until I took a close look at the public side of the site that I started getting worried. Deeply worried. Nauseous worried.

We were closing in on 2 million unique visitors. The jackets were selling so fast, the web-based fulfillment service I was using couldn't keep up. All orders were already going automatically to backorder. We'd sold over 2,000 jackets…and the sales trend was sharply increasing. Our Google Ad Words revenues were running $800 a week – also with a steep growth trend.

We'd become a sensation! Would the media start paying attention? What if they wanted to do a story? Would they get even more interested when they couldn't find an office or an owner or anyone involved with the site?

I'd never thought about it. Success created its own problems. I guess I'd never assumed we'd have such huge success. I thought we'd be lucky to get several hundred people to visit our site.

That night when I checked Amir's batphone (we were on the #3 batphone now), he had left an urgent message for me to call him the next day. I barely slept.

Chapter 35

The next day I drove out to Chestnut Ridge Park. I'd call Amir from the casino at the assigned time. Next to no one would be there in the middle of a weekday afternoon. I could talk in relative privacy without freezing my butt off outside.

Again, Amir answered on the first ring. But, this was a different Amir than I'd come to know. His voice was controlled, but I could detect the underlying rage.

"Rachel, what the hell is going on?"

I'd never heard Amir swear before. I was pretty sure "hell" was a big curse word as far as he was concerned.

"Ummm…unexpected success? I'm guessing that people who aren't consciously aware of the Glyphs are somehow unconsciously drawn to them. That's the only way I can explain how we've gotten so much traffic on so little promotion."

"And how is it that there is now money going in to the company bank account?" It sounded like he was spitting out the words between clenched teeth.

"I set the public side up to act more like a commercial site. I contracted for Google Ads thinking we could generate a little income. And, as you've probably noticed, I'm selling jackets. I figured that would also be a really cost effective way to get our message out…every jacket is like a walking billboard. I didn't think it would explode like this. I never in a million years thought we'd be able to generate this much interest." My voice was cracking.

There was silence on the other end of the line.

"I'm sorry, Amir."

"Is there anything else I should know?"

"I'm pretty sure I got the FBI off my tail."

"Anything else?"

"I think you should drop out of all this. I can manage the website with the income it's generating. I don't need your paycheck."

"Perhaps that might be best. Rachel, it is difficult enough to disguise money going out. But, money coming in attracts so much more attention. I cannot afford that attention. It is best I am not associated with this any longer."

"Great. Then. Thanks. I obviously couldn't have gotten this far without you."

"Will you do me a favor?"

"Sure."

"Keep the next batphone on and with you at all times…in case there are any unforeseen complications I need to clear up with you. I will dispose of the phones on this end, so you will have no way to contact me."

"Fine. Sure. No problem."

"And could you please send back the necklace?"

"Certainly." I made a little squeaking sound choking back the tears. I hoped Amir didn't pick it up on his end.

His voice softened ever so slightly. "It is not that I do not wish you to have the necklace. But, it is one of a kind. It could be traced back to me."

"I understand. No need to explain."

"Goodbye, Rachel."

"Goodbye."

And that was it. I was on my own. I went home and went to bed. For three days.

Chapter 36

Once I'd finally pulled myself out of my funk I had a lot of catching up to do. I sent the necklace to the P.O. Box as Amir had requested. Then, I researched additional service providers for even more Glyphs merchandise. If I was going to be on my own, I'd have to maximize my income stream to afford advertising and other promotional costs.

Then, I returned Seer's call. I didn't find him to be nice. He sounded like a creep trying to pretend he was nice. I didn't think he was a Seer at all. From the comments left on the website, it seemed like only nice people got the Glyphs visions. Or did the visions somehow make people nice? Did it matter?

In any event, when I tried to enter into a bit of a Glyphs philosophical conversation with him, it was obvious he didn't get the Glyphs. He said he had information he could only give me in person. I told him he'd need to post it to the website. He argued, offered to come to my city, offered to fly me to his city. I cut him off politely and threw away the phone.

That guy had me worried. He talked like he was well funded…maybe a government or some kind of fringe group (I'm assuming a mainstream group wouldn't be so sneaky)? Since Seer was trying to arrange a meeting, I was guessing he didn't know who I was or how to find me. I hoped it would stay that way.

Since I was all alone in this whole Glyphs thing now, I felt more vulnerable. I considered fessing up to Bill and trying to get some protection from the FBI. But, I really didn't trust the government to do the right thing when it came to the Glyphs. Big oil had so many politicians in their pockets. Heck, they had owned the White House the preceding eight years. I wouldn't be at all surprised if they tried to suppress whatever info came from the Glyphs if it turned out to be for some sort of clean energy. And then how would they go about suppressing *me*? I could end up being in greater danger than I was on my own.

Besides, the stated plan on the website was to make the Glyphs available to everyone, everywhere. That kind of sharing was the feeling that came with the vision. If the FBI higher ups didn't have the vision, they might not be so generous.

So, the only thing I could do was be careful. Being careful was nerve-wracking. Fortunately, it was snowing a lot this winter. I was always studying the footprints in the snow around the house, making sure I could account for all of them.

I noticed that the website had been infiltrated by some users with an agenda of their own. Certain usernames were consistently disagreeing about the correctness of parts of the Glyphs formula. It looked like they were deliberately trying to cause the wrong Glyphs to be posted (I had set up the site so that every part of the formula could be challenged and voted on, with the majority ruling what remained posted.)

I went through the history of our postings. It was easy to spot the visitors who had insightful comments and what I would consider an accurate eye. These users all agreed on the same Glyphs before the troublemakers came in and tried to vote them down.

We were getting so much traffic on the website that it was hard for the infiltrators to keep voting down parts of the formula. Still, I needed an uncontaminated arena. I created a second, private, invitation-only site. I asked all the users I invited to continue to participate in the other site as they always had so the infiltrators wouldn't get suspicious.

It didn't look like there was any infiltration on the invitation-only site. I was hoping that meant my email hadn't been hacked. Still, I was really careful about what I sent out…and I posted a warning letting users know they should be extremely cautious about all Glyphs interactions.

We were making progress, but it was going very slowly. We'd input maybe one new Glyphs symbol a week. That wouldn't be so bad, except that there were over ten pages of formula with about 1,000 Glyphs per page and 25% of those were blanks. With a major ice shelf having unexpectedly broken off not long ago, I was worried we needed to fill the blanks in a lot faster. (In case you're as bad at math as me, we're talking about 50 years to fill in the formula at our present rate.)

Even though it was really expensive, I went forward with production on a Glyphs video. I figured that was our best shot at really getting the message to the widest possible audience.

I was pretty happy with the way I had been able to keep up my regular routine…morning exercise, followed by several solid hours of work at my parents' house or "at large." (Though, when I was "at large," I was careful not to have any regularity to where I went.) The routine allowed me to maintain my sanity.

Working alone, without any human contact, was a bit weirdifying. (Especially since my "job" was bizarre to begin with.) I didn't want to turn into a total nutcase, so I joined a couple organizations. My favorite was a committee planning a section of bike trail that would hopefully stretch from Buffalo to Colden one day. It was probably my favorite because there were a lot of people my age on the committee. Plus, I had to do a lot of coordinating with local government and homeowners' groups. That kept up my people skills. (Mostly negotiating, sucking up, and groveling…all important job skills I had to keep sharp for when I needed a real job again.)

All in all, except for filling in the Glyphs blanks so slowly, things were going pretty well. And the video would be done in a couple weeks, so I had great hopes things would be moving faster soon. My love life was another story.

Even though I previously had a total lack of romantic involvement, it was easier to take before. In the past, I wasn't involved with anyone because I hadn't found a guy who measured up. Now, after having spent some quality time with two guys that measured up, I felt lonelier. I knew exactly what I was missing.

I was feeling particularly depressed about my total lack of a relationship since this was Valentine's Day weekend. Everyone I knew had a date Saturday night. Even my book club meeting was cancelled. And it just seemed to emphasize the fact that I was so alone…there weren't even any "possibles" in the running.

I worked out extra long Friday morning to try to sweat away my blues. It didn't exactly have the effect I was hoping for. Sweating away with my brain largely unoccupied, I kept thinking of Jim and Amir. I quit working on my Glyphs stuff earlier than usual since I was having such a hard time concentrating. I just wanted to go home and wallow in self pity.

Jim and Amir might not be interested in keeping me company, but I knew two guys who were always there for me. I stopped by the store on my way home and picked up Ben & Jerry. Since it was a special date, I got Wegmans Triple Chocolate Dessert Sauce (like, the most amazing chocolate sauce ever…once you've had the Trip, mere hot fudge will never again suffice) and whipped cream. It was sheer decadence, even if I did resist the chopped nuts.

I flipped through my mail on the way up the stairs to my apartment. It looked like I got a couple of Valentine's Day cards –from my parents, from Kim…and from a couple others. Probably no one interesting. Still, I rushed to the kitchen so I could put down my groceries and open my mail. I stopped dead in my tracks.

Chapter 37

The kitchen was at the back of the house. The back entrance to the apartment was at the far end of the kitchen. Since we didn't have driveway access, we never used that door. My roommates and I *always* came in through the front. I don't even think any of us had a key to the outside back door.

But, when I entered the kitchen, the door dog had been pushed practically against the wall. (The door dog was a long, stuffed tube that my roommate's grandmother had knitted in the shape of a dog. We put it at the foot of the door to block the draft from the back hall.) Someone had opened the door, shoving the door dog up by the wall.

I tried to act nonchalant (difficult to do after stopping dead in my tracks). I mumbled, "Oh, damn, I forgot." Then I turned and walked out of the apartment. (Okay, I walked through the apartment, but I ran down the stairs as fast as I could.) I ran to my car and locked myself in. Fortunately, from my parking spot on the street I could keep an eye on the front door. (Unfortunately, I couldn't see the back door.)

It looked like my landlords were still at work, so I doubted they had been in the apartment. I speed-dialed my roommates. Both were still at work and said they would have had nothing to do with opening the back door. I knew the door dog was up against the door this morning. I would have noticed the draft during breakfast if it weren't. (The back hall opened up to a big, enclosed porch with fourteen, 100-year-old windows, "draft" would have been an understatement.)

As far as I knew, whoever came in the apartment could still be there. I called 911. The police arrived in under ten minutes.

When they heard that my only evidence of a break-in was the door dog, they seemed to calm down quite considerably. Still, they went up and searched the apartment with their guns drawn. They also searched the attic and the basement. My landlords' doors were still locked, so they didn't feel the need to search his apartment.

They checked the basement windows, finding one had been forced open. Someone had simply pushed on it hard enough that the screws on the latch had popped right out of the 100-year-old wood. The officer told me there was a rash of break-ins exactly like this in the area. They suspected it was teens.

The police asked me to check around the apartment to see if anything was missing. The only things I noticed that were gone were my roommates and my PCs. (Thankfully, I had my "stealth" computer with me.) That apparently was somewhat consistent with the other break-ins: PCs were a big target as were cameras and jewelry. (Far as I could tell, no cameras or jewelry were missing…but, there was a good chance no one would find any of my stuff worth stealing.)

The cops showed me how easy it was to jimmy open our apartment's back door with a credit card and advised we get deadbolts. Then, they left. Two seconds later, I left.

Home Depot had all kinds of deadbolts. Trouble was, you needed special equipment like hole saws to install them. And I was too paranoid to call a locksmith to install my locks. Locksmiths can be bribed. Or infiltrated. It was exasperating to be so alone and not able to trust anyone. I sure as heck didn't want to worry my parents by telling them about the break in.

I'd just have to ask my landlord to help install the locks. He was handy and had lots of tools. But, he was incredibly lazy – not really a very good landlord. His wife hated him fixing things in our apartment when so many things needed fixed in their own. He was home when I got back from the store. I pressured him into helping me install the locks right away. (One for the front door, too. You can't be too careful.). He already had deadbolts on his doors, so it wasn't too hard to make him feel guilty. He sawed all the holes and I did the rest.

Chapter 38

Ben & Jerry weren't able to cheer me up that night. Not only was I alone, I didn't know if I was a victim of a random robbery or if a Glyphs-related incident.

Kim had a date with Bill that night, but she spent Saturday afternoon trying to cheer me up. She did put me in a much better mood and probably kept me from finishing off the entire pint of B&J.

Kim and I hadn't gotten together nearly enough in the last month or so – which may have been a good thing. I wanted so much to tell her about everything that was going on with me – and I knew I shouldn't. I felt that the more people knew about what I was up to, the more danger they might be in. I just couldn't put anyone else at risk. As it was, the robbery had me worrying I might be putting my roommates at risk, though I had no way to know if that were true.

I didn't have to worry about my roommates for long. The robbery really freaked them out. On Sunday Emma told me she was going to move back into her parents' house. Olivia used the break-in as an excuse to ask her boyfriend to move in with us.

Olivia was one of those girls destined to always date assholes. She was attracted to them. They were attracted to her. She and her current boyfriend were a match made in hell. He treated her like garbage. She acted like a spoiled brat when he was around. I wasn't about to put up with their constant fighting. I nixed the idea of him moving in. So, she made plans to move into his apartment instead.

While I was happy not to have to worry about endangering my roommates, I was going to miss them. Working alone. Living alone. Life was just getting worse by the minute. So, I got a dog.

Ozone was a mutt I picked up from the SPCA. They didn't know anything about his past, but they said he had a nice, calm disposition. I called him Ozone because he insisted on sleeping with me (mostly, on top of me). That kept me nice and warm. I figured "Ozone" was a better name than "Heating Pad."

Ozone was a perfect pet. He was cuddly, but not jumpy or yippy. He obviously had some German Shepherd in his lineage, so he was fairly large and, hopefully, intimidating. It was love at first sight for the both of us.

I'd only had Ozone a few days when I got a call from Bill. He asked if I could meet him for lunch that day. There was something very all-business about his tone. When I arrived, he was waiting for me with an attractive, middle aged woman. I could see the slight bulge of gun under each of their suit jackets.

"Rachel, I'd like you to meet Special Agent Amy Willis of the FBI."

"Nice to meet you, Amy." I tried to look slightly surprised and curious. Since that was the way I was feeling, I think I pulled it off.

"Rachel, I have a confession to make." Bill cleared his throat. I could see this wasn't exactly easy for him.

"My name is Bill Braxton, not Bill Burton. I am also with the FBI. I wasn't able to be completely honest with you and Kim because I was working undercover when I first met the two of you."

I was dazed. Bill was coming clean. What could this possibly be all about?

"You were investigating someone at Kim's office?"

"No, Rachel, Bill was investigating you."

"Me! Why would the FBI be investigating me?"

"Amy didn't mean you personally, Rachel. We're investigating your employer."

"I'm self employed."

"Your client then."

"CussedEmOuterwear.com?"

"Yes."

"Why?"

"We're not at liberty to disclose details of an ongoing investigation. But, we were hoping you could give us some information about your client."

"Such as?"

"Tell us what you know about the people you work for. What their goals are. What you do for them."

"I work strictly through e-mail. And it's all confidential. I have a nondisclosure agreement." I was so glad that Amir's involvement had been cut short so quickly. There should be no trail linking CussedEmOuterwear.com to him in any way.

"We have reason to believe they might be involved in counterintelligence."

"Counterintelligence? Like stealing government secrets?!"

"Exactly."

"Are those Glyphs stolen from the government?"

"No. We don't think that."

"What do you think?"

"We don't know what to think, Rachel. But, the activity on their website appears suspicious."

"Suspicious, how? I designed that website! There shouldn't be anything suspicious about it. "

"It's not the website per se, but the activity on it. There's communication from all over the globe. Some of it is originating from within enemy nations."

"Oh. Well, that's easy to explain. The site allows anyone to post and strives to connect with an international audience. That was one of my given objectives."

"Still, we'd like to ask you some questions."

"I'll try to tell you what I can, but I do have that nondisclosure agreement." "We could get a warrant."

"Great. That would probably allow me to talk to you without risking a lawsuit."

"The problem is, Rachel, that would take time. And we don't feel we have that kind of time."

"You're putting me in an uncomfortable position here, Bill. Clients are very, very picky about leaking information. Besides, I am positive this website has nothing to do with espionage. My client's intentions are completely honorable. She sees these Glyphs things in her head and apparently other people do too. She wants to create an online community where they can compare notes. You should have been able to gather that from looking at the website. I don't see why you need me."

"Rachel, there is a chance that the break-in at your apartment was related to your client's business."

"Am I in danger?" I didn't have to fake the sudden crack in my voice or my shaky hands.

"That's what we'd like to find out."

I agreed to go back to their office so we could talk in private. I excused myself to go repair my watery eyes. I left my blazer hung over my chair at the table while I was in the ladies' room. My micro voice recorder was on in the jacket's breast pocket at the time.

Chapter 39

Back at the FBI offices, it became evident that they had no idea what the Glyphs were all about, though they had been aware of them for several years. Apparently, the Glyphs had surfaced from time to time in the past, drawing the FBI's attention. But no one ever pinpointed what they were.

I told Bill and Amy the truth, with omissions. There was no reason for them to know that my "client" was me. They didn't need to know that Jim or Amir had ever been involved. But, as far as anything else went, I didn't hold back.

I knew Bill was a conservative and analytical guy. I honestly didn't think he'd take the Glyphs seriously once he got the full 411. Frankly, I was worried he'd write me off as a total nutcase. I knew he already felt I was too whacky for his taste.

"So, your client wants you to publicize the website to find as many people as possible with this 'vision'?"

"Exactly."

"And she thinks this vision is being sent from outer space in order to save our civilization?"

"Not necessarily outer space. It could be inner space. They just don't think the Glyphs are coming from Earth."

"Why is that?"

"The general feeling is that the Glyphs hold a message the sender wants us to have. If it were coming from Earth, they'd be in a language someone could understand."

"And what is this message supposedly about?"

"Most people who 'see' the Glyphs believe they have something to do with averting manmade climate change. Maybe a formula for clean energy."

"Why would space aliens be sending a message about clean energy?"

"Most of the Glyphs community believes that our universe exists inside a host organism…and there could be other universes inside of us. On the website, that concept is referred to as the Horton Theory."

"What would clean energy have to do with the 'host organism'?" You could hear the incredulity dripping from Bill's voice.

"The feeling is that our increased development and energy consumption creates a disease situation. For instance, dirty industrialization may be a cancer or a virus to the host organism."

"So, your client thinks we're a virus?"

"Possibly. Have you ever seen a virus? They don't look organic. They look like little space ships. And they change quickly to adapt to conditions. That could be evolution…or that could be a civilization learning."

"And you believe all this malarkey?"

"Is our conversation completely confidential?"

"Believe me, we're not going to the media with *this*."

"Then, yes, I believe it. Because I see the Glyphs, too."

I could see this admission got a rise out of Bill and Amy. Perhaps I was the first real, live Glyphs-Seer the FBI ever had in its clutches. I wondered if I'd just made a huge mistake.

"Okay. From the top. You see the Glyphs?"

"Since I was a child."

"And you think they're a formula for clean energy because…?"

"Because tied up with the vision are certain feelings. Like the feeling that something the Glyphs will fix is tied up with climate change. Most of the Glyphs community members have been obsessed with climate change their entire lives."

"But global warming is a crock of bull. No one's proven global warming has anything to do with carbon emissions. In fact, the temperature of Mars is rising, too. Carbon emissions on this planet couldn't have a damn thing to do with the temperature rising on Mars."

"Well, not unless you ascribe to the Horton Theory."

Bill just blinked at me.

"If our universe is inside another organism...and we're making the organism sick...the organism gets a fever to try to kill the sickness...everything heats up."

"You've got to be kidding me."

"Well, I've read that a sustained six degree rise in our average temperature will virtually kill off the planet."

"And your point is?"

"A six degree fever is about the point where we start to experience cell death."

Bill literally threw up his hands in disgust at my idiocy. I couldn't read Amy's reaction. She had perfected the stone face.

"The bottom line is, I don't think the Glyphs or our website threatens national security. I wouldn't work on the project if I thought it did."

I think they believed I was sincere.

"Now, can you tell me why you think the break-in at my apartment was related to my involvement with the website?"

"In addition to posts from enemy nations, your website is also getting traffic from several known terrorist organizations."

"And you think these terrorists know I'm working for the website?"

"Not necessarily. Your client has done a very good job of making your and her involvement completely opaque. We don't think it's possible to crack that opacity. But, your intruder has given us cause for concern."

"So, the FBI didn't hack the system at CussedEmOuterwear.com?"

"No."

"Then, I'm confused. How did you find *me*?"

"I was on campus one day when you were distributing t-shirts at UB. I recognized the Glyphs as part of an on-going, agency-wide investigation, followed you to your car and took down your license plate number."

"So the investigation you were working on when you first met Kim was an investigation of me?"

"Yes. But, that investigation has been closed."

"And you're talking to me now because…?"

"Because of the break-in at your apartment. With the nefarious characters that visit your website, we became concerned there might be a connection."

"But you don't think the website can be hacked?"

"No."

"Yet you think the break-in and the website might be connected?"

"It could just be a coincidence. But, coincidences always arouse our suspicion."

"But if the website hasn't been hacked, then the only way anyone could know about my connection to it would be through a leak from the FBI."

Amy and Bill both shifted in their seats.

"I think that's highly unlikely. Your case has been handled with the utmost confidentiality."

"Are there any provisions in place to protect me?"

"At this point, we have no indication that you're in any danger."

"What are you doing to find the intruder who broke into my apartment?"

"That's a matter for the police."

"So, you're concerned enough to drag me in here to interrogate me – but not concerned enough to determine if I could really be in danger?"

"Rachel, the probability that you're at risk is incredibly small."

"But any risk I'm in would seem to come from an internal FBI leak regarding your investigation of me. That is unacceptable." I stood up for emphasis.

"What?"

"The police aren't doing a damn thing about the break in. They think they're looking for a couple kids who'll eventually get caught in the act. Nobody's doing any investigating. I want the FBI at my apartment right now, dusting for prints."

"It's been days. The scene's been contaminated."

"I don't give a rat's ass. You said I could be in danger. Your agency could have put me in danger. You are going to collect prints and run them against whatever database of terrorist suspects you have."

"Rachel, we can't do that. It's not our job. Your break in is not a federal case."

"I thought you said this was a counterintelligence concern?"

"We have no solid evidence linking your break-in to the counterintelligence investigation."

"If you dusted for prints, perhaps you'd have that evidence."

"We simply don't have the resources to investigate paths that aren't likely to produce high-level results."

"I'm going to go to my apartment now. I will expect an investigative team to be there within a half an hour. If they don't show up, I'm sure there are a number of national news organizations that would be interested in this situation." I stormed out of the FBI office and drove home hoping they would not call my bluff.

An FBI team arrived in fifteen minutes.

Chapter 40

The prints from my doorknob belonged to a local teenage thug with a record of petty thefts. I got the feeling the FBI was too embarrassed to pass this information along to the police. I didn't mind. I was just glad it was an ordinary, random break-in.

I was also greatly relieved that the FBI thought the Glyphs website was unhackable. That greatly reduced the stress associated with my uncertainty. (Nothing could ever be certain – I had a Rachel's Law for that – but, there were differing degrees of uncertainty. I'd relegated the website's security to a high uncertainty level [translation: worry level] initially. Now I could reasonably downgrade it to a lesser level of uncertainty/stress.)

Hopefully all the nefarious elements Bill and Amy mentioned would never be able to track me down. (Unless they had a mole in the FBI. Or they followed me to my car that one day UB…what other possibilities might I be overlooking?)

I was a little pissed at Bill, but I didn't dwell on it. I figured if he ever found out I was my own Glyphs client, he'd be miffed at me, too.

The conversation captured on my tape recorder while I was in the restroom at the restaurant was rather amusing. Bill asked Amy what she thought of me.

"She seems like a very nice, responsible young woman."

"Yeah, she's a straight arrow. But whacky."

"I wouldn't say she's whacky. She just has a very open mind."

"Yeah. Like I said. Whacky."

It was just a few days after my FBI run-in that the Glyphs video arrived. I put it on every video file sharing service I could find.

Then all hell broke loose.

The video was a sensation. It got millions of hits. Millions! Glyphs merchandise was flying off the shelves. (I stopped counting how many countries orders originated in when I hit 18.) Thousands of visitors worldwide had inputted a correct symbol to gain access to the private side of our site.

While all this was good news for our cause, it was bad news for me. Working 12-hour days, I still couldn't keep up with the postings or email. I thought about hiring help, but I couldn't justify putting someone else at possible risk. And I'd be at greater risk with every person who knew of my involvement.

I decided I'd just skim the postings since, in theory, they could sort of take care of themselves. I concentrated on the email. After about a week of slogging through it practically 24/7, I came across this:

To: Anne.Hawn.Imus@gmail.com
From: rhymeswithterry@gmail.com
Subject: My sister's Glyphs

My sister has a notebook full of Glyphs. I think she has all the blanks filled in. But, I cant be shure. I dont understand them. My sister is blind. She wants to post the Glyphs but I dont no how.

I think my heart momentarily stopped. When it started back up, it was racing. And I was hyperventilating. Could this be for real? Did I dare dream that we'd be successful so soon?

My first worry was that my email could have been hacked and someone else could have read it before me. Or, would they bother? With thousands and thousands of emails to wade through, would an infiltrator have the time to read them all – or just wait and read through my replies? (I only replied personally to a fraction of the emails. The rest, I tried to address in more generalized postings.)

I figured I'd better do everything in my power to make my reply inconspicuous. I created a standard reply thanking the sender for their email and reinforcing our mission. I made this reply long enough to fill up the entire screen when you first open an email. Then, I sent that reply to a couple thousand people. (Can you say carpal tunnel syndrome?)

Buried within those thousands of emails, I sent that same reply to rhymeswithterry, but I tacked this message on the end:

It is extremely important that your sister's Glyphs get posted. Can you scan the entire notebook into your computer and send it to me? Also, photocopy her notebook and mail the copies to my PO Box. I will make sure everything is posted.

Please be aware that you and your sister could be at risk until your Glyphs are posted. Dangerous groups seek this information. I do not believe our email has been hacked, but you need to be extremely cautious just in case.

Trust no one...not even if you think it is me. The only way to remove all risk is to post the Glyphs to the website.

You can call me at 716-555-7784 if you have questions.

I hit "send" and spent most of the night pacing.

Chapter 41

The next night, RhymesWithTerry's mother called me back on the batphone number I included in the e-mail. Apparently RhymesWithTerry and her blind sister were middle schoolers. They hadn't told their mother anything about the Glyphs until they got my email, which scared the begeezus out of them – and their mother.

Do you have any idea how difficult it is to calm down the mother of a child you've told might be in danger? And then to explain that the whole scenario is over a bunch of squiggly drawings that the kid sees in her head?

"Who the hell are you?"

"Please call me Anne. I help coordinate a website devoted to the Glyphs your daughter doodles. One of your daughters visited the website and contacted me."

"Well, how dare you tell a little girl she might be in danger and scare her half to death!"

"First, I wasn't positive I was dealing with a child. Second, she could possibly be in danger."

"What kind of danger?"

"The FBI recently advised me that our website is being targeted by enemy nations and known terrorist groups interested in those squiggly symbols. If you can scan your daughter's drawings into your computer and post them to our website, you'll most likely remove any threat of danger."

"I wanted to burn those drawings, but she's hidden her notebook and won't tell me where."

"Well, she must be a very smart little girl because destroying the drawings could put her in extreme danger."

"How?"

"If you destroy the drawings, the only place they'll exist is in your daughter's head. If these terrorist groups really want the drawings, they'd then be forced to go after your daughter."

"So, those drawings could be valuable?"

"I suppose there's a possibility that someone would be willing to pay for them. Right now, our website is publishing them for free."

"How much do you think they'd be worth?"

From the tone of her voice I could tell that she was actually considering if she could try to squeeze some cash out of someone for her daughter's drawings.

"I don't know how much they might be worth, but I personally don't think they're worth gambling with your daughter's safety."

I didn't say it, but in my head, I added "You stupid, evil bitch."

Her voice turned cold and stiff. "Is that a threat?"

"Not from me. But I can't guarantee the threat isn't out there from God-knows-who. You need to cautious."

"What about the FBI? You said you talked to the FBI. Could I give the drawings to them?"

"They could be interested in them. However, if the FBI doesn't publish the drawings where the world can see them, I would think your daughter would still be at considerable risk if anyone ever identified her as knowing the entire Glyphs code."

"Why are those drawings so important anyway?"

"No one knows for sure, Ma'am. You should ask your daughter. Her answer is most likely as good, or better, than anyone else's."

"She thinks they're something that will save the world."

"That would be the general consensus."

"So, that surely must be worth something."

I could not believe this woman was a.) trying to find a way to profit from saving the world and b.) willing to put her daughter in danger for financial gain. It was against the website's stated policy, but I started wracking my brain for ways I could pay her. I'd invested my entire $50,000 signing bonus, plus a good portion of my first few months' profits into producing the video. The rest was already earmarked for advertising bills that would be due soon. I hadn't been paying myself much of salary. All I had in the bank was $4,000.

"I...I've got $4,000 in my personal savings account..."

"Four thousand! What kind of fool do you think I am? This has got to be worth *millions*."

"I'm sorry. I have no idea where you could get that kind of money."

"I could post an offer on your website, couldn't I?"

"Sure. And you could hope the people who answer your inquiry aren't murdering terrorists. And if whoever buys the drawings from you doesn't post them publicly, your daughter remains at risk."

"Listen. I have to think about this. I'll call you back."

"No."

"No?" I could hear in her voice that she thought I was some nervy little bitch.

"Yeah. No. Because you have me concerned that you will compromise your daughter's safety. And I can't let that happen. You either post your daughter's drawings to the website now...or you overnight photocopies to me. If I don't see one or the other by noon tomorrow, I will go to the authorities...I'm not sure they can protect your daughter, but you'd leave me no choice."

There was a pause.

"Listen. She won't tell me where her notebook is. I've tried everything. She will only hand it over to you."

I guess, with a mother like that, you had to be a very cautious kid.

Chapter 42

I did have the mother call me back, with both of us using different phones...just in case. Her daughter wouldn't give her the notebook and she didn't know how to scan and post anything online anyway. She said she'd be willing to meet me the next day. She lived in New Jersey.

We arranged to meet at a mall and drive to a post office with a photocopier. The post office was in walking distance from her house. Her daughters would walk to the post office with a group of friends. The girl would give me her notebook, I'd photocopy it, and we'd be done.

I had a ridiculous amount of preparations to make and very little time to make them. Worse, this was big. If anyone had somehow listened in or had any inkling what was going on, who knows what kind of danger we be in? I couldn't afford to skimp on the precautions.

That night I checked into a hotel by the airport using one of the false ID's I'd gotten from Jim's brother back at the start of all this. I paid cash. And, for the first time, I turned off the phone that Amir had asked me to keep on...and I left it at home. I was that worried. Stakes were so high, I didn't know who I could trust.

Early the next morning, in a fat suit and black wig, I pulled a carry on out from inside one of my bags and grabbed the airport shuttle. I knew the plane wasn't completely booked, so I didn't buy my ticket until I arrived at the airport. I was going to have to use my real identity for the flight. I couldn't risk my fake IDs getting caught by the TSA.

At the gate, I had a private conversation with the boarding agent. "Listen, ummm...I have a really big favor to ask you."

"What can I do for you, Ms. Shannon?"

"I've been a victim of domestic violence and I just completed my divorce. There are rumors that my ex hired someone to retaliate against me. I'm extremely worried that I'm being stalked. If anyone purchases a ticket for this flight after me…would it be possible to let me know?"

"Yes. I should be able to do that for you."

"Thank you so, so much. I cannot tell you how much I appreciate it."

As I looked for a seat in the waiting area, I noticed Jim sitting over by the window reading the paper. I supposed it wasn't that big of a coincidence. The flight into Newark would be one he'd likely take to visit Kiku in NYC. I wanted so much to go over and say "hi." But, this just wasn't the right time.

I'd been waiting for about twenty minutes when I heard "Paging passenger Shannon. Will passenger Shannon please come to the gate?"

A feeling of intense anxiety gripped me. I could feel myself breaking out into a cold sweat. I had to walk slowly to keep myself steady. At the gate, the agent confirmed my worst fear.

"Ms. Shannon. There was another ticket purchased. Which is rather unusual at this late time."

"Oh, dear."

"The gentleman who purchased it is standing over at the far end of the gate area. He's in a light brown suit and hat with dark glasses."

"Is he looking this way now?"

"No, he's looking out at the window at the Jetway."

"I turned ever so slightly to glance over in the direction she indicated."

"Thank you. Thank you so much."

"He's seated in first class. If you'd like, I can arrange to have a security escort waiting for you upon arrival."

"I think knowing who to keep an eye on should be enough – after all, it's probably nothing. Thank you so much, though."

The gate agent looked skeptical. She may have been doubly concerned by the man's name and complexion. Just from a quick glance at his back, those broad, square shoulders, the fine suit. I recognized Faris right away.

Fortunately, Jim wasn't sitting anywhere near Faris. I plopped down in an empty seat next to Jim, opened a newspaper in front of my face and spoke in a hushed tone.

"Don't look up. Don't look at me. Don't say a word. It's Rachel."

Jim handled this very smoothly. The change is his demeanor was nearly imperceptible.

"I'm sorry to involve you, but if you could help me just this once, I'd appreciate it. There is a man standing by the window in a hat, light brown suit and sunglasses. He is following me. He'll be sitting in first class."

"When I get off the plane, I'll have short blondish hair, khaki pants and a black blazer. If you could try to keep an eye on him and see if he follows me, I would appreciate it. If you can do this for me, please turn the page."

Jim turned the page of his newspaper.

"I have the batphone. Do you remember the number?" I always kept Jim's batphone with me as a little lifeline…even though I knew there was little chance Jim would ever be at the end of that line. I hoped he turned his phone on occasionally, but I doubted that he did.

Jim turned the page of his newspaper again. Then, we both sat there, reading our papers, ignoring each other until our seats were called.

I was in the very back of the plane and was one of the first rows called after pre-board and first class. I noticed that Faris didn't board when first class was called. He just stood there, looking out the window. My guess was that his eyes were actually fixed on the reflections in the window, watching for any sign of me leaving the gate area.

I had actually screwed myself by asking the gate agent to page me. There was a chance Faris would not have recognized the disguise. I was durn lucky to have brought a second getup. Sometimes being paranoid with a need for endless backup plans pays off.

Just before our descent, I went to the restroom at the rear of the plane with my carryon. I came out a tall (platform shoes hidden under long pants), mousy blonde. My chest was bound down as tightly as I could get it – so tight that not a hint of cleavage peaked out of my scooped-neck tee. I slouched badly and hung my head down when I walked. I had pulled a smaller carryon out of my regular carryon. The fat suit was in the regular carryon which I was just going to leave on the plane. I stashed it above an empty seat way in the back but I returned to an empty seat just ahead of Jim –several rows further up the aisle from where I was originally sitting.

When I got off the plane, I followed the flow toward baggage until I found a place to slip into an elevator up to the arrivals area. I jumped into the backseat of a cab that people were just getting out of. Probably not cool with airport rules, but the cabbie was so surprised, he just went with it. I was pretty sure it was a clean getaway. After a few miles I had the cabbie drop me off at a hotel. Jim call about ten minutes Jim later.

"I just got my rental. I think that guy is still running around the concourse in a panic. He definitely did not follow you."

"I feel bad. He might be a good guy, but I couldn't take the chance."

Jim groaned. "You don't know the good guys from the bad guys?"

"Who ever does?" My voice was cracking a bit from the tension I'd built up.

"Can I see you?"

"I would love that. Take US-1 to the Frontage Road exit and go left, I'm at a Holiday Inn about a half mile down on the right."

"I'll be there in ten."

"Thanks. I don't know what I would've done without you."

"From what I can see, you would've done just fine."

"Except that I'd still be a sweating ball of nerves always looking over my shoulder."

"Something tells me, you still are anyway."

"You know me too well."

Chapter 43

"My, you've lost a lot of weight today. And didn't you used to have breasts?" Jim slid into the chair across from me.

"I didn't think you ever noticed my breasts."

Jim looked like he was about to say something. Stopped. Then just smiled, grabbed my hands and said, "I've been worried about you."

I smiled back. "No need to worry. I'm fine."

"Liar."

I guess I showed the stress of living a secret life, immersed in a cloud of paranoia, never able to trust anyone. Even now, could I completely trust Jim with him magically appearing on this day of all days? What was it Bill said about coincidences?

"Are you here to see Kiku?"

Jim's face transformed into a storm of emotions. "No. I'm attending a seminar. Kiku and I broke up."

"I'm so sorry."

"Really?" Jim raised an eyebrow. "I didn't think you liked her."

"I didn't like the way she treated you. But, since you loved her, I hoped you could resolve that. I care about you. I want what is best for you."

"Well, I think you achieved that." There didn't seem to be any sarcasm in his tone.

"Oh?"

"You got me to re-examine my relationship with Kiku. It turns out, we both wanted really different things out of life. I want to work with the needy. Kiku was hoping that was a phase I'd grow out of." Jim stared into the coffee the waitress had brought him.

"You know, I think I may have been more in awe of Kiku than in love with her. I'm still in awe of her. She's an amazing woman. A brilliant researcher. She'll save more lives with her research than I'll ever be able to assist in my practice. But…we're not exactly a match made in heaven." Jim seemed to visibly shake off the turmoil that was clouding his eyes. "Besides, Kiku says I'm in love with you."

"Are you?" I was dumbfounded.

"I might be. Kiku says I've been suppressing my emotional side for most of my life."

"I'd concur with that diagnosis."

"Kiku also thinks you're in love with me."

Wow. That was straightforward. Now I was trapped like a rat. And it just wasn't the time to be getting into this kind of conversation. "If I live through today, I would not be opposed to exploring that possibility."

Jim immediately turned serious. "Are you in real danger? Can't you call the FBI?"

"As usual, I don't know. I don't think there will be danger, but who knows? I think if I called the FBI, I might be placing people in danger. But, this may be it, Jim. This may be the end of the search. I may have discovered a source with a complete set of Glyphs."

"And here you are doing this on your own. You haven't even asked me for help. You can't ask for help can you? You're not wired for it."

"I just asked you for help in the airport!"

"Oh. Yeah. You asked me to watch a guy for a couple minutes. That's not asking for help."

"OK, how about this: I could use a little backup today. When does your seminar start?"

"Not 'til tomorrow."

"What kind of seminar is it?"

"Tropical medicine."

"Tropical medicine?" That response surprised the heck out of me.

"I'm planning to join the Peace Corp after I earn my medical degree. And you're just digging around to see if I had a valid reason to be on that flight."

"You're awfully intuitive for someone who's been suppressing their emotional side."

Jim dug a brochure on the seminar out of his pocket and handed it to me. "You're just easy to read. And I'm keen to the thought processes of paranoid nutcases."

I still had over an hour before I was supposed to meet the Evil-Bitch-Mercenary-Mom. Jim took me to a nearby car rental site and arranged to follow me to the mall and then the post office. I didn't tell him that a little girl would be meeting us at the post office with the notebook. He didn't need to know that. And I felt a huge responsibility for that little girl's safety.

I was glad Jim was coming. I didn't trust that mom as far as I could throw her. It would probably take a good ten minutes to copy the notebook at the post office, which was a lot of time to be vulnerable. Having Jim there to keep an eye on things would make me feel better. I could not wait until everything was safely posted on the web. Maybe then my heart could start beating normally again.

I got to the mall almost ten minutes ahead of schedule, but the Evil-Bitch-Mercenary-Mom was already waiting at the appointed spot, chain smoking like a fiend to judge by the cigarette butts on the sidewalk. I pulled up next to her and rolled down the window, "Brandi?" She snuffed out her cigarette with the pointy toe of her ridiculously high-heeled pumps and jumped in the car without hesitation.

Brandi was thin and extremely nervous. She wore skin-tight jeans and an even tighter, low-cut top. Exactly what you'd expect a "Brandi" to wear. Who the hell names their kid Brandi anyway? Did her parents hope she'd become a stripper? Maybe they got their wish. I sure wasn't looking forward to driving into Brandi's neighborhood.

"Hi. I'm Anne." I tried to smile with as much warmth as I could muster.

"Yeah. Great. Just take a left at the next exit." She reached into her purse and pulled out a pack of Marlboros.

"I'm sorry. Please don't smoke in the car. I'll have an asthma attack." I was already coughing from the residual smoke hovering over her clothes like its own noxious ecosystem. I opened my window a crack.

With a huff of disgust she shoved the pack back in her purse and started fidgeting with her lighter.

"I was thinking, there may be a way your daughter can make some money off her notebook."

She stopped fidgeting and gave me her undivided attention.

"If the Glyphs turn out to be as important as many people think they are, I'd bet that a collector would be willing to pay a good price for the notebook even after the contents are posted the website. The notebook would have historical significance."

"Now you tell me." She threw her hands in the air and started shaking her head.

'Now you tell me,' she says? What the heck did that mean? "Is there anything you need to tell me? Are we still progressing according to plan?"

"Yeah. Everything just like we talked. Don't worry about it." But something in the way she said that made me worry more.

I looked in my rearview mirror. Jim was still behind us, discreetly back a few cars. Near as I could tell, nobody else was following. I tried to breathe deep to relax, but it only made my lungs spasm from the rancid smell of stale smoke. My hands clenched the steering wheel in a death grip. I could not wait for this to be over.

As Brandi directed me toward the post office, I couldn't help but notice that we seemed to be traveling through a nice, middle-class neighborhood. I wondered why Brandi was so desperate for cash that she had been oblivious to her daughter's safety. Maybe she had some weird jewelry fetish she needed to support. She had diamonds on every finger and draped around her neck. I suspected the diamonds were real. I did not have the same suspicions about her boobs. They were mighty perky for a woman with such leathery skin. She had to have kissed 50 goodbye quite some time ago.

As I was parking in front of the post office, I could see a bunch of girls inside. I was glad I wouldn't have to wait around. Brandi made me nervous. I thought she might stop outside to have a smoke, but she came in with me. She immediately snapped at one of the girls, "Gerry, give Anne your notebook."

I tried to put the little girl at ease. She had the demeanor of a dog that had been kicked too many times and was always on the alert for the next boot. "Hi, Gerry. Nice to meet you. You are a very important person to have a notebook with the complete Glyphs."

"Can you finish this sentence first?" She appeared to be trying to look straight at me, but being blind, she was a touch off.

"Sure, what is it?" She was able to redirect from the sound of my voice. If I didn't know she was blind, I'd think she was looking straight into my eyes.

"Four dots over a smile, swirly, double hump, side star, side star." She waited expectantly.

"That's an easy one. It's fulcrum, wavy skis, swirly, umbrella." I wasn't sure if she'd recognize my references. Everyone had their own way of describing the Glyphs based on what they resembled. Being blind, Gerry might have a difficult time translating my descriptions.

"What's a fulcrum?"

"Ummm…it's like a teeter totter."

"Okay. You passed. Terry, give Anne my notebook." Gerry seemed relieved. Doubtless, she may have worried her mother was trying to pull a fast one on her. But, people who saw the Glyphs innately trusted one another. It's hard to explain. That trust was tied with the images somehow.

Terry pulled the notebook out of another girl's backpack. Gerry was pretty security savvy, not carrying the notebook herself where her mother might get at it. I immediately took it to the copy machine. I couldn't get this transaction over with fast enough. I still had a feeling Brandi had something up her sleeve.

"Let's get this copied and uploaded to the net as quickly as possible, so we can all rest easy." I pulled three copies off each page. The quality of the copies was good. I didn't think I'd have any trouble scanning and uploading them. I just prayed we could get through the copying without a paper jam.

I was working so fast, I didn't really have a chance to look at the notebook that closely. But, it did seem she had all the Glyphs in every section. Brandi paced around while I photocopied, stopping every now and then to check on how I was coming. She'd stand at the end of the copy machine, arms folded, jiggling her knee.

Jim stood by the door where he could see what was happening outside the post office as well as inside. Inside didn't appear to be a problem. There were several patrons, but no one seemed too interested in us. I hadn't bothered to tell Brandi about Jim. She didn't need to know I had some extra security. Lord only knows what arrangements she might have made that she wasn't telling me about. I was pretty sure I saw her texting when I got to the last few pages.

The second I was finished, Brandi grabbed the notebook out of my hands.

"Hey, that's Gerry's." Terry protested.

"No it's not. It's mine. I paid for everything you girls have. I own it all. You are just borrowing it." She was looking at a text as she talked.

"It's okay," I tried to comfort the girls, "I have all the pages copied. The notebook shouldn't matter anymore."

"We've got company!" Jim's voice sounded truly alarmed. I quickly shoved one set of copies into the stamped, manila envelope I'd brought and deposited it into the mail slot on the wall.

"Oh, God. There's like five guys with ski masks tumbling out of a van." Jim started quickly backing toward us. "Somebody call 911!" He shouted to the staff.

"I think they're here for me." Brandi started walking toward the door.

"Are you nuts? These guys don't look friendly." Jim had grabbed Brandi's arm.

Brandi indignantly shook him loose. "They're going to buy the notebook."

"Even if they do buy it, once they find out the information is public, they're going to be mad as hell. What's to stop them from tracking you down?"

"They don't know me. How they gonna find me?"

"Is there a back way out of here?" I shouted over to the postmaster.

"Yes. And I called 911."

By this time, all the patrons realized something was going down and had the sense to look nervous.

"They've got guns!" Jim shouted. "Everybody outta here."

Everyone except Brandi and Jim raced to the back door. Fortunately, the post office was one of a row of connected buildings. No one in front could see us pouring out the back. I told the girls to scatter. I was going to run with Terry and Gerry to make sure they were safe, but I instantly realized, I'd only slow them down. All those girls had speed! Terry guided Gerry expertly and they ran like the wind. All the girls were quickly around the corner, into other building or otherwise out of sight in seconds. I poked my head back in the post office. Jim was trying to drag Brandi toward the back, but she bit him hard and broke loose, running out the door, notebook raised in her hand.

There was nothing we could do at that point. Jim and I slipped into the back alley and then in through an unlocked back door of a restaurant a couple shops down. We heard distant sirens. Then shots. Multiple shots. Then tires squealing.

Chapter 44

I could barely drag myself out front. My feet felt like giant blocks of concrete that my wobbly legs couldn't attempt to lift. Once I heard the shots, I felt like I slipped into an alternate universe. Surely this couldn't be *my* world. People did not shoot guns in my world.

I simply wanted to crawl into a corner, curl up in a ball and disappear. I'd been running on adrenalin when I thought that just maybe, there might be some way I could help. But now that the shooting had stopped, the thought of facing the aftermath had me paralyzed with fear. I didn't want to see what happened. If I didn't see it, I could cling to the hope that everyone might be all right. But, deep inside, I feared the worst. I imagined innocent people sprawled bleeding and dead across the sidewalk. All because of me. Because of my stupid website.

I can't begin to describe the level of dread I felt walking toward that restaurant door. Would there be children crying for the dead mommies? Or mothers for their children? Would Jim's involvement in all this cost him his opportunity to get a medical license? I would have been very happy to have the earth explode. For those endless seconds it took to reach the door, the future seemed too difficult to bear.

We peeked out the door. Any sign of physical threat appeared to have ended. The van with the masked gunmen was gone. Three bleeding bodies were strewn across the pavement. A half dozen or more people were out there. One was bent over the evil mother, trying to stop her bleeding. A couple of the others were holding guns on two masked men, which seemed unnecessary. Except for the blood pouring out of them, they were motionless on the pavement.

Jim rushed over to the mother and started tending her wound. He yelled instructions for the others on how to stop the bleeding of the masked men. No one moved, so I went over to apply pressure as Jim directed. One of the others followed suit.

The guy I tried to help appeared to leaking rather than actively bleeding. "Jim, I think he might be dead."

Jim asked the woman next to him to apply pressure to the evil mom's side. He came over, pulled off the mask of the guy at my knees and began administering CPR...mostly chest pumps, but he asked me to deliver a few breaths. It looked like the guy was starting to breathe again. Then the police and ambulances arrived and took over.

An officer helped me to my feet. I was so shaky I could barely say what I had to say. "Tttthh....ttthat lady's kids," I realized I was hyperventilating as I gulped for air, "could be in danger...gotta find them."

"What kind of danger? Where are they?" The officer's hand on my arm seemed more aggressive than supportive.

I motioned toward the guys on the ground. "There are more – in a van – could be looking for the girls." I was gaining my composure a bit. "I told the girls to run. They live around here someplace."

The officer dragged me over to the ambulance they were loading Brandi into. They had her purse. He rifled through it for ID, then radioed for a car to pick up the girls at her address.

Once I knew the girls were going to be taken care of, my brain seemed to spin itself into a daze. Every time I could gather the wherewithal to focus, more police were arriving on the scene. The officer that had me by the arm never let go. It occurred to me that I was being treated like a suspect.

Finally, a detective took me off the officer's hands. He pulled me aside and started hurling questions at me. He had already interviewed the gun-toting bystanders. (Okay, I guess they weren't exactly bystanders if they were toting guns.) So, he quickly concluded I knew nothing of the shooting itself. I hadn't actually seen a thing. I didn't have a gun. And he didn't seem to like my explanation as to what led up to the shooting. Apparently, I was the least informed person he'd talked to. Which shocked the heck out of me.

The police seemed not to know what to do with me. They couldn't charge me with a crime, but they were reluctant to let me go when I had no local address. After much discussion and a couple phone calls, they asked me to sit in a patrol car. The FBI wanted to talk to me. They were on their way.

While sitting alone in the patrol car, I took the opportunity to photograph the photocopies of the notebook with my cell phone. I hoped I was doing an acceptable job. Even though it had grown less pronounced, my hands were still shaking uncontrollably. I had only gotten about half way through the photographing when Agent Adams came to retrieve me.

I shoved my phone and the papers into my jacket pocket before I got out of the car. Agent Adams spoke to me perfunctorily. I think he was totally confused about the whole situation. He didn't know whether I was a bad guy or a good guy, but I think he was leaning toward "bad guy." I couldn't blame him. I mean, I was involved in an incident that left three people shot.

"Ms. Shannon, I need you to come down to headquarters and answer some questions for me." Agent Adams gave no indication that this was a request rather than a demand.

"I'd be happy to, but first, I really need make sure that the little girls are safe. Could you find out if the police have them?"

"I'll get that information for you on our drive downtown." I could tell that he wasn't concerned at all about the girls.

"No, you don't understand. I think these girls could be in danger. I can't go anywhere until I know they're safe."

He gave me a totally exasperated look, but went over to consult with the police, keeping a wary eye on me the entire time. He reported back to me that the police had the girls at their station and were waiting for social services to come and pick them up.

"Social services? What are you nuts!" I couldn't believe that I had the nerve to raise my voice to this guy. But, I was so worried over the incompetence of everyone involved that I just couldn't help myself. "The guys that were here –the van full of masked men with automatic machine guns – they could be after the girls. You know, I'm really not going to be comfortable unless those girls are with me. Can you arrange for them to get an armed escort down to the FBI headquarters?"

"That's out of the question. The girls belong with social services. It's out of my jurisdiction."

"Then I'm afraid I won't be able to join you downtown. I have to go to the police station and see what I can do about getting those girls some protection."

Adams literally threw his hands up in the air. "There's nothing you can do. It's a matter for social services. They'll find the girls' relatives."

"I doubt social services or the girls' relatives will be able to handle an armed assault. They won't understand what they're up against. *You* don't understand what *you're* up against."

"Then why don't you tell me?" Adams' voice was dripping with sarcasm.

"The guys in the van probably aren't local thugs. They're likely either terrorists or have ties to enemy nations. They shot the girls' mother. They may want the girls dead as well. If they do, they may stop at nothing."

To Agent Adams credit, he seemed to then appreciate the severity of the situation. He had two police cars take the girls to the FBI office in Newark. Jim and I, along with all the armed bystanders, were shepherded to the FBI office in separate patrol cars. I managed to finish photographing and uploading Gerry's pages during the ride. They might not be entirely legible…but the more info in the public domain, the safer we all would be.

At the FBI headquarters, each of us was interviewed in a separate room. I told them everything I felt they needed to know. It didn't take long – I really didn't know that much. All I could tell them was that I thought Brandi was trying to make money off a Glyphs notebook in her possession. I didn't know how she made arrangements with the armed entourage. Mostly, I just had questions about what actually happened. It seemed like the agents knew a lot more than I did, but they weren't telling me.

"The police mentioned that you had some papers. Where are they now?" Agent Adams was still treating me like a bad guy.

"In my pocket."

"What are they?"

"Photocopies of the notebook."

"I see. I'll take those." Agent Adams held out his hand.

"I'm afraid I can't give them to you." I wondered if they could force me to hand them over. I wasn't too worried. In addition to the copies I mailed myself, I had shoved another set of photocopies into my bra. I was determined to treat each of the three sets like gold.

"I'm afraid you have no choice. Please give them to me."

"I believe I do have a choice. I've done nothing wrong. They are my private property."

"It's a matter of national security, which overrides personal property." Adams continued to hold out his hand.

"I don't believe it's a matter of national security."

"That's not for you to decide."

"Well, I have to post clear copies of these papers online, first. Until I post the papers online, I believe everyone involved is in danger. Myself, the girls, their mother…even you. You can have the papers right after I post them."

"No, I need them now."

"Tell you what. Let me make photocopies and then I'll give you the originals."

"No, I'm afraid that won't be acceptable."

"Did you hear the part about those little girls being in danger?"

"The gunmen appear to have taken the original notebook before they fled. No one is in danger."

"Do you know if there is only one set of bad guys after the notebook? Because I don't know. I don't see how anyone can know. None of this ends until the Glyphs are posted for the world to see." I stood up. I figured it was time to force my hand. "I'm sorry. I've told you what I know. I have to go now."

Agent Adams stood up to block my path. "You can't go right now. Homeland Security wants to interview you."

"Homeland Security?" I sank back down into my chair and held my head in my hands. Those were the guys with the waterboards, weren't they? The guys with the warrantless arrests? I needed to get someone who understood the legal system on my side – and fast – before some government agency could make me disappear. "I would like to call an attorney."

At that moment there was a knock at the door. "Ms. Shannon's attorney is here." The agents exchanged comments in whispers I could not hear.

"Hello, Ms. Shannon, I'm Dana McKenny. I'll be representing you. Are you being treated well?" The attorney offered me her hand. I grasped it as if grabbing a lifeline.

"Are you my court appointed attorney?" My voice was a little shaky. The mention of Homeland Security had really thrown me for a loop.

Dana seemed to be repressing a smile, but Adams let out a full-blow guffaw. "No. A friend of yours requested that I represent you."

"That must be some friend you have there, Ms. Shannon." Adams seemed to be smirking. It turned out that Dana McKenny was one of the best, most well-respected lawyers in the tri-state area. I think he equated the powerfulness of my attorney with the likeliness of my guilt.

"I think I may have a lot of friends. The trouble is, I don't know who they are." I hoped no one noticed that I was fighting back tears. The overwhelming weight of the truth of that last sentence had come crushing down on me. I didn't know who my friends were. I didn't know who I could trust. It was an unbearable way to live.

"You have no grounds for holding Ms. Shannon. If you have no further questions, we'll be on our way." Dana hadn't even bothered to sit down.

"Homeland Security would like to interview Ms. Shannon. They're on their way."

A look of concern crossed Dana's face. She leaned down and asked me what was going on. I informed her about the papers and my urgent need to post them to the Internet.

"Tell Homeland Security to meet us in my office in an hour. They can talk to Ms. Shannon there." With that, she abruptly pulled my chair back and started escorting me out of the office.

Agent Adams blocked our path. "It could be very dangerous out there for you with those papers in your pocket."

"No one knows I have them."

"I do."

"Agent Adams, are you threatening to release information that could put my client in danger?" Her tone was steely.

"I'm just saying that information is never secure. It leaks out. It travels fast. Any number of people could know that Ms. Shannon has those papers on her person. And by her own admission, that could place her in a great deal of danger."

Dana and Adams stared each other down.

"It's true. If anyone knew I had these, I could be in a lot of danger. Can I get a police escort?"

"I could arrange that if you give me the papers."

Dana looked at me with a worried eye. I tried to give her a look that said I knew what I was doing. "Fine," I said. "I'll give you the papers. I want four police cars."

"Deal."

I handed Adams the papers. He looked genuinely befuddled. "This is what all the shooting was about?"

"Yep."

Dana grabbed my arm, "Let's get out of here." Over her shoulder she shouted back at Adams, "Have those patrol cars down by my limo. Now!"

Dana passed on the first elevator that stopped, but had us hop on the next. It was a very short run out to her limo. And we did sort of run. I wondered how much Dana knew about the whole situation. Fortunately, the patrol cars were magically there as she requested and we were on the move in no time.

Riding in the back of the limo, Dana began a furious series of phone calls. I paid little attention as I was busy uploading new photos from my phone to the Web. I knew several of the first batch had been a little too fuzzy, so I dug the photocopies out of my bra and re-photographed them (actually, it was more like I dug them from the binding I had going over my bra – I was still in my disguise from the plane that morning. Geesh. That plane ride felt like it was weeks ago – and my poor, squished boobs felt like it was months ago.)

Once everything was successfully uploaded, I began to relax a bit. Dana seemed finished with her phone calls so I asked her if she could check up on Jim and the girls. Apparently, they had released Jim a while ago and still had the girls in protective custody. I told her the girls would be in less danger soon as I had just uploaded all the documents.

Chapter 45

It was a fairly short ride to Dana's office in Manhattan. I filled her in on what I knew and she filled me in on what she knew. She knew a lot more about today's incident than I did.

Apparently, Brandi had posted Gerry's notebook for sale on CussedEmOuterwear.com just before I picked her up at the mall. The gunmen were believed to be from a Mid-Eastern terrorist cell. Brandi had run out to them waving the notebook in her hand. One of them grabbed it with no exchange of money. As Brandi ran after the guy who grabbed the notebook (apparently she was stupid as well as greedy and evil), another aimed to fire at her. At that point, one (or more, it still wasn't clear) of the bystanders shot the guy, so the shots he got off at Brandi were not well aimed.

That started the gunfight between the terrorists and the bystanders (though they weren't exactly bystanding...they took cover behind cars and mailboxes). All of the bystanders were there and armed because they had read Brandi's post about the notebook transaction on the Internet. (Stupid me, I had thought everyone in New Jersey was just heavily armed and helpful.)

Brandi was not actually the twins' mother. She was their foster parent of only a few months. It appeared she was probably going to pull through, but would face months of recovery.

Dana didn't know who hired her to represent me. And the Homeland Security thing had her worried. She wasn't sure those guys felt bound by the rule of law. So, she had arranged for me to give a press conference before I was interviewed. She figured they wouldn't screw with me if I was in the public eye.

The public eye! That was the last place I wanted to be. What the heck was going on with my life? I spend months trying to make myself undetectable to protect myself– and, in like 10 minutes, I was going to be jumping into the public eye to protect myself. Who lived like this?

I tried to squirm out of the press conference, but Dana was adamant. She was really worried for me. She did think we could get away without releasing my real name. She'd bill me as "the Anne Hawn-Imus of the now famous, CussedEmOuterwear.com."

I was glad I was still in disguise and had a pair of large, dark glasses with me. Dana had arranged to have fresh clothes waiting for me at the office (the ones I had on were covered in blood from my attempts to help after the shooting.) I figured I'd do a southern accent, even though the thought of using a fake accent made me feel like a nutcase. The entire situation was just too ridiculous to believe.

The press conference didn't go too badly. Perhaps because the press really didn't know the right questions to ask. Mostly, they just asked me about the shootout that morning and what provoked it. And I was able to get the word out that the contents of the notebook had been posted, helping to secure the safety of everyone concerned. I was amazed at how many reporters showed up. There was someone from every nearby newspaper and all the TV networks. That's New York City for you.

The Homeland Security guys were pissed that I posted the pages from the Glyphs notebook. But, there wasn't much they could do about it except for letting me know they were angry. They said they'd be watching me, but I kind of doubted that. Now that the Glyphs were posted, I couldn't think of any reason why anyone would want to watch me. It was time for me to walk away. I was no longer of any value to anyone as far as the Glyphs were concerned. Or, at least, that's what I thought.

However, the reporters had other ideas. There was a media frenzy outside Dana's office waiting for me to emerge. Dana had security move the crowd out of the building. I thought getting past them was going to be tricky, but Dana had it all worked out.

I gave my clothes, wig and sunglasses to Dana's secretary, whom she escorted out of the office and rushed into a waiting limo, yelling out "no comment" the entire time. After that, the crowd of media broke up. Once a messenger brought me back a bag with my wig and glasses, I left the building, unrecognized in new clothes (with unbound breasts...boy, did that feel good) and my own hair. A limo was supposed to be waiting two blocks down to whisk me to a hotel. (By that time, I'd missed my return flight. And the police wanted me to stick around for a few days.)

Chapter 46

As I got closer to the limo, I recognized Faris standing on the sidewalk next to it. He was grinning ear-to-ear and sort of bouncing back from one foot to another like a child about to receive a present.

"Faris!"

He practically bounded over to me, not his usual formal self at all. In fact, quite surprisingly, he gave me a big, almost uncomfortably strong, fatherly sort of hug.

"Oh, Miss, I am so happy to see you so well. When I saw you kneeling on the ground, covered in blood, my heart leapt from my body. I thought I would have to throw myself off a bridge to stop my pain."

I literally had to break his hold on me so I could breathe. "You were at the post office?"

"I arrived as the police were pulling in."

"How did you know to go there?" I was totally confused.

"Amir told me." That made sense. Amir had probably logged in and seen Brandi's posting about the notebook for sale.

"I'm so sorry if I caused you worry, Faris. But, please, promise me you will never throw yourself off a bridge on my account."

"I promise, Miss."

Faris didn't appear to realize that I knew he was following me on the plane. Good. I didn't want to hurt his feelings. He had no way of knowing I couldn't trust anyone in my miserable, solitary existence. An existence that it seemed I might now be able to leave behind. Just a few loose ends to tie up and I could start imagining a normal life again.

At the hotel, Faris insisted on escorting me to my room. He was not going to leave me alone for a second. I was touched by his concern.

The hotel was, of course, quite swanky. Faris told me I was already checked in and pushed the button to the penthouse in the elevator. Typical Amir, I thought, first class all the way.

While the extravagance of the penthouse suite didn't surprise me, what I found when I opened the door shocked the hell out of me. Standing there, arms outstretched to greet me, was Amir. And, as if that weren't enough, as I hugged Amir, I saw over his shoulder that Jim was there, too.

I was speechless. And then all the emotions that I'd suppressed all day came welling up at once. I started shaking and crying, unable to get an intelligible word out through my sobs.

Amir and Jim sat me on the couch. Jim put a jacket over my shoulders and Amir brought me a cup of hot tea. There I sat, between the two men I adored, and the thought of that made me sob all the more.

"As long as you're already upset, you might as well appreciate all three rings in this circus." Jim picked up the TV remote while Amir passed me a box of tissues. There, plastered on every news channel, were scenes from my day – including huge close-ups of me from my press conference.

Once I gained my composure, I checked my home phone. No messages. It seemed no one had recognized me as the now famous, or perhaps infamous (depending on your point of view), blonde, Southern belle, Anne Hawn-Imus. I programmed my calls to forward to my cell just in case. No one knew I was in New York City. Maybe I could keep it that way.

Then, I got the other bad news. All the media outlets wanted me to appear on their talk shows or be interviewed for publication. And Jim and Amir had come to an agreement that we needed all that free publicity. We still had to get those Glyphs translated and that would require an entirely new audience: the academic and scientific communities.

That sank me into my own personal nightmare. Just the thought of all that public attention focused on me (even as my alter ego) sent my stomach into acrobatics. And how was I going to protect my anonymity with news hounds barking at my heels?

Jim and Amir tried to cheer me up. They had apparently gotten together quite some time before I arrived and had really hit it off. They were joking around trying to make light of the situation as best they could. Jim was better at the sarcasm. I think perhaps in Amir's world sarcasm may have been meant to bite more than delight. He tread lightly on this assumedly new territory.

Room service brought a fabulous dinner, but I could barely eat (and you know things are bad when *I* can't eat). I found out that Dana had assurances that neither the police nor the FBI would be releasing my real name to the public. They decided that I was technically a witness in need of protection. (Wanting to keep me all to themselves as a future source of information was likelier closer to the truth.) That was good news. Plus, Jim was heading back to Buffalo the following evening so he could check me out of the hotel and pick up Ozone from the kennel.

Amir had to fly out soon. Apparently he was already in NYC and about to leave for Chicago when Faris called to say he'd lost track of me. Cala searched all credit card transactions, airline manifests, any and all avenues available through Amir's vast holdings. When she found I was flying to NYC, Amir delayed his departure, figuring something huge was occurring based on my subterfuge. Now that he knew I was safe, he had to get to Chicago ASAP. I walked him to the door.

"It was so good to find you in one piece, Rachel. This afternoon, with the possibility you may have been shot…those were the longest minutes of my life."

"I'm sorry for putting you through all this."

"No. I am sorry for leaving you to carry the burden alone. I shall never forgive myself for being so selfish."

I didn't believe Amir was selfish in the least, but I was too emotionally exhausted to argue. "Goodnight, Amir. Thank you for the attorney, the room, for having Farris watch over me…for everything."

"There is a separate security suite in the anteroom. Farris will be there if you need him."

"Thank you."

"Your friend, Jim, is a good man. I like him very much." Amir brushed my hair from my cheek. His hand lingered for a split second on my face. "I have missed you."

"Same here."

He turned and left.

Chapter 47

"Amir is quite the guy." Jim stood as I returned from the door.

"Funny, he said the same about you."

"I suppose I really should be going. I've got an early seminar. And you look exhausted."

I was exhausted. And confused. And somewhere in the back of my head I was wondering when Jim planned on joining the Peace Corps and how long he'd be gone. I was in no shape to deal with all the conflicting emotions wreaking havoc on my body at the moment.

I walked Jim to the door. "Good night. And thank you. I'm so sorry I dragged you into all this."

"I'm just glad I was there."

"Me, too. And that's an understatement."

Jim gave me a long, long hug. Then he bent his head and gave me the sweetest, gentlest, most tender little kiss. Our first kiss. And he left.

I took a long shower, gulped a couple aspirins and went to bed.

Chapter 48

I didn't sleep well. The reality of how incredibly stupid I had been sunk in while I tossed and turned all night. I was lucky to be alive. I was lucky no innocent people got killed. But, that's where my luck ended. Three people had been shot because of a situation I created.

Sometimes, after a difficult day, I'd wake up in the morning able to shake things off and start anew with a positive attitude. This wasn't one of those times. I didn't want to get up and face the world. However, I saw that the message light on my phone was blinking. (I didn't know how I could have slept through a ringing phone...could Amir have asked the desk to hold my calls?)

The message was from my attorney. Dana had a list of media looking for interviews and wanted to know if she could go ahead and schedule them for me. And she said the twins wanted to talk to me.

I immediately contacted the twins. We spoke for a long time. It turns out that the girls were not happy to be Brandi's foster kids. With Brandi in the hospital, they needed a new foster home and were hoping I'd be it. Plus, Gerry had been fretting over how I had called one of the Glyphs "wavy skis." She knew what I was referring to, but couldn't understand why I didn't call it what it was: a river. Apparently there were some Glyphs she recognized as standing for something specific: river, ocean, sun, etc.

I didn't think I had the qualifications to be a foster parent, but the girls told me horror stories. Apparently there weren't enough decent foster families around so social services seemed to accept just about anyone. Mostly, the families the girls ended up with were people looking for the cash the foster system paid – and some free labor from the kids. They felt Brandi was just interested in the money, but she was one of the better homes they'd had: They were together and weren't being abused.

Their story of being split up and shuffled around to abusive and unloving homes was heartbreaking. I couldn't bear being responsible for the girls getting placed in an even worse situation. Plus, I wasn't entirely sure they were completely safe. There might be some nutcase group out there who'd think Gerry had some kind of additional insight into the Glyphs. (Obviously, based on her comment about the river, she might.)

I called Dana and got her started on whatever I had to do to foster the twins. She assured me that I could bring them back to Buffalo with me. (I was thinking it would probably be best for them to finish out the school year in New Jersey. I'd have to figure that one out.)

Dana also told me I had two talk show appearances scheduled the next day. I went out to get a few things to wear. I had t-shirts printed up with the web address splashed across the chest in big type. (Such irony! I hated people staring at my big chest. I was going to be binding it down to a reasonable size, but I still needed to draw attention to it. Life isn't fair.)

I'd wear the t-shirts on the talk shows to help get more people visiting our website. The mission had changed now. I needed to get the general public aware of the Glyphs and seriously interested in decoding them. Once the Glyphs were decoded, my job would be done and I could try to live a normal life again. (Or at least as normal as a 24-year-old single woman with two teenage foster kids could aspire to.)

Chapter 49

The talk shows were a mixed bag. Some were tolerable, some painful. It was really, really hard to try to word things carefully so quotes couldn't be lifted out of context.

Of course, the biggest problem was that the interviewers had a different agenda than I did. Some wanted to focus on the terrorist angle and talk about the shooting. Some wanted to label the Glyphs community as some kind of a nutty cult. Others wanted me to address the fanatics (all non-Seers, it seemed) who were taking the Glyphs vision as a sign for their own particular brands of religion.

All I wanted to do was set the story straight and get people interested in deciphering the Glyphs. I skirted answering questions that would divulge personal information. I kept a Southern drawl going, but that was really, really difficult. I hoped it was believable.

The toughest show to do was with an arrogant, loudmouth who was pretending to be a news anchor when he was really just an opinionated blowhard. I had to admit I was predisposed to dislike (okay, detest) the guy. My sweet, caring grandmother was a fan of his. I'd seen how the venom he spewed – under the guise of "reporting the truth" – had been successfully filling Grams with the particular brand of hatred he championed.

Of course, the guy also employed nasty tactics. I figured he was going to try to make me look like a nutcase. I was right. He knew how to push all my buttons. He was real pro at being an aggravating jerk and I was an inexperienced lamb going in for the slaughter.

His opening line was, "It seems to me that these ridiculous Glyphs, as you call them, are your way of undermining American beliefs with some sort of mystical hoo-ha in the same vein as L. Ron Hubbard or Jim Jones?"

How was I supposed to answer an attack like that? He intoned it like a question, but it wasn't a question. I was totally unprepared. I've never been one to think fast on my feet.

"I'm sorry. I thought this was a new show. Do you want information from me, or do you want me to sit here while you deliver your own opinion?"

"Listen, Missie, just answer the question. Fair enough?"

"'Missie?' What kind of way is that to address a guest? When I agreed to this interview, I thought I'd at least be treated with common respect."

"Could you just answer the question? Huh? I ask the questions. You answer the questions. That's the way a news interview goes." He was really perturbed.

"But, you didn't ask me a question, you just made a broad derogatory statement with no basis in fact. There was no question there."

I must have hit him on a really bad day because he absolutely exploded and started screaming for someone to "get her the @#$# out of here."

I have to admit, I was relieved not to have to complete that interview. Still, it was hundreds of thousands of dollars in free publicity down the drain. My only hope was that details of my imploded interview would leak out and become a news story in its own right. If that happened, perhaps it would generate enough attention to make up for loss of the interview audience.

As I walked out of the building, some of the employees gave me subtle signs of support. I couldn't understand how they could work there if they didn't believe in what they were supporting. I hoped I'd never be reduced to being a whore like that.

Chapter 50

An interview for a weekly news magazine show didn't go much better the next day. But, at least the interviewer was being fair and respectful. It was her job to shoot holes and boy, did she know how to shoot:

"So, these pictures in your head come with a feeling that they are of earth-shattering importance. But, you don't actually know why they're important?"

"No. I assume that it has something to do with clean energy, but that is just a guess."

"Complete conjecture?"

"Well…it's a sort of feeling that comes with the visions."

"But, these Glyphs could just as easily prove to represent something destructive?"

"I suppose. Though, that would mean the sender of the message was being deliberately deceptive. And, realistically, I don't see what purpose it would serve to try to get a destructive formula in the hands of every person."

"You said you've seen the Glyphs since you were a child. If there's such a powerful feeling that the Glyphs need to be shared with the entire world, why did it take you 24 years to do that?"

"I was afraid that I'd be locked away as insane if I told anyone about the Glyphs. And I thought maybe I was insane. It wasn't until I discovered that other people saw the Glyphs, too, that I got the confidence to act on them. I suppose it's similar to people who have synesthesia. If they think their experience is unique, they tend to hide their experience. Once they discover there are others like them, they're more likely to admit to their condition."

"Perhaps you should share with our audience what synesthesia is."

Oh, hell, why-oh-why did I just say that? "As I understand it, synesthesia is when people experience certain things to be always associated with some sensory experience. For instance, when they see an 'A' it may always be red. When they see a '6' it may always be blue. But, I'm no expert. I was just making an analogy."

"So, are you saying synesthesia has something to do with the Glyphs?"

"Oh, no. No. I was just using the analogy to demonstrate that people are prone to hide sensory experiences that they think are unique to them…in answer to your question as to why I didn't follow the urge to share the Glyphs with the world sooner."

Could I have clouded things up any worse? Me and my analogies! One of the art directors at work had labeled them: Shannonalogies. I think the term inferred that I saw connections where no reasonable person would. The synesthesia analogy clouded the issue and made me sound like an idiot. The only thing that stopped me from crawling into a large hole and dying was that, at least for now, only a handful of people knew it was Rachel Shannon talking. Hopefully they weren't watching.

After three days of interviews, I was ready to go home. I'd proved to myself that I was totally incapable of being a spokesperson. When I resumed my regular career, I'd have to make sure I always had a "behind the scenes" job. I always thought that was the case. It was just hard to face how incredibly true it was.

I'd been in constant contact with Dana and the twins. The twins convinced me that they did not mind finishing the year at a new school. They said they were used to shuffling from one school to another. That didn't make it right to switch them yet another time, but I couldn't think of any other option. Even if I could figure out a way to afford living in New Jersey for the next three months, I thought it was risky to stay where so many people would know the twins were involved with the Glyphs shootout. In Buffalo, no one would know them or their connection to the shootout. Their names and faces were never released to the media.

That didn't relieve my guilt in moving them. Especially since I was pretty sure the school they'd be going to in Buffalo was not the greatest. I lived in a moderate-to-low-income area. There were a lot of good kids, but also a lot of thugs. I knew Buffalo had at least one magnet school that was one of top schools in the country, but I doubted I could get the kids into it this year. And I wondered if Gerry would be better off going to a special school for the blind. Man, it was tough having to think like a parent.

I'd been in touch with Kim and my parents. They still weren't aware that I wasn't home. I didn't know how I was going to explain the twins to them. Or to anyone, really.

Chapter 51

The minute I was back home, I called Jim under the pretense of getting Ozone back. But, deep down, I knew what I most craved was Jim's moral support. He was the one person I could talk to who knew what had happened. He would be the one person who could understand why I had to foster Terry and Gerry. Plus, I was hoping he was still serious about starting a relationship. Now that I had the responsibility of the twins, in some way I felt more alone than ever.

Jim said he'd bring Ozone right over. I didn't mention the twins; I just told him I had a big surprise.

"A surprise? With any other person, that would be something to look forward to. With you, Rae, I'm not so sure." His voice was smiling, but I was pretty sure I heard an anxious undertone.

"Yeah, well, with me – life is interesting."

"Isn't that a Chinese curse? 'May you lead an interesting life?'"

"Didn't Confucius say 'He who asks too many questions before delivering dog becomes annoying?'?"

"See you in an hour."

"You are so good at taking a hint."

The girls got settled in quickly. They didn't own much stuff and I had no bedroom furniture for them to unpack anything into. Fortunately, I had a sleeper couch. They'd have to make do with that until we could go shopping the next day. There was so freaking much I had to do! Buy bedroom furniture. Get some real food in the house. Enroll the twins in school. Get back to the website. Get a real job.

I was so overwhelmed, I was paralyzed. Tonight I'd just decompress with Jim and the twins over pizza. Maybe tomorrow I'd be able to prioritize and move forward.

I heard Ozone barking with joy as soon as he entered the entrance hall. The girls were really excited to have a dog and couldn't wait to meet him. They went barreling down the stairs to answer the door before I could hold them back. I'd certainly not have let Gerry run blindly down an unfamiliar set of stairs if I could help it. (Okay, there it was, I was definitely already in mother mode.)

This was not exactly the way I wanted Jim to find out I'd brought the twins home, but there probably was no good way to say "hey, the girl you're interested in dating now has two teenage daughters."

I met Jim halfway up the stairs. I wasn't sure what the look he gave me said, but my guess was that may have been because he didn't know exactly what he thought of the situation yet.

"So, are these lovely young ladies your surprise?"

"Yep. Bet you never would have guessed this one."

"Not in a million years."

Jim presented me a bunch of flowers and carried my bags upstairs. (Not only had he gotten my bag from the hotel, he had checked at the airport and found the carry-on I'd abandoned on my flight. He was such a pragmatist. And so thoughtful.)

We sat in the living room and played cards (Gerry had a set of Braille cards she brought with her) until the pizza arrived. The girls pretty much demolished the pizza in seconds. (Mental note: remember those ravenous appetites on my next trip to the grocery store.) After dinner the girls went to watch TV in the living room while Jim and I chatted in the kitchen. The two rooms were on opposite ends of the flat, so we'd have complete privacy.

I explained the girls' foster parent horror stories and my concern for their safety. Jim agreed I'd done the right thing, though he didn't think doing the right thing was necessarily a good move for me or the girls. But, he couldn't see any other option either. I think he was proud of me in a way. This fit in with his altruistic ideals. Though, he certainly wasn't altruistic when he spent the rest of the night mocking my talk show appearances. He hadn't missed a one. And he said he had them all on tape to better torture me for eternity. I neglected to tell him that his VCR was destined to become a dinosaur he'd never be able to replace – and I foresaw a tragic accident befalling it in the near future.

Jim couldn't stay late. He had to work the night shift at the hospital.

"I'll be working 'til 4 tomorrow afternoon. After that, I can swing by and help you shop for furniture or whatever else you might need."

"No. Don't you worry. The girls and I can do all our shopping in the morning. With luck, we'll have everything delivered and set up before you even get off work."

"You're incapable of accepting help aren't you?" Jim wasn't kidding. Those earnest, sparkling eyes were trying to delve down through mine and deep into my soul. And he'd hit the nail right on the head. I could not ask for help. Had a hard time accepting it when it was foist upon me.

"Just accept that it's the way I'm wired."

"I'll be on the lookout for a good electrician then."

"Uh-uh-uh. Ain't nobody gonna go messin' with my faults. Might screw my positives up."

"I am fond of those positives."

"Then maybe you can come by for dinner on Sunday? I'm going to have Kim and her FBI man over…and my parents, too."

"And you're going to spring me and the twins on everyone at the same time?"

"Am I that transparent?"

"Definitely."

"Good. I'm glad you can definitely be there. This time, I really do need backup. See, you've already fixed me. I've arranged for your help."

"I think maybe asking for help and tricking someone into helping you are two different things."

"Perhaps it's the way us non-askers cope."

Jim had to run to work and the girls were in the next room, so our goodbyes weren't exactly romantic. But, Jim hadn't balked at meeting my parents. To me, that meant he was still interested in doing the boyfriend/girlfriend thing. I couldn't be happier. Or more exhausted.

Chapter 52

Shopping went great. We found some really nice, high-quality bedroom furniture at Gently Used Home Furnishings. I wasn't sure the girls appreciated that the used furniture was actually better quality than anything we'd be able to get new. But, they did seem to love what they picked out. And they went nuts when we went shopping for accessories at Target. I even got a good deal on new mattresses at the mattress shop. To top it all off, I found some friends of friends who had a truck and were willing to pick up and deliver everything that day for $75.

That night, after we got their bedrooms all arranged and had a halfway (emphasis on half) nutritious dinner, we were definitely starting to feel like we were living in a real home, not just some temporary way station. At least, that's how *I* felt. It was a nice, warm feeling that helped calm my underlying sense of desperation.

I'd been prepping the girls on the absolute necessity of never, ever telling anyone about the Glyphs or how we came to be together. I didn't know if we'd truly be able to pull off hiding the Glyphs debacle. I mean, they were only 12 and they had this incredible story of shootouts and terrorists. How long would they be able to resist impressing their new schoolmates with that tale? But, I told them that, for their own safety, I might not be able to keep them if the story leaked out. And I emphasized that *no one* except Jim knew and *no one* was to know. Especially not the new foster grandparents they were going to meet that night.

Jim arrived early, bless his heart. I had already filled him in our cover story. Bill was also already aware that he was supposed to know nothing. Though, I wasn't exactly sure of how much Bill did know. (I hoped he didn't know Jim was at the shoot out with me.) What a comedy this was. So many people not being able to tell the entire truth to people close to them. And this was supposed to be the start of my return to normalcy!

Considering I sprang a couple foster kids on Kim and my parents, dinner went rather well. I could tell my folks were concerned that I was taking on more than I could handle. But, they seemed mighty pleased that I was dating Jim. (They might not have been as enthusiastic if they knew our first date was a shootout.)

While my parents might have been reconciled to the idea that I was on my own and making my own decisions, Kim seemed a tad offended that I'd made such a major life change without even mentioning that I was considering it. But, she sounded enthusiastic about developing a friendship with Terry and Gerry. In fact, we made a date for her to come over later that week to teach Terry some drawing techniques.

I was glad Kim seemed so interested in the twins. Through the entire Glyphs ordeal one of the things that bothered me the most was the growing distance between Kim and me. It was a nightmare having to live a charade of normalcy when I was caught up in so much turmoil. Not being able to share such an important part of my life with my best friend put a strain on our relationship.

Now, while I couldn't yet tell Kim all that had gone on, I could at least hope to move forward as we had before: friends sharing everything. (Okay, the fact that her boyfriend knew so much about my life that she didn't know was still going to be tough, but I was going to totally suppress that thought.)

After everyone went home, the "post game" calls started rolling in. The calls all started with the pretense of thanking me for dinner, but they quickly got to their underlying agendas. My mother asked me if I understood what a huge responsibility raising two teens was going to be. My father asked if I needed money. Kim wanted to know if I was okay. Jim wanted a recap of what I thought everyone really thought. Bill assured me that the FBI considered my case confidential and that he'd never divulge any details to anyone not involved in the investigation…and he reminded me that I was never to tell Kim that he started dating her as a pretense to investigate me.

I finally hung up the phone for the last time and it was just me and the twins. They selected outfits for school the next day and loaded their backpacks with the supplies I'd gotten them. (I really hadn't a clue what they'd need. I pretty much just tried to grab a few of everything in the office supplies aisle.) Then, I fell into bed, exhausted.

The next morning we all got up bright and early. Gerry was like me, not really a morning person. It was work to get her up and ready for school. It was also problematic that we only had one small bathroom. I'd forgotten how long young girls can take getting ready – longer than my former roommates!

Even though I'd allowed plenty of extra time so we could get to the school early and get all the paperwork done before classes started, they barely made it. The school wasn't happy about the two being in the same classes. The principal had a policy of splitting up siblings. But, since Gerry was blind and they didn't yet have an aide for her – and there were only 3 months of school left – she said she'd keep them together for this year.

It broke my heart to leave the girls at school. I could see that under their tough façade, they were nervous. I did break down and cry a bit in the car on the way home.

Then, I logged into CussedEmOuterwear.com for the first time in days. Wow. What a shock. There was more activity on the site than ever. And the orders for the t-shirts were through the roof. I guess I wouldn't be looking for a regular job for awhile. I found a freelance webmaster to help me revamp the site for our current needs. And I found a fulfillment house that could process and ship the overflow of orders for merchandise.

I wanted to talk to David Moore about adding t-shirt designs, but it was time to pick the girls up from school before I knew it. They looked pretty glum when they got in the car, but said their day was "fine." I offered to stop somewhere for a treat, but they weren't interested. I took that as a bad sign.

When we got home, they each went to their room to change…and never came out. A bit later, I heard sobs coming from Terry's room. After a frustrating exchange, Terry finally agreed to let me come in and talk to her. I stroked her hair as I dragged the story of her day out of her. All the kids mocked the girls' Jersey accents and their clothes (apparently, what was hot in the tri-state area was not hot in Buffalo).

Oh dear. What to do? I figured the girls would eventually blend in and find some friends. I didn't want to run out and buy them new clothes right away, though I was tempted. But, I figured they wouldn't know the "in" things after just one day. Plus, I hated reinforcing the petty notion that "fashion equals acceptance." We went through their belongings and picked out some unassuming, yet attractive outfits for the next day.

I made the girls a special dinner and the three of us talked over their schooling options. I told them they could transfer to a nearby Catholic school if they weren't happy with their situation by the end of the week. Just knowing they had a way out if things didn't improve seemed to make a big difference in their mood.

After dinner I tried to help them with their homework. (Emphasis on "tried" – I didn't remember nearly as much math as I thought I had.) And then, poof, it was bedtime. Where had the day gone?

And so the days went on, all pretty much disappearing before I could accomplish what I needed to. The girls made some friends and ended up deciding to stay at the public school. But, every week or so there was a new crisis: a slight by a friend, harassment from one of the tough cliques, homework meltdowns, crushes and broken hearts, sports defeats…the list was a mile long. Plus, there were rides needed to games, trips to the mall, arguments over makeup, requests for sleepovers and even a big fight about a tattoo. The parenting gig was definitely no walk in the park.

During all the preteen drama, I had to figure out how to cook healthy meals for girls who pretty much detested any food even the slightest shade of green. (How Gerry knew what was green, I'll never know. She seemed to be able to taste the color.) I had laundry up to my ears. I was always chauffeuring this one or chaperoning for that one or attending a recital or a game.

There was no end to the demands on my time. And Jim's time, too. On the two days a week that we actually got to spend some time together, we were often running the girls in two different directions for part of it. And when we were all together, we always seemed to fall into the same pattern: watching TV with Jim in the easy chair and the girls flanking me on the couch. After the girls went to bed, Jim would join me on the couch, but one or both of us would invariably fall asleep after a few minutes.

Plus, with no time to get to the gym, I was getting a little pudgy around the edges. Jim never mentioned it, but the extra flab put me in a defeated mood.

Kim was a big help, though. She loved the girls and stopped over for dinner at least twice a week. After dinner the girls would go off to do their own thing and Kim would get me to laugh while we sipped tea at the kitchen table. If it weren't for Kim, I may have gone insane.

Kim felt that her relationship with Bill was definitely cooling off. She was beginning to see that he was way too rigid for her. And he hated her spending so much time with me. He considered me to be totally whacked. (I hoped that was why he didn't like Kim hanging with me…but I couldn't rule out the possibility that he thought I could still be a target of "known subversive elements." I hoped he didn't know something I didn't know.)

Kim and Bill were still dating, but less frequently. Kim felt more like they were just keeping each other company until someone better suited came along. She felt that feeling was mutual. That's why I was so surprised when Kim asked Jim and me to go out with them and another couple one Saturday in early June.

That Saturday was absolutely beautiful. We don't get tons of sun during spring, so the days when we do always raise your spirits. The sky was brilliant blue. It was delightfully warm. The breeze was just enough to blow a skirt in swirls around your knees. The twins were having a sleepover at my parents' house. I was in heaven.

Poor Jim was a little less so. He was just getting off an 18-hour shift at the hospital, so he was really tired. I told him I didn't expect him to contribute much to the conversation. He could just sit there and look handsome.

When we got to the restaurant, I was surprised to find that the other couple was Amy and her husband. (Amy was the FBI agent with Bill when he first approached me about the Glyphs.)

I was desperately trying to remember who knew what about my meeting with Amy and Bill and how to handle introductions. Fortunately, Bill solved my dilemma by taking the lead and introducing Amy as if we had never met.

We had a wonderfully relaxing time at Root Five, overlooking Lake Erie. We had drinks on the outdoor patio, but it was still a little too early in the season to have dinner outdoors. The lake was still cold and once the sun went down, the air would get chilly fast. But, we did manage to eat dinner at an indoor table by the window. There's something about watching the sun set over the water that puts me into a euphoria zone.

That's where I was mentally when Amy dropped the bomb. She and her husband, Marcus, were hoping that I would consider giving them the chance to take over as foster parents for the twins.

As much as I didn't feel prepared to be a foster mom when Terry and Gerry first asked me, I didn't see how I could let them go now. We were a family. I loved the girls. I was pretty sure they loved me.

I had planned on having a very romantic evening when Jim and I got back to my place. (Or at least as romantic as possible with a guy who'd worked an 18 hour shift then been forced to socialize.) But, Amy's offer sort of blew that all to pieces. Jim was definitely in Amy's camp.

"You know, this would be the best thing that could ever happen to the twins. Amy and Marcus are older and more experienced. They live in a great school district. There'd be two parents there for the girls. And Amy is a trained FBI agent. If there is danger — and there definitely could still be danger — Amy is a lot better prepared to handle it than you."

"Well, you know what? You could say there are a lot of kids that would be better off with different parents. But, they're a family, so they stay with their family." Jim didn't seem to be seeing both sides of this coin and that was really irritating me.

"But, you and the girls have only been a family for a few months. And you're too young and inexperienced to be an effective parent. You're more like a big sister. And kids need parents, not a big sister."

"What they really need is love and stability. Yanking them around yet another time will not help."

"If they go with Amy and Marcus, it would be the last time they get yanked around. If they stay with you, who knows how much yanking will occur? You don't know where your future lies. You don't know what kind of job you'll be doing in six months. You might have to move. You might get married. You might have kids. And if, God forbid, something happens to you, the twins are completely alone again."

The way Jim was talking was upsetting. It didn't sound like he was talking about himself when he talked about whether I'd get married. He certainly wasn't indicating that he'd be there for the girls.

"Rachel, it would be the best thing for you as well as the girls. You're not up to handling your work and parenting two teenagers. You're running yourself down. You're not having any fun."

"I have some fun. You just haven't been around when the girls and I are out having family fun."

"That's because I'm not part of the family. I don't want the girls to get attached to me only to have me go off to the Middle East and never see them again."

Never see them again? Then he wasn't planning on seeing me again either? Could it be that Jim was just using his exhaustion as an excuse to stay distant because he didn't want this relationship to last?

"I didn't realize you were going to go off never to be seen again."

His voice softened. "That wasn't my plan. My plan was to have you come with me."

"To the third world?"

"Uh huh."

I'd had no idea that was what Jim had had in mind. But, I knew it would never work. I was not a third world kind of person. I didn't think I could thrive so far away from my friends and family. I didn't think I could deal with the hardships. I didn't want to raise a family in an underdeveloped country. And there would certainly be no place for my job skills.

"Even if the twins went with Amy and Marcus, I couldn't go off to the third world. Couldn't you work here in the inner city?"

"I don't know how to explain it. I have this…calling. I feel like I *have* to go to the lowest of the low. I feel like that's where I'm needed most. I feel like that's where I could make the most difference."

"Rachel's First Law of Efficiency." I half laughed to myself.

"What's that?"

"Concentrate your efforts where they'll do the most good."

"Your laws are pretty gosh, darn spot on."

"Except, I couldn't do any good in the third world. I'd be a basket case. And I think it would be unfair to raise children so far away from modern civilization."

"I don't think it's a good place to raise a family, either."

"So, you'd come home when it's time to raise a family?"

"No…I was thinking it would be too selfish of me to have children of my own. I guess our futures don't exactly jive."

"Understatement."

I couldn't hold back the tears any longer. They started spilling over my face in buckets. Jim put his arms around me and gently rocked me, stroking my hair.

He kept whispering the same thing over and over. "I'm sorry, Rae. I'm so very sorry."

Chapter 53

The next morning Amy called bright and early and asked me to come to her house for lunch. She had a beautifully restored older home in East Aurora – complete with a barn and horses. Her husband was a school teacher. Her neighbors had a 13 year old daughter. The girls would have to share a room, but it was huge and beautiful.

I was beginning to feel defeated. Especially when Amy told me she and Marcus had lost their own daughter five years before. She had been at a sleepover at a friend's house and died from carbon monoxide poisoning from a malfunctioning furnace in the adjacent room. She had been 10.

Then Amy told me something she'd never told anyone. She saw the Glyphs, too. I knew it took a lot for her to share that with me. Even though my PR work had tended to legitimize the Glyphs, Amy feared that a lot of people in the top echelon of the FBI still felt those who claimed to see the Glyphs were some kind of lunatics.

"Don't you think it's odd that there are so few people who see Glyphs at the top layers of the government? I mean, wouldn't you think the ability to empathize and sort of see through people would be a skill that would lead you to the top?"

"You'd think, Rachel. But, working in the government as long as I have, I can tell you so much of it is political. Especially at the top. And I don't think intuitive people are motivated to play that game."

"Do you think the twins and I are at risk?"

"I…we…nobody knows for sure. I think you've done an impressive job of protecting your identity. We certainly don't know who else you're working with – and I know you've got to be working with someone. I don't think you have the computer skills necessary for the kind of subterfuge you've engaged in. If someone were after you, I don't think they'd be able to trace you using the Web – at least, not if you keep operating the same way. As far as I know, the FBI doesn't have any information that would indicate you're at risk. Unless the situation changes, I have no reason to believe harming you would be of any value to anyone. However, I think Gerry may still be of interest to people…and I've seen motivated groups improvise all sorts of ways to find what they're after."

We walked to the end of Amy's beautiful perennial garden abloom in late tulips, clematis, and bluebells. The garden ended at the horse pasture and Amy's two fillies sauntered over to greet us. One nuzzled its nose into my neck as I rubbed her forehead.

Two weeks later, school was out. I told the girls about Amy and Marcus.

"What if we don't like it there?" Terry was definitely not too keen on the idea.

"If you don't like living with Amy and Marcus, you can come back and live with me. I've been very happy having you girls with me. But, there's always the worry that someone might try to track Gerry down. And you'll be harder to find – and better protected – there than you would be here."

"So, like, the only reason you're sending us away is because of me?"

"No, honey. Of course not. First, I'm not sending you away. I'm giving you an amazing opportunity to have a family with a mother and a father. A family with a permanent home where you can enjoy some stability. A family with better financial resources than I can offer. I love you girls. I'm not sending you away; I'm letting you try out someplace better."

"I like it here, with you. I don't need to try out someplace better. I don't want to go." Terry was fighting back tears.

"You *have* to go. For two weeks. If you want to come back after two weeks, you can. But, I'm not going to let you pass this up without at least giving it a try."

"They have *horses*, Terry. It's worth a try. It will be like a vacation." Gerry's enthusiasm was a welcome surprise.

"And you promise we can come back after two weeks?"

"Yes, Terry, I promise. But I want you to promise me you'll give it a real try. Not just a sit-there-and-pout-until-I-can-go-home try."

"Okay."

"Don't worry. I'll make sure Terry gives it a fair chance."

There was something about Gerry's reaction to the situation that put a blip on my internal radar screen. I cornered her alone later. "Gerry, you seem almost anxious to get away from here. Is anything wrong?"

"Not now."

"What does that mean?"

"I really like it here. I like having you for our foster mom. But..."

"But?" Gerry's amazing ability to "see" the Glyphs so clearly made me give a lot of credence to her intuition.

"Moving in with Amy and Marcus feels safer."

"So...you've been worried?"

"Maybe a little."

"I wish you would have told me about that before. Is there anything else you're not telling me?"

Was it me, or did Gerry hesitate a split second before she said, "no?"

Chapter 54

Jim and I kept in contact as friends, but we never let our relationship flame to the romance level. That would just complicate a sad situation. After the girls moved out, Jim and Kim spent the entire day with me trying to keep my mind off things. I appreciated the distraction. As soon as the twins left, I felt the most incredible relief and the most overwhelming sadness I'd ever experienced.

Kim suggested we go sailing in her dad's boat. That was an excellent choice. I alternated between complete fear (I can't swim) and complete and utter relaxation (somehow being near the water washes away my stress). There is something freeing about flying over the water on a cooling breeze. It's easy to "be in the moment" and let all your other cares slip away.

That carefree feeling lasted exactly one day. The next morning, all my worries and guilt were back. I jumped back into my Glyphs mission to distract myself. I'd kept the Glyphs in the news by writing articles for various publications and websites, but now I could really ramp up my efforts. As yet, it didn't appear that anyone had solved the puzzle. (Or, if they had, they were keeping it to themselves.)

I was, in fact, a bit worried that someone would solve the Glyphs and keep it to themselves. After all, if they weren't "Seers" to begin with, they wouldn't have that urgency to share what they knew. They'd be more likely to want to exploit what they could for their own gain. Greed did seem to be a basic human motivation.

It had also occurred to me that whatever the Glyphs revealed might have a nefarious application as well as a beneficial one. I mean, look how the energy unleashed by an atom could be used. It could light a city, or blow it to pieces. It didn't seem like a clean energy source would have a lot of destructive potential, but you never know. And it could also be something other than an energy source. (The "feeling" with the Glyphs was tied to climate re-stabilization, but the feeling didn't specify a means.)

Why had it taken me so long to realize the possible downsides? Was it because the drive to nail down the Glyphs was so overwhelming? Or had I just assumed the translation would be fast and easy? I wasn't sure, but I tended to lean toward the former. When it came to the Glyphs, my actions seemed compelled by a force beyond my control.

Unfortunately, it seemed like the analytical skills required to decode the Glyphs didn't come naturally to the intuitive types that could see them. Beyond the very first page, which was quite obviously an introduction to a numeric system, not one solid decoding contribution came from any of the original Seers on CussedEmOuterwear.com. Some of the new recruits had some promising possibilities, but the deciphering was going nowhere fast.

I guessed that the US government was working on the Glyphs. Ditto the enemy nations and terrorists that had been visiting the site. But, I had no idea whether anyone else was making any serious attempts at deciphering.

I didn't trust the government to do the right thing. And I worried what the bad guys might do. It seemed like my only option was to see the Glyphs through. I had to throw all my resources into an effort to crack the code.

I decided I'd launch a three-pronged approach. I'd continue to generate as much free publicity as I could by writing articles. (That's what I had been doing, and I was still getting a steady stream of new visitors to the website, so it was effective.) I'd also create some sort of a contest with a big cash prize to encourage individuals to try their hand at deciphering the Glyphs. (A long shot, but you never know. And it would create a deadline that might motivate procrastinators.) And, I'd flat out hire the best people I could find to work on the deciphering full time.

When it came to hiring people, I didn't have any connections in the scientific world and wasn't even sure what field I should look at. Should I find a physicist? A chemist? A language expert? A cryptographer? And where would I find them? I figured I'd reach out to Amir on this one. Amir seemed to have connections everywhere and likely knew key people in the scientific world. If he didn't have the answers, he could probably guide me to the people who would.

Even though I appeared to have successfully avoided any public connection between myself and CussedEmOuterwear.com, I still had to be cautious about contacting Amir. He still had a lot to lose. But, I thought I knew a way he could participate without putting himself at risk.

I sent a letter to the address I had returned the necklace to. Though, I thought about simply putting a sign that said "Hey Faris, I need you." in my window. I had no idea if Faris was still keeping an eye on me. There really wasn't any reason for him to be doing that. But it seemed Amir was even more cautious than me. Apparently smarter than me, too. He'd known everything about me since our first encounter. And I still knew virtually nothing about him. I wasn't even sure if his name really was Amir Kezal. (I was still too worried about exposing his connection to me to even consider googling his name.)

Chapter 55 Gerry's Story

Okay, like, this is the story of my life: First there was light and happiness and then there was darkness an' hell. The only thing I can remember from the light and happiness was just that. I remember a sense of brightness. I remember a feelin' of being safe an' comfortable an' happy. That's it.

I can't remember faces or colors. I try real hard to remember what my mother looked like. Or sounded like. But, there's nothin'. The only memory I have a her is the sensation of my sticky hands and face being washed. The face part is not entirely pleasant. I have a remembered feelin' of screwing up my face and tryin' to turn away. The hands part is better. I remember the feelin' of my hand being covered in a soft, warm, wet washcloth and rubbed from both sides – with each finger bein' individually wiped down.

That's about it as far as anything havin' to do with my birth mother is concerned. And I only have a tiny bit more memory a the world at large. I have, like, this vague idea of what everyday things look like, but I think I'm mostly makin' that up in my head. I think that because all I have is this sense of the shape of things. I have no sense of what color they are or what their texture looks like.

Anythin' else I know from that time of light and happiness is what I been told. And that's not much. Mostly, I been told about the day it all ended. The day the light and happiness turned to my dark hell.

My mother moved to New Jersey just a coupla months earlier. We were livin' with her brother. The neighbors told police he was friendly, but, like, quiet. He had a thick accent that they thought was maybe Russian or some other "Eastern Block" country. He did odd jobs for people in the neighborhood for cash. Nobody knew where he worked or what kind of job he had. They only knew his first name: Yuri.

He was excited about his sister and us comin' ta live with him. He talked about her an' her twins. No one remembered the sister's name or our names. Me and Terry were named by our first foster family. Their last name was Foster. Whatta big, cosmic joke. They named us Teresa an' Geraldine Foster.

Anyways, no one knew our mother or much about us except that we were twins. Social services figured we were around two on the night everything changed. That night, a giant sinkhole opened up and swallowed the duplex we were living in. I must have gotten outta bed to see what the noise was all about. I can't remember seeing the house swallowed up by. I sort of remember the blast. I opened the bedroom door and there was a big, white flash. The next thing I remember was wakin' up in a hospital days later.

The flash was a gas explosion set off when the sinkhole swallowed the house. The explosion knocked me clear across the room an' against the wall. The heat from the explosion blinded me.

The blast didn't hurt Terry. Our bedroom was an old concrete addition. I was told that a long, long time ago the original owner operated a pelt tannin' business in that room. Since Terry wasn't near the door, the concrete walls shielded her from the blast.

After the explosion, I was in the hospital for, like, months. I had burns on my face an' hands an' a cracked skull an' broken bones. Terry says you can't even see the scars 'cept maybe a little bit on my forehead. That's why I wear bangs.

No one could find out much about us after the blast. My mother an' Uncle Yuri were dead. Our landlords, who lived in the other unit in the duplex, were dead. I heard they were old an' stayed to themselves. Their son in California didn't talk to 'em much an' didn't know anything about their tenants. With the house completely destroyed, there were no papers or records. Everything was gone. They didn't even find any bodies. That is, if they even bothered to look for 'em. I don't think they did. Millions of tons of World Trade Center debris they'll sift through forever for tiny bits of DNA. A 50-ft. hole in New Jersey, they just fill in with a bulldozer.

Not that I begrudge the Trade Center families havin' their loved ones searched for. If the state a New York or the Federal Government is willing ta devote that kinda effort ta finding body parts, like, good for them. You just think New Jersey could spend a fraction of that time and money recovering my mother, Uncle Yuri and the landlords. I mean, I wish I had a grave I could visit. Or, I dunno, *something*.

The police, post office an' social services kept watchin' for clues 'bout who we might be. But, nothin' came a it. No paychecks. No tax statements. No mail.

Far as anyone could tell, my mother an' Uncle Yuri didn't have bank accounts, cars or even a phone. The utilities were included in the rent, so Uncle Yuri didn't even have an account with the electric company. Nobody knew our last name or if we had any family. They didn't even know what country our mother was from or if we were born in the United States. We only said a few words, "mama' being the main word.

Far as I know, they're still looking for any mail that might come with a clue to our identity. But, after more than ten years, I'm not holding my breath. I don't like it, but I've accepted the fact that I'm a ward a the state. An' let me tell you, the state sucks at takin' care a its wards.

Chapter 56 Gerry's Story

Terry went ta live with the Fosters while I was in the hospital. The Fosters weren't bad; I think they were just in over their heads. They didn't have kids an' Terry was the first kid they fostered. They brought Terry around to visit me at the hospital on weekends in the beginnin', but after a few weeks, that dropped off.

The nurses at the hospital were really nice, but they were too busy to spend much time with me. I was alone most of the time. Like, totally and utterly alone for hours on end for days an' days. Blind an' alone.

When I got out of intensive care, I at least had roommates. Sometimes they were kids old enough to talk. Sometimes they had visitors that would talk to me. Sometimes the roommate would watch TV an' I could listen. I don't remember if I knew English or some other language then. I just remember I liked ta hear people talk.

I went ta live with Terry an' the Fosters when I got outta the hospital. I had dressings that needed changed every day an' I had to go for therapy an' doctor visits all the time. It was more than the Fosters could handle an' they had ta give me back. They said it would be cruel ta separate me an' Terry, so they put her back in the system, too. I think they just realized they didn't really want a kid around 'cuz me an' Terry were, like, split up mosta the time. They coulda kept Terry an' it wouldna made a difference.

It was hard to get a family that'd take two toddlers, especially when one was blind. Most people who took toddlers were "auditioning" the kid for adoption. But, since Terry had a blind twin, no one wanted to adopt her. I figure they had too much guilt over not adoptin' me, too. Once Terry could talk, she asked for me all the time. An' I asked for her. I heard it drove people nuts.

My second foster family, the Austins, was pretty good. I was there a long time. They had a lotta foster kids. All a them were handicapped in some way. They were like the saint family that social services relied on ta take the hardest cases. I liked it there. With so many brothers and sisters, I was never alone.

At the Austins, every kid was paired with another kid so we could help each other. I helped Elise. She was paralyzed an' couldn't use her arms or legs. It was my job to feed her an' push her wheelchair around.

Elise was older, maybe 9, when I started livin' at the Austins. She was good at makin' people laugh, especially me. Her job was to be my eyes. She'd tell me where things were an' how to steer the wheelchair when I was pushin' her.

I learned ta, like, take care a myself at the Austins. I was making breakfast before I could speak full sentences. At least, that's what Elise told me. She said I was the best breakfast maker in the family. Course, I always made what she wanted because she was the one who guided me through it.

It's not like the Austins were slave drivers. Everybody just had to do whatever they could ta keep the family functioning. There were 12 kids living at home, all with bodies that were defective in some way.

The Austins were, like, super religious. They carted all 12 a us ta church every Sunday an' we had family prayers every night. Elise said people stared at us when we walked inta church. She said they didn't stare in a bad way, but she didn't like ta be stared at just the same.

When I found out Elise an' the other kids didn't have visions like I did, I told Mama Austin about 'em. I didn't just see the symbols. I saw terrible things. Fires an' floods. An' famine. Horrible famine. Mama thought the visions sounded biblical an' asked if Jesus was in the visions. I told her no, but she thought they still might be comin' from Jesus. She had me talk ta Pastor about 'em.

Pastor told me my visions were the devil's work and I should block 'em from my mind an' never speak a them again. He said they would come ta no good. Mama thought Pastor was being rash, so she prayed ta Jesus ta show a sign. She said she never did see a sign either way. She said the visions probably weren't bad if they didn't tell me ta do bad things. Still, she said it might be best not ta speak about the visions ta anyone outside the family.

I lived with the Austins until right before I started kindergarten. That summer Mama Austin was in a terrible car accident. She was in a coma for a month an' then she died. Some ladies from church came ta the house ta help out while Mama was in the hospital. They came two atta time in shifts. But, after Mama died, they came less an' less.

Papa Austin tried to take care a us by himself, but it wasn't workin' out. I heard him cryin' at night when he thought everyone was sleepin'. I think he was cryin' partly because he missed Mama an' partly because he, like, couldn't cope. When he told us he wasn't gonna be able ta take care a us anymore, he was bawling his eyes out.

I heard a lotta the Austin kids ended up at the County Home. People talked about the County Home like it was a bad thing. But, after being in a few foster homes, I wonder if, like, the County Home wasn't a better place ta be.

The foster home after the Austins started out okay. Mama Papadik was a real good cook an' Papa Papadik read me bedtime stories every night. But, after awhile, Papa Papadik started getting closer an' closer ta me when he read me the stories. He stroked my hair an' patted my leg in a way that, like, was totally skeevy. Then, one night he stopped strokin' my hair an' put his hand over my mouth. An' his other hand slid up my leg. He told me that if I ever told anyone, he'd hurt me real bad.

Soon, Papa Papadik was doin' even more horrible things ta me. Sometimes when he was heavin' on toppa me, I couldn't breathe. I thought maybe I'd die an' it would all be over. But, I didn't die. So, I ran away.

Runnin' away was easy. I just lived at school. I was on the program where I got breakfast an' lunch for free. For dinner, I snuck inta the kitchen an' took whatever food I needed from the school's refrigerator. There were plenty a places ta hide from the janitor.

I coulda lived at school all year. But, after about two weeks, my teacher called Mama Papadik ta say that I was smelly an' dirty. Mama Papadik told my teacher what Papa Papadik told her: that social services found my real mother an' took me away. I heard that turned out ta be, like, the end for Papa Papadik. The police an' social services an' everyone got involved.

After that, I lived atta string a foster homes. Some were okay. Most were bad. There was the shithole. That was a slobby family that smelled bad. They had cats an' dogs that peed all over the carpet an' no one ever cleaned it up. I slept in a closet, which was probably the best place in the house because nothing ever peed in it.

My foster families were mostly just interested in the money they got for taking care a me. One family hardly fed me. They, like, flat out said things like "the county don't give us enough money ta feed you meat." After the Papadiks, I was afraid to complain about my foster families. I mean, like, who knew how bad the next one might be? But when I was at the starvers' house, I lost a lotta weight fast. My case worker noticed an' pulled me outta there.

Terry had it worse. Being able-bodied an' all, she was always in demand. People wanted healthy foster kids ta help with the housework along with bringin' in a side income. Some families worked her ta the bone. She didn't have time ta do her homework or play or nothin'.

Chapter 57 Gerry's Story

Every now an' then, Terry an' I would be in a foster home together. That was the best, even when the families, like, sucked. With Terry around, my random life didn't seem so random. I didn't have ta worry about how she was doing. An' she could help me with things I needed ta do.

One a the things I needed Terry for was findin' hiding places for food. I was worried about the famine. I figured someone would be able to take us someplace safe if the fires or the floods came, but no one would be able ta get food if there was a famine. An' after livin' at the starvers' house, I was scareda famine more than anything.

Terry could, like, keep an eye out ta see if anyone ever went near the spots I picked out as hiding places. Once she said they were okay, I'd start squirrelin' away jars a peanut butter, cans a baked beans an' stuff like that. I figured there was nothin' worse than slowly starvin' ta death. Knowin' me an' Terry hadda food stash made me feel better.

Terry an' I were livin' in separate foster homes for almost two years before we got ta Brandi's house. Brandi was different than your typical foster mom. For one thing, she didn't have any other children. For another, she didn't seem ta want us for the free labor or the money. I think Brandi wanted us as sorta, like, fashion accessories.

Be Randy (that's what me an' Terry called her behind her back), was, like, a serial dater. She would go directly from one man ta the next. It's like she didn't exist if she wasn't being adored by some guy. She would date a guy 'til they got ta know each other, then they'd break up. I think Be Randy would drop the guy if he stopped givin' her, like, jewelry an' stuff. Or, the guy would drop Be Randy if he figured out what she was really like.

Be Randy thought she wanted a husband. I think that's why she wanted us. We made her look all respectable an', like, human. I think she thought she'd attract a better class of guy that way. But, I don't think Be Randy would ever be happy as a wife, no matter how classy her husband was. What she really wanted was the thrill an' the gifts from a new relationship. But, I sure as hell wasn't gonna tell her that.

Me an' Terry had it good at Be Randy's. As parta being her perfect accessories, she bought us nice clothes for, like, the first time ever in our lives. She got 'em from the Goodwill, but she knew how ta pick 'em out. One thing you had ta say for Be Randy, she knew about style.

The clothes Be Randy got us were always the latest fashions from the top brands. She wouldn't let us wear sexy clothes like she wore. But, it wasn't like she picked out convent clothes for us. They were exactly like the fashion magazines showed nice kids from good families wearin'.

It was a good thing Be Randy dressed us good, too. She lived at the edge of an okay neighborhood next ta the rich section of town. You hadta have good clothes in that school if ya wanted anyone ta talk ta ya.

It was nice ta go to a school an' live ina neighborhood where ya didn't have ta fear for your life all the time. It was nice ta finally be able ta make friends an' go ta their houses an' listen ta music in their fancy bedrooms. We didn't bring friends ta Be Randy's house much. It was dinky an' worn out compared ta everyone else's. Plus, Be Randy, was kinda embarrassing with her tarty clothes an' all her jewels an' troweled-on makeup. I don't think Be Randy would want ta put up with havin' other kids around, anyway.

Be Randy wasn't very motherly, which was fine by us. Me an' Terry learned to be, like, independent a long time ago. Be Randy told us ta call her "Aunt Brandi." I think she didn't want people ta think she was old enough ta be our mother. But, she liked ta lecture us about motherly stuff like nutrition an' grades. That was just a small annoyance compared ta what me an' Terry were used to.

For the most part, Be Randy kept outta our business an' we kept outta hers. That is, until the whole notebook thing.

Chapter 58 Gerry's Story

Be Randy was such a bitch about the notebook. It was MY notebook. I had it with me before I got ta Be Randy's house. An' all of a sudden she's supposedly worried about danger? What about when she brings home a guy she's, like, known for an hour drunk in a bar? He could be a serial killer for all she knows.

Then, when she thinks she might make some money, then all of a sudden the danger doesn't bother her. She's lucky she didn't get killed. I'm glad she didn't get killed. I mean, she wasn't all that bad.

At first, I thought she did get killed. I heard her scream when the shooting started. It was the kind of scream you knew meant she was hit. And then, there wasn't any more. Just that one scream.

I never ran so fast in my life. I mean I, like, can't run. When you can't see, ya don't run. An' even a little bit a uneven ground can send you flyin' on your face. But, when Terry grabbed my hand, it was almost like I could feel what was ahead of me. 'Course, she told me every step a the way. She's, like, the best sister anyone could have.

After the shootout the police came to Be Randy's house. I could hear on their radios that Rachel (only then I thought her name was Anne) was worried about us an' bargaining for our safety. I, like, hadn't had anyone except Terry really care about me like that in forever.

Livin' with Rae was pretty cool. She wasn't like a mom. I mean, she was tryin' to be a mom, but she didn't exactly pull it off. It was more like livin' with a bossy girlfriend. She, like, took us to all kindsa awesome places. She told us we HAD to join a team or a dance class or somethin' like that. Our other fosters wouldn't LET us do that kind of stuff. None a the other families'd waste their time cartin' us around.

Rae was obsessed with gettin' the symbols we saw translated. An' she was obsessed with security. That put me in a bad place. I could tell I knew a lot more about those symbols than was on the website. But, if I was the only one who knew that stuff – an' anyone else found out – we could be in danger. I decided to keep things to myself for the time bein'. But, IDK, I wondered if I said something if that might help stop the fires an' the floods an' the famine?

The other big problem was that I had this, like, bad feeling. I knew livin' with Rae would mean something terrible would happen someday. I felt bad about that. I didn't want anything terrible ta happen. But, I figured whatever happened might not be as bad as what could happen to me an' Terry in the foster system.

That's why I was psyched when Amy wanted ta adopt us. I had, like, no bad feelings about livin' with Amy. An' she had effin' horses! Amy an' Marcus ended up bein' cool, too. Marcus could cook real good. An' Amy had the visions. Anyone who had the visions seemed ta end up bein' an okay person.

Chapter 59

At the end of the twins' second week with Amy and Marcus, Amy took me out to lunch. The twins wanted to stay with her longer. No big surprise.

"You shouldn't look at this as a failure, Rachel."

"I know that in my head."

"But not in your heart?"

"It's just difficult to admit to myself that I couldn't provide them with the perfect home."

"No one expects a person of your young age to be able to instantly mother two preteens. Under the circumstances, you did a terrific job. Truth is, they'd be fine with you if there weren't security concerns."

I almost told Amy about Gerry's safety worries if we'd stayed together, but decided against it. "How big do you think the risk really is?"

"It's difficult to say, Rachel. Some of the groups who feel they have a stake in the outcome of the translations…well, they aren't people who act rationally. But, I have connections in Homeland Security and other intelligence quarters. Connections that will alert me when a threat is perceived. Officially and unofficially alert me."

"I know the girls will be safer with you than they could ever be with me. Heck, you're armed."

"Hopefully it will never come to that. We'll try to stay one step ahead of trouble."

Those "official and unofficial notifications" from sources that had their fingers on the pulse of all known terrorist groups and hostile nations would go a long way toward keeping the girls secure. I knew the girls deserved parents like Amy and Marcus. They deserved a home like the one they could have in East Aurora. They deserved some stability in their lives. Jim was right. I couldn't give them stability.

But, I also felt just a little, well, guilty. Somewhere, deep down, it was a relief not to shoulder the responsibilities of parenthood. I'd never been one to shy away from a challenge. Getting out from under that enormous challenge was like getting a "Get Out Of Jail Free" card in Monopoly®. I hadn't earned that reprieve. And I felt terrible about feeling relieved.

The conflicting emotions of missing the twins desperately while experiencing the near-elation of no longer shouldering responsibility for them – well, it made me an emotional mess. It didn't help that I had also lost my boyfriend and my dog. (Ozone was with the twins. It didn't seem right to separate them.)

Deep down I was worried that I had invented a reason to seek out Amir. Was it just my loneliness that made me reach out to him once again for the Glyphs? With each passing day, I could tell I was growing more anxious and excited at the possibility of talking to him again.

Finally, I came home to find a note slipped under my door. It read, "*Ms. Rachel, please to meet me at the mall Tuesday at noon. You know the dressing room. Cala*"

Wow! It looked like Amir was going to meet me in person. I hadn't counted on that. I thought we'd talk over the phone. The thought of seeing him both excited and frightened me. After all, the stress from my recent months of parenting had left me frumpish and plumpish. I'd gained nearly two sizes. I much preferred Amir having an image of the old Rachel when he thought about me.

The prospect of seeing Amir again got me motivated to go to the gym. I wouldn't be able to lose any serious poundage by Tuesday, but maybe I could get in good enough shape to avoid panting if we walked fast.

Tuesday seemed both excruciatingly far away and dangerously close. When it arrived, I was a nervous wreck. I met Cala outside the Urban Outfitters dressing room, we went straight to her car, dispensing with a bit of the cloak-and-dagger routine (though I'd taken a city bus to the mall and I'd shopped around for a good 40 minutes before meeting Cala…just in case). We didn't bother with disguises.

Cala took me to her car. I wanted to ask where Faris was, but it seemed that might be rude. We drove to Niagara Falls, parked the car and walked over the Rainbow Bridge. Separately. With me a good 10 minutes ahead of Cala. I got a table at the Hard Rock Cafe and she joined me after she cleared customs. After lunch we walked around seeing some of the sights. (I don't think Cala had been there before, and the Falls really are something to experience.)

I was getting curious as to what our plan might be when Faris pulled up in a Town Car. Cala seemed embarrassed when she realized that she hadn't mentioned we were going to Toronto for a late afternoon meeting with Amir.

"I did not reveal our destination and timetable? Oh, please to forgive me! In my fun, my mind turned to mush. And you were too polite to point out my neglect. You are too good a friend."

"It's fine, Cala. I was having fun, too. And a little mystery adds to the adventure."

"It is my job to make things run smoothly. Mystery should not be on the agenda."

I squelched the urge to mention that everything about Amir was mysterious to me. I was tempted to ask her whether Amir was meeting me in person simply because he was so close to Buffalo. Or could he have arranged to be in Toronto as an excuse to meet with me in person? I hoped he was as anxious to see me as I was to see him. I so wished I was 20 pounds thinner.

In Toronto, Faris dropped us off at a towering office building. Cala led me into a large, corner office with a breathtaking view of Lake Ontario and took her leave. Amir was seated behind a beautiful, ornately carved wooden desk. He rose to greet me, but remained behind the desk, extending his hand. He grasped my hand in both of his. It was warm, but nothing more.

"Rachel! I am so happy to see you."

He did look genuinely pleased to see me. I'd say he looked a little sheepish, too.

"It's good to see you, too, Amir...I've missed you." I must have been desperate for companionship. It wasn't like me to let my feelings hang out there like that, with no signal they were reciprocated.

"I owe you my deepest apologies," Amir hung his head in what I can only describe as an attitude of shame. "When we last met, I was so happy to see you well after such a scare. I neglected to feel the shame that dogs me."

I could tell this was extremely difficult for Amir. And I was confused about what was going on. He continued in the same conciliatory tone.

"I haven't been able to forgive myself for the way our business relationship ended. I was a fool not to consider how successful you might be at our endeavor."

A slight smile briefly crossed his lips. "I had assumed my biggest problem might be you spending our money like – what is the phrase – a drunken sailor? And instead, my frugal little Rachel, you find a way to make money! Money going out is difficult enough to disguise...money coming in is, well, it is a red flag screaming for attention."

"It was so stupid of me, Amir, not to have realized the problem I was creating."

"No. You are the marketing genius. Finances were my responsibility. I should have foreseen every possibility and I did not. That is the past. Water under the bridge."

Amir's gaze dropped from my eyes to the top of his desk. "But, it would be cowardly for me not to apologize in person for seeking the return of your necklace."

I could see Amir forcing himself to meet my gaze. "I should never have given you such a traceable gift. But, I had been overwhelmed by you. My only thought was to find something worthy of you. And nothing could fit that task except for something unique and dazzling. Asking you to return that necklace was…humiliating for me."

"Oh, Amir. I was never happy about accepting that necklace in the first place. I don't even know how to own something of such value. I just didn't know how to refuse it without insulting you."

"Well, let us put that whole unhappy episode behind us, shall we? I am grateful for you to so graciously accept my apology. And I am quite intrigued by your new proposal."

He liked my proposal! Excellent! I almost didn't include it in my letter. I thought it was such a long shot. "I just think it would make a lot of sense for you – for all of the Middle East – to think of yourselves as energy producers rather than oil producers. Oil won't always be the cash cow it is today. Everyone is working on new technologies – clean technologies – to replace it. If the Mid East doesn't lead in developing those new technologies, you will become dinosaurs struggling to survive."

"As you said in your letter, we should learn from the railroads. They believed they were in the rail business rather than the transportation business, no? And the airlines made them obsolete? Such an old reference. You are as anachronistic as your friend Jim told me."

"I'm not the anachronistic one," I laughed. "Jim is anachronistic. If you'd like a more recent example, look at Kodak. They must have assumed they were in the film business rather than the image business. Digital photography was invented at Kodak. And they did nothing with it. Now, they are struggling to remain relevant in the digital age."

"Ah, now I remember...you were not the anachronistic one, you are the encyclopedic one."

I made a mental note to myself to never leave Jim and Amir alone together again. Amir chuckled at what must have been the consternation on my face. It appeared the men in my life could gang up to poke fun at me even when they were in separate cities...heck, separate countries.

"If you're buying into the idea of investing in alternative energy, how are you going to move forward? Will you be able to openly fund that undertaking? Or can I help front that operation for you?"

Amir became suddenly serious. He bit his lip, then spoke haltingly. "I...cannot again risk any involvement with you in an endeavor that may well – and hopefully so – have strong, positive financial outcomes. It would simply draw too much attention to our connection. While your anonymity miraculously remains in place...that may not always be the case."

I hoped Amir couldn't see the dejection I felt. I thought that the situation might have now allowed us to become open friends. Wishful thinking on my part.

"I am forming a corporation to develop alternative energies. I've interested other leading Arab businesses to join me. We will employ researchers to study the Glyphs as a part – a very small part – of our enterprise. It won't be a main focus, as I'm sure that might attract unwanted attention from international authorities. And, from a profit perspective, it is a long shot."

Amir shuffled nervously through the papers on top of his desk. "But, I wanted you to know that there will be substantial resources devoted to it. I only regret that I cannot hire you to play a role in that enterprise. You have much to offer. Lurking beneath that altruistic heart of yours is a very savvy business mind indeed. I am incredibly saddened that I cannot leverage your skills."

"It didn't work out so well the last time you hired me. Probably wise not to make the same mistake.

Amir did not seem to appreciate my self-deprecating humor, perhaps because it was also at his expense. A dark cloud passed briefly over his face.

I awkwardly tried to lighten the mood. "I'm joking, Amir. I hold nothing against you. It truly was liberating for me to not feel beholden to you. Your large expenditures frightened me. I am much more comfortable when there's an income as well as an outflow. It's easier to gauge my effectiveness."

"I am relieved that there are no hard feelings."

"It would be rather silly of me to hold a grudge against someone who has apparently been providing me with my own bodyguard."

"Protecting your interests is also in my good interest, Ms. Shannon."

"Well, you've helped me add a new entry onto my list of Rachel's Laws."

A bemused expression crossed Amir's mouth. Why did men find my laws so amusing?

"And what law might that be?"

"Always look for the downside in unexpected gifts."

Amir raised an eyebrow, "and how exactly did I inspire this law?"

"The valet driver who took my car when we first met. I hadn't expected it…so…I never examined that surprise for the downside. It hadn't occurred to me that you'd be checking out my license plates and running an entire background on me. And once I met you, it was even less likely to occur to me that it was anything more than an incredibly thoughtful and practical move on your part."

"And have you performed a background check on me?"

"I wanted to. But, I felt googling your name would be too big a risk. If Amir Kezal is, in fact, your real name."

"Ever the altruist. More concerned over the safety of another than of yourself. There should be a Rachel's Law against that."

"I'll take it under consideration. But, I'm curious, Amir... If we won't be working in partnership, why did do you bring me here today?"

Amir's expression was slightly pained, "I wanted to apologize in person for our past misunderstanding. While dealing with that over the phone was necessary at the time, it was also exceedingly rude. And...I have some news I wanted to deliver in person."

Amir appeared to struggle to find just the right words. "I am engaged to be married."

"Oh...how wonderful for you." I hoped that sounded more enthusiastic than I felt.

"I actually have you to thank for the engagement. As I was soliciting partners for this new venture, the marriage was proposed as a way of sealing one of the partnerships. My betrothed is a princess from an extremely wealthy and powerful family. I have yet to meet her, but she is said to be quite charming and very intelligent."

I was floored. This was the last thing I could have ever expected. "Do you think you can be happy in an arranged marriage?"

"Yes, I believe I can. It is, of course, a long-standing tradition in my country. And the marriages there statistically last longer than marriages in countries where that tradition does not exist. The arrangement pleases my father greatly."

Amir sighed. "Sometimes, with a great deal of power comes a great deal of powerlessness. This arrangement is good for business. It is good for politics. It is good for my family. It was not my role to protest such a perfect alignment of the stars."

"I'd like to be happy for you, Amir. Though, I'm not sure I can be unless I feel that you are happy as well."

"Happiness is an elusive state. It would be dangerous for me to pursue the woman I would like to pursue. And even if I chose to take that risk, this woman does not choose me. Because of politics. So, you see, politics was already in charge of my love life…I just allowed it to remain so. I hope this marriage brings me happiness. But if it does not, perhaps it will at least not bring the pain that love has already awarded me."

"I feel that pain, too."

"And that strengthens our friendship. We both know the price one must pay for certain things. We both know the fates can be kind. And they can be cruel."

"You seem more comfortable with the finality of these fates than I am."

"The secret is…once you accept the fate…shed the hope. The pain lessens when the hope dies."

"I…I don't know if I can do that."

"You, my dear Rachel, are a person who holds onto hope to the very end. But, I know you. I can assure you of the alternate path you would take. You would decide to throw Rachel's law to the winds. Perhaps we would fool ourselves into believing we could have a future together. But, at the moment of finality, you would realize the obstacles are insurmountable."

Amir looked into my eyes, seeking verification that I understood the truth of his scenario. My answer was barely a whisper.

"Damn you for being so rational."

"Curse you for being so desirable, yet unattainable."

Amir insisted that I spend the night in Toronto and accompany Cala to the theater (or theatre, since we were in Canada). I couldn't decide whether the purpose of his insistence was to give Cala a nice night out, or to relieve his guilt for dragging me up here just to drop me.

I could tell poor Cala was lonely for female companionship. She traveled so often with Amir, she really didn't have much of a personal life. And most of her business dealings were with men. She had no one to let loose with.

We had a spectacular dinner and saw "Jersey Boys," which was fabulous. We giggled quite a bit. And Cala shared some of Amir's faults with me, making me just a wee bit less sad. It turns out Amir was so fastidious, he had his socks and underwear pressed (or, at least, he thought his socks were pressed…she ignored that request and he was none the wiser). I couldn't see me ever sharing a household with such a neat freak. I seemed to create a mess every time I attempted to do anything – even to clean. And my style was so casual and relaxed, I didn't even own an iron.

Chapter 60

The meeting with Amir had certainly left me in shock. But, he was right. Now that I'd lost the ridiculous hope that somehow a miracle would allow Amir and me to be together, the pain was fading. I could move on.

Unfortunately, I wasn't sure where I was going professionally. Could I rely on Amir's company to unlock the secrets of the Glyphs? Or should I pursue that separately as well?

With so many outside interests involved in Amir's company, any breakthroughs there would remain private. Perhaps Amir specifically told me about those partnerships so I'd be aware that any Glyphs revelations wouldn't be shared with the world?

That put me right where I was before. No scientific contacts. No independent financing. Just a quandary as to how to proceed. But, at least my personal quandary was laid to rest. Unfortunately, I now felt more like having a bowl of Cherry Garcia than like going to the gym. But, somewhere deep inside I found the resolve to head out for at least one Zumba class. I knew that after I made it through, I'd feel better. The music would lift my spirits. The exercise would invigorate me. Maybe it would clear my head.

I'd been letting my guard down little by little ever since the Glyphs became a public phenomenon. I still couldn't tell Kim everything, but I did share with her that I had met someone and that it just didn't work out between the two of us. She didn't need to know the details to appreciate my sense of loss. My one last hope for a meaningful relationship had dried up.

Kim set about taking my mind off my woes. She joined the Y and arranged to meet me at a Zumba class three nights a week. That was pretty major for Kim. She wasn't one to exercise. I must really be a basket case if she was willing to mambo for me.

Those workouts really did help. I started feeling like I had some energy. I was in a better mood. Even just having someplace to be three times a week gave my schedule a needed sense of normalcy. (Though, in the back of my mind, I was nervous about sticking to a routine. What was good for my sanity might not be so good for my safety.)

Kim and I started "trolling for men" in all the most ridiculous places. We went to the library, the two major art museums, we even took a drive down to the Corning Museum of Glass, stopping at all the little wineries along the way. We had a blast, but neither of us came up with any romantic prospects. (A couple guys at Heron Hill winery seemed promising, but they quickly became appalled at our low wine IQ…right around the same time their wine snobbery reduced us to uncontrollable fits of laughter.)

I was starting to relax and enjoy myself despite my lack of male companionship. But, the good times soon came to – not exactly to an end – but a drastic slowdown. Kim met someone at one of her office baseball games. (She kept score for the team.) Most everyone in the league would go out to shoot darts and have a beer after the Tuesday night games. That's where she met Curtis.

He was a really nice guy: charming, handsome, intelligent and a real gentleman. He treated Kim like a queen. He actually went a little bit overboard in that regard.

"I shouldn't let Curtis spoil me the way he does," Kim giggled, "but I know this kind of treatment won't last, so I figured I'd enjoy it while I can."

"Just make sure you don't hurt yourself when you fall off that pedestal."

"Nothing to worry about. It's not that high a pedestal."

"I was getting a little spoiled with all the time we were spending together."

"It's not like I'm seeing Curt all the time…"

"I know. Don't be silly. I'm just yanking your chain."

"Well, I'm not abandoning you altogether. I just have to squeeze in a little time for Curt."

"I'm fine. Really. Besides, I'm sure I'll be seeing more of you once Curtis starts scratching his butt and asking you to make him a sandwich."

"I think he has that scheduled for next week."

"He's a keeper if he can hold out that long." We both giggled

I was truly happy for Kim. I had gotten past all my own self-pity. In fact, I realized the one I missed most of all was Ozone. He was always happier to see me than any boyfriend was. And he could sort of be replaced. I was getting in my car to leave for the SPCA when Amy pulled –tires squealing – into my driveway with the twins.

"Rachel, upstairs fast." Amy was in a panic. I dashed up the stairs in no time. Amy was on my heels the entire way.

"There's been a breakthrough. The team working on the Glyphs has determined part of the code includes plans for a weapon."

My jaw must've just about dropped on the floor. A weapon! It was too bizarre to comprehend.

"Are they sure? I can't believe…"

"There's no time to talk. I'll take your computer down to the car. You grab your cell phone and anything you don't want to fall into the wrong hands. Put a couple days worth of clothes in a shopping bag – not a suitcase. I'm going to pull around to the next street. Cut through the backyards and meet me. And do it fast."

I flew through the apartment, grabbing up my phones and throwing clothes in a bag. I ran down the back stairs and out the door. When I was halfway through the neighbor's backyard, I heard tires pulling into my driveway. I sprinted to the far side of the neighbor's house and slunk along the wall. Even if my "visitors" came to the back door, they wouldn't see me. Once in front, I dashed over to Amy's car, got in, and pulled the door closed oh-so-quietly.

"They're here!"

"Don't worry, they won't find us." Amy drove further into the neighborhood, not toward the main road. We continued to drive along side streets as much as possible. Finally we arrived at a truck stop adjacent to a Thruway entrance.

"Do you have your regular cell phone with you?"

"Yes. It's right here." I pulled out my phone

"Is it on?"

"No. I turned it off back at my apartment."

"Turn it on now and put it on "silent." I'm going to pull up next to that truck with the motor running. I want you to slip your cell phone somewhere on the truck. Someplace it won't be seen. But someplace secure, where it won't fall off."

Amy pulled up. I slipped out and tossed the cell through an open window in the truck's cab. It landed behind the seat. That should be perfect. I got back in the car and Amy took off again – but, not onto the Thruway. We took the country roads.

"I'm going to take you and the girls someplace out of the way until things calm down. I don't know what's going to happen. But I think you all need to lay low until we see how things shake out."

"How long will that be?"

"I have no idea. Hopefully not too long. But, I'm guessing it will be at least a few weeks."

The girls were giggling in the backseat. They thought this was an exciting adventure. I don't think they really had a sense that they might be at risk…that the government might want them in protective custody…or might even want to keep them as some sort of guinea pigs.

I was having a hard time assimilating all that had just occurred. Would I be wanted for questioning? Could a warrant be put out for my arrest even though I hadn't done anything illegal? I didn't want to burden Amy with my questions, at least not while the girls were in earshot. She likely didn't know much at this point anyway. I was guessing no one did.

Chapter 61

I was surprised when I found out that Amy had no plans to accompany us.

"It will be better if I stay at home. I have a job I can't leave. And that job provides information vital to your safety."

"I think I'd feel safer if you were with us."

"I don't think you would be. To begin, my staying should buy you time. If I disappeared, it might trigger an immediate search for the girls. If I stay put, it may take them quite some time before anyone realizes the girls are gone. They won't want to question Gerry right away. They wouldn't know what to ask. If they look for you now, they'll be looking for a woman traveling alone…not a woman with two children."

We drove for 14 hours straight, with Amy and I spelling each other behind the wheel. We didn't even stop to eat in a proper restaurant. We loaded up on prepared sandwiches at convenience stores. Finally, we arrived on the Atlantic coast. Amy hustled us onto a yacht. We cut Gerry's hair, transforming her into a boy with some clothes we picked up at Wal-Mart. Amy gave the girls kisses and hugs and tried not to cry as our boat pulled away.

Chapter 62

If we had to be on the lam, at least we were doing it in style. It was a really, really nice yacht. Or maybe all yachts were this nice? What would I know?

Amy's brother-in-law, Sam, was skippering the boat. He apparently owned a yacht of his own, but he traded his for a friend's boat for the month..."just for fun." If anyone went looking for his yacht, they'd find it right where it belonged. Hopefully that would end any investigation into his whereabouts – if there was one.

We were headed for Tortola, one of the British Virgin Islands. But, we hooked up with a catamaran in open water just outside the U.S. Virgin Islands. That boat was from Tortola. I didn't know how much it's Captain, Jonathan, knew. I suspected he didn't know much. But, he was a close friend of Amy's. He trusted her enough to smuggle the three of us onto the island.

This boat was larger than the tiny catamarans I was familiar with. It had an inside cabin! I didn't even know they made catamarans that big. It was such a different experience from being on the yacht, which had no sails. So quiet and peaceful. If I weren't totally freaking out about sneaking into another country, I would've really found that ride relaxing.

Jonathan timed it so we arrived at Tortola near dusk. He pulled the catamaran next to a place called Smugglers Cove. (How apropos.) He loaded the girls and me onto a little dinghy and took us ashore. In the twilight, Smugglers Cove lived up to its name. It was dense with coconut palms. A cacophony of sounds was coming from the tree tops. Loud chirping and whistling – completely exotic sounds echoing off the surrounding hills. Jonathon said most of the chirps were coming from tiny tree frogs. That gave the girls and me no comfort. The entire scene was just too eerie.

Jonathan guided us across the beach and into the coconut grove. It didn't help that we passed between a burned-out car and an eerie, abandoned nightclub. I suspected the club, with its missing wall, was the victim of a hurricane or poor economic times. The burned-out car was another story…and I sure didn't want to hear it just then.

We didn't have to go far. Jonathan's wife was waiting in a car in what must have been the parking lot for the derelict bar.

"Judy will take you up to your place. It's quite nice. I think you'll be very happy there." Jonathon's British accent gave him such a sophisticated edge, but no one could be more folksy and down-to-earth. He could tell we were nervous.

"Don't fret for your security. There's virtually no crime against visitors on this island. And no one's going to be bothering you up at your villa."

"It's not just people I'm worried about."

"Even less to fear then. There are no poisonous snakes, no deadly spiders, not even any predators that could take down more than a chicken. We have lots of feral chickens, though. Goats, too. Don't let those give you a scare."

"We'll be fine."

"I know you will. Judy will settle you in good. And we're just a phone call away."

Judy, was a pleasant as Jonathon was. I didn't know how she kept so relaxed and composed on that road. The deep ruts had the Jeep bouncing us right off our seats every few seconds. I'd imagined the road was long abandoned. And as soon as we got on what you might call a main road, the terrain became incredibly steep, with even steeper drop-offs on the side.

Judy deposited us in a huge villa near the top of a mountain. She came in to help us turn on the lights and get acclimated. It was a gorgeous villa, but arriving at night...not knowing the surroundings...with all those surreal sounds emanating from the jungle...it felt creepy. I don't know about the girls, but I didn't get much sleep that night.

The morning was a different story. I woke up to discover we'd landed in paradise. It was difficult to say which was more spectacular, the villa or the views. Tortola rose up from the ocean in a series of mountain peaks. The mountains were covered in lush greenery and rimmed along most edges by gleaming, white, sandy beaches. The water near the shoreline was crystal clear and the most amazingly vivid color of turquoise you could imagine.

The villa was huge and decorated in bright colors and bold patterns. It had a swimming pool, a guest cottage, and tennis courts. (The courts were useless to me...I'd invariably hit the ball over the fence and it would roll hundreds of feet down the steep hillside into the dense vegetation.)

Summer was the off-season here. Many of the villas on the surrounding hillsides were empty. Even so, the island was big enough that we didn't attract much attention. Our villa was at the end of a long, steep road of loose gravel. That gravel would crunch loudly under the wheels of any vehicle that dared to brave the incline. No one could drive up without us knowing about it.

The girls and I marveled at the beauty of Tortola. Even though the summer weather was hot and humid, the villa's elevation treated us to temperatures that were amazingly pleasant. As long as the breeze kept up – and it was almost always there – we had no need for air conditioning. Which was good, because fancy as this villa was, there was no air-conditioning.

One day when Terry took a nap, I had a little heart-to-heart with Gerry.

"You said before you had a bad feeling about staying together as a family. Do you have a bad feeling about us being a family right now?"

"Un-uh."

"Care to use an actual word…maybe even a sentence?"

"The bad feelin' I had before is gone. It went away when we went to stay at Amy an' Marcus's house. It never came back."

"Are you sure about that?"

"Yep. That was a really big, really bad feeling. I'd know if it was back."

That was worrisome. A really big, really bad feeling and she hadn't mentioned it until the cause was gone? Yipes!

"Are there any other really big feelings you want to tell me about?"

"No."

"Why didn't you tell me about the bad feeling about us staying together when we were together the first time?"

"I worried that might make things get worse."

"You know, I trust your feelings. And I care about you and Terry. I wouldn't make things worse for you. Even if it made things better for me." I hoped that was the truth. I thought it was.

"Uh huh."

"Is there anything at all you want to tell me?"

"Un-uh."

"Think hard, is there anything you know – or feel – that might be important?"

Gerry hesitated.

"Even if it's just something little. Or something you're not sure about."

"The Glyphs aren't bad. They're good."

"I feel that way, too."

"I don't just feel it. I know it."

"I know it, too." Gerry let me give her a big hug. She fell asleep on my lap as I stroked her hair.

Chapter 63

Life in Tortola wasn't bad. A Jeep came with the villa, so I'd take the girls down to the beach for a bit most days. We discovered that, by day, Smuggler's Cove wasn't scary at all. In fact, it was one of the best beaches on the island. The water was tranquil. The snorkeling was superb. And you could get a great barbeque lunch on the beach. Far from being abandoned, the rutted road to the beach was just par for the course when it came to Tortola's side roads.

The scary scenario we encountered on our first night was just beyond the main beach area. I imagine the tourists were totally unaware the abandoned nightclub was even there.

Being off season, we often had huge sections of the beaches almost to ourselves. Especially Smuggler's Cove, since there was no resort nearby. Occasionally a church group or family reunion at the beach would provide the girls with opportunities to talk to kids their own age. I stayed to myself. I figured the closer people got to me, the more questions would arise. Better to be perceived as a haughty stranger than to have to weave a web of lies.

Except for the isolation, life was good in Tortola. There was the chance of a potential hurricane through November. But, the villa had "hurricane proof" windows and doors and its own generator, so we were set to weather anything that came our way – in theory.

Chapter 64

It was closing in on the end of August. We'd been in Tortola for weeks. I assumed we might be staying much longer since I hadn't heard a single word from Amy.

While the weather had been unbelievably gorgeous the entire time, the forecast threatened the possibility of a tropical storm or even a hurricane within the next several days. I figured we could handle a tropical storm. I supposed it couldn't be worse than some of the more intense blizzards we'd had in Buffalo. But the prospect of hurricane made me nervous.

I felt so cut off from the world in our villa. If we didn't drive down to the beach, days would go by when we'd never see another human being. I considered the visits from the housekeeper and gardener to be like presents of humanity. If anything terrible happened to us, how long would it be before anyone would even know we needed help?

If there was a hurricane, I could gas up the generator so we wouldn't have to sit in the dark feeling helpless. (Sitting in the light feeling helpless wasn't that much better, but every little advantage would help.)

The next day the forecast made it sound even more certain that a hurricane would be coming our way. They still hadn't upgraded the "tropical depression" to a "tropical storm," but they were talking like that would happen at any time. I took the girls down to the grocery store and we stocked up on supplies.

I tried to pick out things that wouldn't require refrigeration, just in case the whole generator scenario didn't work out. I let the girls pick out whatever snacks they wanted. As I remembered from storms in Buffalo, snacking was one of the prime family activities during a storm. Snacking and baking cookies. But, I was pretty sure we wouldn't want to be turning on the oven in this tropical heat. With all the windows and doors shut against the storm, that villa would be transformed into a steamy nightmare.

The next day they did upgrade the tropical depression to a tropical storm. And they continued to forecast that it would pass directly over Tortola – most likely as a category 3 hurricane. I searched around for all the supplies I could find. Fortunately they were pretty well organized. Flashlights, candles, matches, board games, even an extra supply of bottled water were all stowed in obvious places. I supposed if you lived in the Caribbean, summer hurricanes were a common threat.

I was stunned the next day when there was a knock at the door. I hadn't heard a car come up the road. And it wasn't like a car could come up silently. Heck, I could hear cars coming up a road that was halfway over on the other side of the mountain.

There weren't a lot of privacy measures at the villa. It was all about the view. Large expanses of windows substituted for walls . Even the door was glass. And there was nary a drape in sight. I was totally unnerved as I approached the door. But, then my heart leapt! It was Jim! What was he doing here?

I flung open the door. "Jim!" I threw my arms around his neck. Had it been that long since I'd seen him? He seemed to have filled out and changed so much. I wasn't sure how I felt about his scruffy, new beard.

"Hey, hey, hey, hey!" Jim backed up to release my grasp on his neck "sorry to disappoint you, but the doctor is not in."

I backed farther away. It looked like Jim. But it certainly didn't sound like Jim.

"Rachel, it's Pete!" He stuck out his hand in greeting.

"Pete! What on earth are you doing here?" It had to be Jim's brother, Pete. I felt like I knew him from all the help he gave us setting up the CussedEmOuterwear.com site.

The girls had come in from the pool deck to see what all the fuss was about. "Girls, you remember Jim? This is his brother, Pete!" The girls were thrilled to have visitor.

"Hey, now, just because I'm related to Jim don't hold it against me." Pete smiled broadly at the girls.

"Pete this is Gerry and Terry. Or, as they're now known Chris and Pat."

"Please to meet you, Chris and Pat." Pete shook the girls' hands.

"Well, come on in and sit down. You look like you're about to drop from heat exhaustion. You didn't walk up that hill, did you?"

"It was more like crawled. That's no hill. That's one steep mother of a mountain."

The girls giggled. Pete was certainly not the "gosh, golly" kind of guy that his brother was. "Well, that helps us keep out the riffraff."

"Let one slip by today."

"Quite."

I poured Pete an ice-cold lemonade and we all sat around the kitchen table. "So, how is it that you're here?"

"Your friend, Amy, had been talking to Jim about how worried she was for you and the girls. Jim told her about me and Amy had him track me down. I think she's worried you might be a bad influence on her girls. She figured I might be able to keep you in line."

"And you just dropped everything and came? That's pretty amazing."

"I didn't exactly drop everything. I brought it with me." He hefted his backpack up on the table. "As long as I have my computer, I'm good to go."

"Well, I really appreciate your coming with that hurricane on the way."

"Fortunately, it's really easy to get a seat on a plane headed toward a hurricane zone."

Pete got up to pour himself a second lemonade. I liked a man that so quickly made himself at home and was self-sufficient. But, when he rounded the corner into the pantry area, he was a tad surprised. "Holy crap! Did a junk food bomb explode in here?"

"Are you criticizing our hurricane supplies?" There hadn't been room in the cupboards for the bulky bags of chips and cookies, so I left them on the counter.

"I think you can be arrested for contributing to the delinquency of minors. Or maybe child abuse. It looks like you could be the cause of America's childhood obesity epidemic."

"Since we're not in America, that can't possibly be true. Do we have your favorite snacks? There's still time to run to the store."

"Does this finely tuned hunk of manhood look like it consumes snacks?"

"Forgive me for failing to notice your abs," I lied. It occurred to me that he had failed to ogle my boobs. Just like Jim. I wondered if rather than being gentlemanly, the Kirkwood brothers just weren't boob men.

"How's Jim doing?"

"The subject turns to abs and the first thing you think of is my brother? That wouldn't be the Jim I know." A slight smile crossed Pete's lips. "He seems to be having the time of his life plotting his course to saving the world. You know, if you'd tried dying of an incurable disease, you may have been able to get him to stick around instead of plotting a medical assault on the third world."

"Yeah, well, there's something about dying of an incurable disease that doesn't totally appeal."

"Just as I suspected. You're a selfish bitch."

I looked pointedly at the girls hoping Pete got the idea that I didn't use words like "bitch" around them. "I'm afraid that compared to your brother, I am."

"Yeah, well, same for Mother Theresa."

I laughed. "I take it you don't take after him?"

"No. He's a real buzz kill. I'm much more fun at a party."

Pete then went on to prove just how much fun he was. He had the girls and me in stitches.

Chapter 65

The next day the predicted hurricane fizzled. When the storm finally hit us, it was just two days of rain and a stiffer breeze than usual. Pete said that he was with us for the long run, even though he'd rushed here specifically for the hurricane.

It had really killed Pete to go "on the grid." I felt a little guilty about that, but I didn't think it would do him any harm. He didn't seem like the type who would ever be on the run from the law. Of course, neither did I. "Pete, do you know if there's a warrant out for my arrest?"

"Last I heard, there was no warrant. But they are actively seeking you for questioning."

"Hmm…how active is actively?"

"As I understand it, they've interviewed everyone who knows you well. I know they talked to Jim. But, I don't think the search has gone international – or even national. I mean, your face hasn't been on the news or anything."

"That's a relief. While your goal might be to stay off the grid, my goal is to stay off the news." I wondered if Jim had shared the secret identity of Anne Hawn-Imus with his brother. If he had, Pete certainly wouldn't miss an opportunity to torture me about it now.

"This seems to be a pretty good place to stay off the news. I doubt they even have a news camera on the island."

It looked like Pete wasn't aware of my blonde, publicity-hungry alter ego. Good. The fewer people who knew, the better. "I never thought to ask…those BVI passports you brought for the girls…are they listed as females on those?"

"Yeah. Amy figured the closer to the truth, the better. And you should realize that you're not 'Belongers.' I think that means you can't vote. The classifications for citizenship in British territories are unbelievably complicated."

"Dang. I was hoping to make a difference in the next election. They're thinking about putting restrooms down by the beach and I have strong views on that."

"Typical spoiled American with an affinity for modern plumbing."

I snorted resentfully at his pompous, outhouse-embracing self.

"Hopefully, now that I'm here to complete the happy family, it's less likely that you'll draw the attention of anyone looking for you. Hell, I don't even think the authorities know you have the girls."

"Oh?"

"Yeah, Amy has been laying low. She hasn't let anyone know the girls aren't home. Sooner or later, someone's bound to figure it out. But, for now, she says no one's come looking for them."

Amy's FBI connection likely made that agency reluctant to interview the girls. She said she had connections with Homeland Security and other agencies. Maybe they, too, would hold off as long as possible in deference to her – if her connections were powerful enough.

I don't think they'd even be able to come up with relevant questions for the girls. It was pretty obvious the girls knew nothing about weapons. In fact, none of the Seers seemed to know anything about weapons. We'd never imagined the Glyphs to be about anything other than saving humanity.

"Did they release any information on what kind of weapons we're talking about?"

"No. The Feds have been pretty tightlipped about the details. They were really pissed that the weapons information was leaked. I don't think they want the world to know how much Glyphs code they've been able to make sense of. They're probably afraid someone's further ahead at deciphering than they are. Don't you get any of this on the news here?"

"There's no reception. I think they may let their cable go for the summer. If they even have cable here."

"That explains why I never see the television on. I thought you might've banned it. And I couldn't imagine a softy like you enforcing that kind of ban with the girls. But, you do have cable here. I've been flicking on the tube after you're all in bed. You just have to know how to work the remotes."

I was as embarrassed about being called out for being soft with the girls as I was about not knowing how to work a damn TV set. But, I never claimed to be a technical whiz and I just didn't have the heart to enforce super-strict rules after all those poor girls had been through.

Unlike me, Pete was a disciplinarian. He had the twins getting onto a strict regimen of chores and reading. They might have rebelled if they didn't adore him so.

Pete was just as disciplined about his own habits. I felt like a degenerate in comparison. In this tropical paradise, I spent a lot of time liming (the islanders' word for lazing around).

That changed when the school year officially began. I started the girls on a formal homeschooling program. They were such excellent students, it really only took a couple hours a day to cover the material. I delivered lessons by the pool so we could cool off now and then. September was the hottest month of the year here.

Pete worked several hours a day at his computer. He wouldn't tell me what he was working on. After he was done with his own work each day, he'd show the girls how to perform some of his computer magic. At my request, those lessons were low on espionage tactics and high on things like Photoshop®, animation, and website development.

Visitors could only stay in the BVI a month before needing additional documentation. So, Pete hopped the ferry to St. Thomas in the US Virgin Islands, planning to make his way back surreptitiously.

I was anxious about Pete leaving. Having him here took away so much of my stress. If it took him a while to get back, I'd be under double stress: Dealing with the girls by myself, and worrying about what might have happened to Pete. September was a big month for hurricanes in the Caribbean, too…even more reason to worry about Pete making a speedy return.

All that worry was for nothing. Everything went according to Pete's plan. He was back on Tortola in less than two days.

I was worried he might want to move into the guest cottage so he could have more privacy. When he first arrived, he took one of the spare bedrooms in the house because the hurricane was supposed to be on the way. But, whether he sensed I liked him close for security, or he didn't mind the lack of privacy, or he was just a creature of habit – he moved right back in to the room he had vacated.

Pete assured me that my computer was set up in such a way that I was virtually untraceable.

"That word, 'virtually,' means 'not quite,' doesn't it?"

"Look Warts, when it comes to not wanting to be found, I am the king of paranoia. And I assure you, I have no qualms about you using your computer. It's as safe as mine. Probably safer."

Pete had taken to calling me "Warts." He said I needed a nickname so he wouldn't get confused and call me the wrong name in public. My BVI passport had me listed as "Sharon." "Warts" was short for "worrywart."

"Why would my computer be safer than your computer?"

"Because part of the safety is in the motivation of those seeking you. Right now, the only ones who appear to have any interest in talking to you are all agencies of the U. S. Government. They don't have a warrant for your arrest, nor do they have what could be considered a reasonable reason to get one. Tracking you down through your computer would take warrants from multiple countries. It just ain't going to happen. They don't have the money, manpower, or political capital to waste on you."

"So, someone is after you that might be more motivated?"

"No. But if someone were after me, they might have more resources, stronger motivation, and no need to play by the rules. But, at the moment, that isn't the case."

"But it might be the case at some point in time?" Pete was starting worry me.

"Not at any time while I'm here Ms. Worrywart."

"And you still don't care to share with me any clue about why anyone would want to track you down ever…even in the future?"

"Nope." And he made clear that that was the end of the conversation.

Chapter 66

It felt good to be able to hop back on the computer. I felt more connected with the world. There wasn't much happening on the CussedEmOuterwear.com site. Everyone was abuzz about the "weapon." Most felt it had to be a misinterpretation. Some felt the whole weapons issue was invented just to throw others off the real track. I knew that would be unlikely. Amy would have sent for the girls if that were the case.

The long, hot days of relative isolation were wearing on us. Pete and I were such opposites in so many ways. And the girls really hadn't had anything to look forward to in so long. Funny how after weeks in paradise, the pool lost its allure. These days, jumping in the pool was more necessity than a playful break.

I don't think Pete felt the strain quite as much as we did. He hadn't been here as long. He was a loner to begin with. Mr. Survival Skills was off building contraptions in the forest for hours at a time several days a week. Maybe having that alone time made it less likely that I got on his nerves. (Though, I'd like to believe that I'm just the kind of person that doesn't get on people's nerves.)

Pete never offered to take us with him or show us whatever he was working on. He refused the twins' requests to help him.

I suspected that whatever he was working on wasn't designed for us. I imagined Pete might have some use in mind for a much later date. For all I knew, he could be planning to spend years out there in the woods living like some Robinson Crusoe, completely off the grid. There didn't appear to be any buildable land in the forest above us, so I'm guessing Pete could exist undisturbed up there for decades.

He was a lot like his brother after all. Both of them were seeking their own sort of refuge, far from modern civilization.

Chapter 67

Pete came back from one of his little sojourns in the forest with a nasty cut one afternoon. I cleaned it up as best I could and splashed it with iodine. I tried to bandage it in such a way that the scab would not tear off when the dressing needed to be changed.

But my unsatisfactory nursing skills became apparent when Pete came down with a severe fever the next day. The wound was infected. I cleaned it more thoroughly and applied some topical antibiotics I found in a first aid kit. When Pete's fever hit 103°, I gave him some acetaminophen.

Bringing the fever down proved to be no easy task. I was worried Pete might have tetanus, but the symptoms didn't quite match what I found online. Pete swore he kept up on his tetanus shots. (Though he was starting to hallucinate, so I wasn't sure if I could completely believe anything he told me.)

Pete had been adamant that I not call an ambulance or otherwise try to get him to the hospital. He was off the grid. He intended to remain off the grid. And I wasn't sure exactly what might happen to him – or to us – if they found out he was here illegally.

I did manage to identify a prescription antibiotic that might be of benefit. I also managed to find a condition that I could realistically complain about to get those antibiotics prescribed for me. I worried if Pete could last long enough for me to see a doctor, though. It was late at night. The island didn't have a 24-hour clinic. I was afraid that if I went to the emergency room, they might try to admit me to the hospital instead of sending me home with the antibiotics.

Pete's fever was creeping up over 104°.

"Can you walk?"

"Been walkin' since I was a baby." Pete's speech was slow and slurred.

"Okay, then. Let's go to the bathroom. You need to take a bath." I slipped his arm around my shoulders and started to ease him out of bed.

"Do I stink? Sorry…want…smell nice for you." His legs were buckling under his own weight. I let him drop back into bed and called for the girls. It took the three of us to drag Pete to the bathroom. I filled the tub with water and ice. It was really wrenching to watch him shiver so. But even soaking in the ice water barely kept his temperature at 103°.

In the morning, I left early so I'd be at the clinic the minute it opened. I gave the girls strict orders to keep adding ice to the bathtub and to monitor his temperature. If it stayed over 105° for more than 20 minutes, they were to call an ambulance. I hated leaving them with such a huge responsibility. But, I didn't feel I had a choice.

Fortunately, the doctor prescribed the exact antibiotic I was hoping for. They had a supply right there at the clinic, so I was on my way back to the villa in under 45 minutes. Pete's temp was still hovering between 103° and 104° when I gave him the pills. Within two hours, he was edging toward 102° and starting to become lucid.

"Holy crap, woman! Are you trying to give me pneumonia?"

"I thought you'd be easier to take on the rocks. Might cool that hot temper."

I helped him out of the tub and wrapped him in a big, fluffy beach towel.

"Why was I bathing in my boxers?"

"I didn't want the girls to get any more of an education than absolutely necessary."

"Girls? Oh, yeah…the twins."

He was still weak and leaned heavily on me as I walked him to his bed. I was amazed at how some microscopic organism could render Pete's huge muscles so useless. Did the bacteria have any sense it was harming its environment? Or was it just going about its business, living its life with no inkling that it was living inside – and destroying – another creature?

If we were inside some sort of Horton, was the human race capable of causing him deadly harm? Were the Glyphs Horton's way of getting us to obliterate ourselves before we killed him? That would certainly be in keeping with the overwhelming feeling that the Glyphs needed to be shared with the entire world. A unilateral weapon wouldn't keep us down…but if everyone were equally armed – with an unimaginably powerful weapon – how long would it take for us to wipe most of civilization off the map?

I couldn't help but wonder how religion figured into all of this. Could Horton be God? If not, did God care about Horton (or whomever it was who sent the Glyphs) as much as He cared about us? Could He have cared about the bacteria raging through Pete's system as much as He cared about us? The bacteria I just helped kill?

Such huge questions. And they seemed so ridiculous. I suppose the notion of bacteria would have seemed equally ridiculous a thousand years ago: invisible organisms living inside us, even capable of killing us. How unbelievable would that be if we didn't have microscopes? I wondered what even more incredulous possibilities might be uncovered a thousand years from now.

Those questions were beyond me. Did the answers even matter? After all, we'd existed for centuries without those answers. I suppose we'd existed for centuries without antibiotics, too – but they were good to know about. Pete may not have been around much longer without them.

The Glyphs appeared to be a new wrinkle. But, why weapons? And why now?

Chapter 68

At one point during the night while Pete was in the ice bath, he appeared to be somewhat lucid. I had been sitting with him all night, making sure he didn't drown and holding a large bag of ice on his head. He reached over and grabbed my hand, looked into my eyes and said, "Do you know I love you madly and passionately?"

I assumed that even though he appeared lucid, he was still delusional at that point. But, I wondered...could he have meant what he said?

As Pete quickly started to become his old self, I tended to doubt he even remembered that exchange.

"Why the hell didn't you call an ambulance?"

"You'd asked me not to."

"I was delusional. Don't you think it's unwise to follow the orders of a delusional person?"

"You asked me not to before you became delusional."

"Yes, well, I wasn't on death's door then was I?"

"I was going to call for help if you sustained 105° for any period of time."

"105°! Good Lord, that's slicing it mighty thin don't you think?"

"Don't worry, next time I'll seek medical assistance if you have but a splinter."

Pete seemed to be kidding during these exchanges. But, I think there was some smidge of seriousness to his tone. Apparently he might have the good sense to be more concerned for his health than his anonymity. Nonetheless, I was glad that we didn't have to blow our cover.

I did convince Pete that he needed to at least show me how to get to his little survivalist sanctuary. That way, if he didn't return one night, I'd have a clue as to where to go looking for him. He said he'd take me most (but not all) of the way there the next time he felt well enough to hike up.

Was it my imagination, or were my interactions with Pete just the slightest bit weird now? Maybe was just me, since I was now always on the lookout for any hidden meaning or sign of affection.

To be honest, I wasn't sure what I'd do if Pete had romantic feelings for me. He was incredibly handsome, built like a rock, funny as heck, and a really helpful guy to have around. But, I hadn't thought about him in a romantic way before. He was certainly wackier than your average human being. But then, maybe I was too. Not too many sane people worked full time figuring out visions in their head.

Since I couldn't put my finger on how I felt about Pete, I decided to consciously avoid thinking about it. Whenever he'd say something terribly cute, or look straight into my eyes with that little twinkle thing going in his eyes, I'd put any inkling of feeling right out of my mind. I'd replace the thought by fixating on a tall, cold, margarita. I made a mean frozen tropical beverage.

Chapter 69

Pete still wasn't quite feeling his old self when we got a message from Amy. Well, not exactly from Amy, but about Amy. Jonathon called to tell us Amy was being questioned in the disappearance of the twins.

"They can't really believe Amy would have harmed the girls, could they, Pete?"

"I doubt it. The bastards are just trying to force you out of hiding."

"I wonder if some new development made them crank up the heat?"

"Might be. Some of the guys I follow online think the Feds' chatter is ramping up."

"People are tracking federal chatter?"

"As best they can."

"And you didn't tell me about this because?"

"Who knows how accurate their assessments are? And who knows what it could be about? They could be planning a big state dinner."

"Anything else you're not telling me?"

"Nothing pertaining to you."

Pete and his secrets could be so maddening. But, that penchant for privacy was what kept my involvement with the website off the public radar.

"Maybe it would be best if you didn't use your computer for awhile."

Pete losing faith in the nontraceability of the website really scared me.

"Do you think they suspect I'm with you?"

"There's a possibility. Your little shootout made them aware you're friends with Jim. If they get real serious about investigating, they'll start looking into relatives and friends of friends. If that happens they'll connect the dots that lead to Tortola."

"Tortola's small. If they check it out, it won't take long to find us. Maybe you should leave, Pete." I hated the idea of him leaving, but there was no reason for him to expose himself to trouble. He was on the island illegally. Who knew what consequences that might create?

"You're right. It's not like I'll do you any good if the Feds show up."

I was hurt that Pete jumped on the chance of leaving. But, he was extremely practical. He packed his backpack in preparation to leave at daybreak. I woke up extra early to make him a nice breakfast and drive him down the hill, but he was already gone. He left a note: "*I meant what I said.*" Then he drew a little heart and signed it "*Pete.*"

Chapter 70

After Pete left, I was an anxious wreck. Without the Internet, I felt like I had no contact with the outside world. I didn't know what the government might be doing to pressure my friends and family into divulging my whereabouts (not that they knew). And I was constantly on edge, expecting the authorities to turn up at any minute. It was almost maddening when they *didn't* show up.

Pete had been gone for a week and I'd heard no news from – or about – Amy. I'd just tucked the girls into bed and happened to turn on CNN. Anderson Cooper stopped me in my tracks. There was an update regarding the Glyphs weaponry. Homeland Security had released a statement: The weapon would be of absolutely no value on earthbound targets. It was strictly designed for objects in deep space.

I turned off the TV and called Amy.

Autumn, 2009
The End of Book One

Additional books by Sue Knott include:

TwiLITE A Parody

Vampire The Transformation of Trinity Jones, a novella with adult content

The H.Unger Games Gone Wild, A Parody (with Lardyard Hempoon)

(Look for a 50 Shades parody coming soon)

Catching On Fire was originally slated to be titled **Do You See What I See**, but research revealed that title to be in use too many times for the author's comfort. The author intends this book to be the first in a series. The release date for the next book has not yet been set (as of Spring, 2012).

ACKNOWLEDGEMENTS

This novel was vastly improved by the contributions of a number of people to whom I am eternally grateful. Among them, Agnes, Carol Wente, Jean, Sharon Ludwig, Sue Ho and several others who have not indicated they wish to be mentioned...but you know who you are.

ABOUT THE AUTHOR

Sue Knott is the doting mother of a teen son and the long-suffering wife of an equally long-suffering (but much crankier) husband. She has also been "mom" to a bunny (now deceased) and an extremely energetic Siberian Husky.

She has had a varied and successful career as an advertising copywriter. She has lived in Pittsburgh, PA; NYC; LaCrosse, WI; Scranton, PA; and currently makes her home in upstate NY. Occasionally she tries her hand at stand-up comedy, though she is in complete and total terror whenever she takes the stage. She prefers to write, rather than perform, humor and has published multiple parodies of popular fiction.

Sue is an avid gardener and wishes she had time to pursue craft projects (or even just to clean her house). Sue has a sweet tooth. She wears a size 9 shoe. She collects art glass. She recycles. She sewed her own wedding gown (big mistake). She revels in the outdoors and longs to be on the beach. She prattles on at the keyboard. She is a safety nutcase. And she loves to Zumba.